Barrington Family Saga

VOLUME THREE

AT HEAVEN'S DOOR

ANITA STANSFIELD

Covenant Communications, Inc.

Cover: *Familiar Bend* © Daniel F. Gerhartz
Cover design by Jessica A. Warner, © 2007 by Covenant Communications, Inc.

Published by Covenant Communications, Inc.
American Fork, Utah

Printed in Canada
First Printing: November 2007

13 12 11 10 09 08 07   10 9 8 7 6 5 4 3 2 1

ISBN-13: 978-1-59811-468-3
ISBN-10: 1-59811-468-9

For Charles Barney,

my father's great-great-grandfather, who was

endowed in the Nauvoo Temple during the evacuation.

And for Louisa Maria Hall Harris,

my mother's grandmother, who as a child went back after

being driven from her home by a mob to get her pewter teapot,

so the enemy wouldn't melt it down and make bullets.

And then she saw the house burn.

❧ ❧

Because of them and many others,

the spirit of Elijah has led me to Nauvoo.

And there I find my greatest legacy.

Chapter One
DRIVEN

Iowa City—1846

Eleanore Barrington hurried from the post office, returning to the buggy she'd left parked nearby. A playful breeze urged the dying leaves of autumn from trees where they reluctantly clung. But the afternoon sky was clear and the air pleasant. Once seated, Eleanore hurried to open the letter she'd just received from her dear friend Sally Jensen, who was residing with her family in Nauvoo, Illinois. Eleanore had felt uneasy about the situation with her friend for nearly a year now, since she'd sent word that the Saints were leaving Nauvoo in order to avoid the growing unrest and persecution that inevitably followed the Mormons wherever they might choose to settle. Miriam Plummer, a mutual friend to Sally and to Eleanore, also lived in Nauvoo with her family. While Eleanore worried for all of the Saints who shared her religion, Sally and Miriam were dear friends, making her concern more personal. And now she had in her hands the first letter she'd received in many weeks. Or was it months? She opened it frantically, praying the news would be good.

Eleanore, my dear friend, It is with a heavy heart that I pen this letter, not certain when or how I will mail it. We are among the last to be leaving Nauvoo. Only those who have struggled with illness or couldn't afford the necessary provisions to go remained behind, and there were only five or six hundred of us left, I would estimate. We've had our provisions ready, but our youngest has not been well, and we've hesitated to take her from our home. Andy and Miriam and their children are with us. They

*too have struggled with illness and have waited. Now, we have no choice.
We've waited far too long. We should have left with the early companies.
Tears that I have fought bravely are now refusing to hold back as I share
my deepest sorrows with you, my friend. The peace of Nauvoo is
completely gone, my dear Eleanore. The worst has happened. The city was
overtaken by cannon fire and . . .*

Eleanore gasped and put a fist to her pounding heart. She couldn't
believe it! She wiped the tears from her own eyes to continue reading.

*. . . And a battle ensued. In the end we were forced to surrender our
city and our temple.*

"No!" Eleanore muttered, then glanced around, grateful to find
no one nearby to hear her outburst. Then she looked at the words
again, unable to believe it, sick and horrified at the very thought of
this beautiful, sacred building in the hands of people who would only
defile it. She read on.

*We were assured that we could go in peace, but Mark and Andy had us
packing up immediately, not trusting that the enemy wouldn't do us harm
if given a chance. We were some of the first of this final company across
the river, where we are now back to living in tents as we were when we
first came to Nauvoo. Now, as I write this, I look across the river to our
beautiful city while an endless line of wagons, people, and livestock
continue to cross over to safety. We will soon move on to Winter Quarters
to join with the rest of the Saints for the winter while preparations are
made to go west. I'm not certain when I'll be able to post this letter, but I
needed to pour my heart out to you now. I hope this letter finds you all
well, and I don't want you to worry for us. We are in God's hands, and we
are together. All will be well. I will write again when I can. Your friend
and sister in the gospel, Sally.*

Eleanore just sat there, the letter frozen in her hands, struggling
to accept the horror of what she'd just learned, wondering how it
had come to this. She could fill buckets with the sorrow she'd felt
on behalf of her friends and thousands of others who had been

unable to find peace, in spite of their hard work and enormous suffering. Eleanore and members of her household had lived their religion alone and very quietly for years, hoping to avoid the persecution that was so common wherever members of the Church settled. She'd been more than willing to join the Saints and go wherever God asked her to. Her husband, James, while initially choosing not to embrace her religion, had supported it wholly. He'd agreed that if God wanted them to move to Nauvoo, he would do it. But they'd both prayed and had received the same answer numerous times. For reasons they could not understand, God meant for them to stay in Iowa and keep their beliefs quiet for the sake of their own safety. James had finally entered the waters of baptism last year, and he'd personally become more zealous about joining the Saints; he wanted to help build the temple. But again the answer had come that they should stay. So they secretly found joy in sharing their beliefs beneath their own roof, waiting for the time when God might allow them to join the body of the Church. Even as settled in Iowa as they were, they had anxiously waited for word that the temple was completed so they could go there long enough to reap the eternal blessings that had been promised by the Prophet Joseph before his death.

Eleanore's strongest connection to the members was through her regular correspondence with Sally and Miriam, and she'd often envied her friends for being able to live in Nauvoo, even though she knew that it had come at a very high price. Eleanore clearly recalled her one visit to Nauvoo. The city had been thriving and beautiful, one of the largest in Illinois. And its highlight had been the temple being built in the midst of it, rising like a beacon of devotion to God. In most visible ways, the persecution and illness that had caused so much suffering had been in the past. At the time, Eleanore had desperately longed to live there, but her own path had been made clear, so she'd remained content with the regular exchange of letters. Then word had come that Nauvoo was being left behind, that Brigham Young intended to lead the Saints west to a place where they could build, and live, and thrive in peace, and never again be uprooted. The Saints had increased their work effort to complete the temple, in spite of knowing they were leaving. Just thinking of their commitment and sacrifice often moved Eleanore to tears. And now this. How could it be? She just couldn't believe it.

Eleanore was brought back to the moment by a sudden wave of nausea. Just this morning it had occurred to her that she might be pregnant. Little Jamie was only seventeen months old and getting into everything. The thought of keeping up with him and enduring the illness of pregnancy left her unsettled. But she could never begrudge having another baby, even if she didn't feel ready. And she reminded herself that there were many people in her home who would help care for her *and* for Jamie.

Looking again at the letter in her hands, Eleanore wanted to sit where she was and cry like a baby. But she was too far from home, and too conspicuous. She tucked the letter into her satchel and snapped the reins, driving the horse through town and some miles farther. Going off the main road and over a bridge, her home came into view, set against a background of trees with a river flowing past it, surrounded by a well-groomed yard that merged into the more natural woods and prairie that constituted the acreage they owned. The stately, two-story house was painted white, with a porch that wrapped around. Nearby were a huge red barn, a large garden, and corrals. It was beautiful, and she loved living here. But at the moment her mind was elsewhere. She halted the buggy near the barn and jumped down, trying to figure where James might be. Then she heard the crack of wood splitting and followed the noise. She found her husband on the far side of the barn, chopping wood. The striped shirt he wore with suspenders over his shoulders had the sleeves rolled to just below his elbows. A hint of sweat glistened on his face. For a long moment she just watched him, feeling all at once the circumference of the life they'd shared—and how the news she had to give him would alter plans they had made. Now there was no way of knowing when or how they would be able to go to the temple together. And the heartbreak she felt on behalf of those adversely affected by this was devastating.

"Hello," she said with some nonchalance, wanting to delay telling him, but at the same time needing to share her grief.

He turned in surprise and stuck the axe into the chopping block. "Hello," he replied, then his smile faded, and his brow furrowed, as if he had only to look at her to know something wasn't right, in spite of her efforts to appear composed. "Is something wrong?" he asked.

Eleanore ignored the question and stood before him, pushing her fingers into the thick, dark hair that was combed back off his face, except for a few stray locks that had fallen over his forehead during the course of his work. She put her arms around him and nestled her head against his shoulder, if only to hide her expression as tears crept close to the surface once again.

"Eleanore?" he asked and eased her away, taking hold of her shoulders to look into her eyes. The concern in his expression intensified. She held up the letter, and the lines in his brow deepened. "Bad news?" he asked, taking it from her with some trepidation.

"Just read it," she said.

James considered his wife's mood and hesitated a long moment before unfolding Sally's letter. He read only the salutation before he lifted his gaze again to Eleanore, his concern deepening. Her dark auburn hair looked more mussed then usual, as if the pins holding it in place at the back of her head had waged battle with a fierce wind. But there had been no such wind today. Her eyes looked traumatized, her expression strained. She paced back and forth slowly, distracted and agitated. She pushed trembling fingers into her hair, giving him a clue to the cause of its untidy state and letting him know that her initial greeting had been suppressing the effect of whatever Sally had written that had upset her so thoroughly.

James focused on the letter, fear clenching his heart even before the words took hold in his mind. He felt suddenly unsteady as the deeper implications settled in. He staggered backward and sat on the stump beside the axe. He had to reread certain phrases to assure himself it really did say that Nauvoo was lost, the Saints driven out, the temple overtaken. Although they'd known for some time that the Saints had been slowly leaving the City Beautiful, they'd also known that the temple was being completed. The last they had heard, the temple was finished, and work was being done there, but it had been in haste, and then Brother Brigham had left Nauvoo. They'd waited and hoped for word that it was safe to come to Nauvoo and participate in the blessings of the temple. But they'd heard practically nothing from Sally for months. And now the worst had happened. His heart cracked to consider that his deepest wish to be bound eternally to his wife and children would now be postponed indefinitely. There was no way of knowing where the Saints might find safety and security enough to build another temple, or how long it might take.

Eleanore waited for a reaction, then nearly crumbled when he hung his head and pressed a hand over his eyes. She heard him sob then moan as the letter fell to the ground, and he pushed both hands through his hair.

"Oh, Ellie," he murmured and sniffled loudly, "we should have gone sooner; we should have been *living* there—and then we could have gone to the temple when the chance was there and—"

"We know we're supposed to be living *here,*" she said. "And we've been very blessed."

"Yes, well . . ." his voice hinted at anger, "apparently living in safety has a price . . . perhaps one with eternal consequences."

"We haven't stayed here out of fear or willfulness, James. We both know God wanted us to stay, and surely He would have prompted us to go there before now if He knew there would be no other way."

He looked up at her, his eyes brimming with fresh tears. "But what if something happens to one of us, Eleanore, before we have the chance to—"

"God will not deprive us of being together eternally, James, if we remain faithful. And we will. We must trust in Him." James could hear her faith firmly etched in her voice, and he could see it in her countenance, and he marveled that she could be so strong. She was an inspiration to him. "I'm just so . . . worried," she went on, "for Sally and Miriam, for their families—for all of them. It's so horrible." The determination in her expression deepened before she added, "We must go to Nauvoo."

"Why?" he demanded. "There's nothing there, Eleanore."

"Maybe they're still camped across the river. If they're there we can help them. We can—"

"We have no idea how long it's been since she wrote that letter. It's not dated. They're probably long gone and—"

"I have to go!" Eleanore insisted, startled by the urgency she felt. "If only to . . ." Tears crept into her voice, "to . . . see the temple and to—"

"It's in the hands of our enemies, Eleanore." He stood and took hold of her shoulders. "We can't just . . . walk in there to have a look around."

"Please, James," she said more gently. "I can't explain it. I just know I have to go."

He sighed and stepped back, struggling for words to convince her of the ridiculousness of this request. "Just . . . pray about it," she added. "And I will too." He drew a deep breath. It had been standard procedure in their relationship, right from the start, to pray over their decisions and do whatever they felt unanimously right about. Even before the gospel had come into their lives, they'd both been the kind of people to pray and listen and strive to follow God's desires for them. It was one of the greatest common bonds that had brought them together. He couldn't disagree with her request, even though he wanted to. Still, he couldn't figure why God would want them to travel all those miles just to see a desecrated temple. And he couldn't fathom that any of the Saints would still be camped by the river if Brigham Young was gathering them elsewhere.

"Very well, I'll pray about it," he said and sighed as he took her into his arms, holding her desperately close, finding comfort in the way she held to him just as tightly. Whatever they had to face, they were in it together. He couldn't imagine what he would ever do without her.

Eleanore picked up the letter, grateful to feel her husband's strength beside her as they walked together toward the house. Coming around the barn they found eighteen-year-old Ralph unharnessing the buggy. Ralph Leichty had worked for the Barrington family ever since they'd arrived from England in 1839. He'd initially tagged along with his mother, Amanda, who had been widowed prior to that time. Amanda and Ralph lived a short distance away, but both spent far more time in the Barrington home than they did in their own. They were like family. They were also both members of the Church and joined them each Sunday for a private worship service at home after they all attended church in town to keep up appearances and avoid suspicion from those who opposed Mormonism. Ralph was tall and robust and he was a hard worker. He'd been a good friend to James and Eleanore's son David, in spite of his being five years older. But David had died of pneumonia the previous spring, and Ralph had been affected by the loss almost as much as David's parents. For that reason, they shared a deep unspoken bond. There were moments when

Ralph's presence made Eleanore miss David more, and others when having him around eased the emptiness caused by David's absence.

"Thank you, Ralph," James said to the boy at the same time as Jack, the family dog, ran to greet James. He nonchalantly scratched the dog's ears.

"Not a problem," Ralph said and smiled before he disappeared into the barn, but Eleanore saw a glimmer of concern in his eyes, as if he'd sensed that something was wrong.

Jack followed them into the house and curled up in his usual spot in the kitchen where they found Amanda busily engaged in supper preparations. She enjoyed cooking and was very good at it. Seeing her at it always left Eleanore with a sense of security and constancy. Amanda was a tremendous blessing in their home, not only for her hard work and abilities with cooking and cleaning, but with her tender heart and generous spirit.

"Frederick and Lizzie are still cleaning the attic," Amanda reported. "The children were in the parlor, last I checked."

"Thank you," James said and followed his wife to the parlor while he wondered how the attic project was coming along, although it seemed a paltry concern in contrast to the news they'd just received. Frederick and Lizzie were husband and wife and had come with James and Eleanore from England. They had served James faithfully in his household there, and now they were as much family as they were employees. They lived in a smaller home nearby that had been built on the same property, but they all shared meals and worked and worshiped together. It was Lizzie who had declared that the attic was in need of a good cleaning. The children loved to play or just sit and read up there, especially when the weather was not too hot or cold. Right now in the cool of autumn it was relatively pleasant in the attic, and Lizzie had declared it the perfect time to get rid of some dust, and put in better order the trunks and boxes and other odds and ends that were up there.

In the parlor, Iris, who was relatively mature for twelve, sat reading aloud to Mary Jane, the six-year-old daughter of Frederick and Lizzie. Iris was also watching out for Jamie, who was playing with a set of wooden blocks on the carpet. James rarely saw his daughter without being aware that she was as kind and sensitive as she was beautiful. Her blonde hair was long and thick and usually hung in a smooth braid down her back. Her features were almost doll-like, and she mostly favored her birth mother in appearance, although Eleanore declared regularly that she had a remarkable resemblance to her father. James was grateful to see Iris only as herself. He couldn't see any similarity to himself, and he had no desire to see any likeness to his first wife. David and Iris's mother had been a difficult woman at best, who had left a great deal of heartache and destruction behind at her death. Life had been better for James since Caroline had passed away, and he had married Eleanore the following year. She had taken him and his children into her heart so readily that he continued to be amazed. Right from the start, she had loved and cared for the children more than their own mother ever had, and David's death had been every bit as hard for Eleanore as it had been for him. Little Jamie had helped fill the void that David had left behind. While no child could ever replace another, Jamie had brought great joy into their home that helped compensate for the tragic death of his half-brother. Eleanore had lost three babies before they'd been blessed with Jamie, and they considered his existence a miracle.

Iris was gifted at looking after the younger children, and her general attitude of helpfulness was almost uncanny. James and Eleanore had discussed the possibility that the hardships of her young life had left her more keenly appreciative and humble than most children. But surely her spirit had a natural strength that lured her toward gratitude as opposed to bitterness. Or perhaps Eleanore's loving example of faith and strength had helped Iris overcome the effects of a harsh mother and her brother's death. Whatever the reasons, James was grateful for his sweet little daughter. Her smile helped soothe his present heartache as they entered the room. Jamie jumped up and ran excitedly into his mother's arms, jabbering nonsense as if he were telling her a great oratory of his activities during her absence. The boy had the slightest hint of red in his dark hair, much like Eleanore's. With the depth of love James felt for his wife and children, his deepest desire was to share eternity with them. The thought stabbed at him with this latest news from Nauvoo, but he smiled and greeted his children as brightly as he could manage. He and Eleanore spent almost an hour with them before Amanda sent Ralph to tell them that supper was nearly ready. James sent Iris and Mary Jane to set the table. He followed to help them while Eleanore went upstairs to change the baby's diaper.

Over the supper table Frederick and Lizzie reported that the attic was now clean enough to be inhabitable once again, and Ralph told them about a girl near his age that he'd met at church. The two of them had conspired to meet in town a couple of times to visit, and he was considering a visit to her home, but felt nervous. Iris talked of a novel she was reading, which was one of Eleanore's favorites. Reading was a common bond between Iris and her parents, and they never ran out of things to talk about as long as there were lots of books to read. James listened and observed, occasionally holding Eleanore's hand across the corner of the table, while his mind dwelled on the letter from Sally and what it meant. He considered his wife's request to travel to Nauvoo, and couldn't imagine what purpose might be served by such a trip. But he uttered a brief, silent prayer on behalf of their friends and asked if going to Nauvoo was the right course.

"Are you all right?" Frederick asked James, startling him from his thoughts. "You've been awfully quiet."

"The both of you have," Lizzie commented with concern, reaching for Frederick's hand in a way that was common between them.

James caught Eleanore's glance. They both knew the others needed to know. He didn't want to be the one to tell them, but he took his role as head of the household very seriously, and he knew it was his place to share the unpleasant news.

"Um." He cleared his throat and straightened his back, tightening his hold on Eleanore's hand. "We got a letter from Sally. I'm afraid the news isn't good."

"Oh, no!" Amanda muttered and set down her fork.

The others followed her example, and the meal was officially interrupted while James repeated what Sally had written. Amanda and Lizzie both shed tears but had nothing to say. Iris broke the pall of silence by asking, "Are they going to be all right, Papa? Where *is* Winter Quarters? Do they have what they need? And—"

"One question at a time, precious," he said gently. "We don't know if they're all right, or if they have what they need. I believe Winter Quarters is on the Nebraska border, but I don't know exactly."

"And what about the temple, Papa?" she asked with tears glistening in her eyes.

James didn't realize he was crying until he felt moisture trickle down his face. He saw compassion in Eleanore's eyes as she wiped his tears with a napkin. He cleared his throat and said hoarsely, "I don't know." And he couldn't say anything more.

Later that evening, James tucked Iris into bed with a kiss to her brow, grateful that she didn't consider herself too old to be kissed goodnight by her father. He doused the lamp in her room and crossed the hall to Jamie's room. He leaned in the open doorway and watched as Eleanore stood from the rocking chair with the boy sleeping in her arms. She carefully laid him in the crib and brushed a mother's hand over his wispy, dark hair before she took James's hand and walked with him to their own room. He sat on the edge of the bed to pull off his boots while Eleanore sat in front of the mirror to take down her hair. He watched as she unpinned the thick braid and let it fall, then she untied the ribbon at the bottom and worked her fingers through the weaving to undo it. For as long as he'd known her she'd worn her hair this way. He loved the way it represented her simple nature and her gentle beauty. She was the greatest thing that had ever happened to him. In spite of her being more than twenty years younger than him, he'd never felt anything more than equal to her, or perhaps more in awe of her. He'd often wondered how a woman so young could be so wise, so full of faith and insight.

Nothing was said between them as they prepared for bed. He knew her thoughts were the same as his, but they felt too heavy to articulate. He didn't know what to say. But he wasn't surprised by the words with which she broke the silence after she'd crawled into bed and settled her head on his shoulder.

"I feel an urgency to go to Nauvoo, James. I feel driven. I don't know why, but . . . the idea won't leave me."

James couldn't deny his own feelings. "I fear that going there will only break your heart."

"Only mine?"

"And mine," he admitted.

"Perhaps I need to see for myself that it's true."

"It's a long way to go to be assured that Sally's not lying to you."

"Of course she's not lying to me."

"Then why?"

"I don't know. I can't explain it. I just . . . need to."

James sighed. "We'll talk about it tomorrow." He fell asleep praying about this seemingly ludicrous journey to Nauvoo and woke up with the impression that he should take his wife there. He resisted cursing under his breath, then resisted again when the first words out of Eleanore's mouth were the repetition of her request.

"I am *amazed,*" he responded with exasperation, "at what you and God manage to talk me into doing." She laughed, but he couldn't tell if she found his statement humorous, or if she were truly that relieved at being able to go. He added firmly, "I think we should just go by horseback in order to go more quickly, and we should leave this morning. Hopefully we can get there and back before bad weather sets in. We're not staying. It's there and back. Agreed?"

"Agreed," she said and kissed him. Then she vigorously began packing.

Eleanore was taken aback by a wave of nausea. Her earlier suspicions of being pregnant had become lost in the news from Sally. And now she wondered if James might call off the trip if he knew what she suspected. But she felt driven to make this journey and firmly decided to keep her thoughts to herself for now.

Eleanore felt deeply relieved as they set out right after breakfast. And, as on many occasions in the past, she was grateful to have Lizzie and Amanda available to look after the children. She knew all would be well in their absence, even though they weren't certain how many days they'd be gone.

They rode east to the Mississippi, where they crossed on a ferry, then continued north. They rode for hours. Eleanore was grateful for sunshine, and she managed to keep eating bits and pieces of biscuits she had in her saddlebags in order to avoid the increasing nausea. And James didn't seem to notice. They stayed at a hotel on the river that night, then set out again after breakfast. They'd not been riding long when Eleanore had no choice but to halt and quickly dismount, barely in time to find a place to throw up. She found James beside her before the heaving stopped. She'd long ago gone beyond feeling embarrassed over such things. She couldn't count the times he'd seen her throw up.

"Are you all right?" he asked.

"I'm fine," she insisted and walked back to the horse.

James considered the incident, and more importantly, the subtle hint of guilt in her eyes. She was keeping something from him. He followed her and took hold of her arm before she could mount. "You're pregnant," he said firmly. She looked down but didn't answer. "You're *pregnant,* and you didn't *tell* me? We're out on this ridiculous, *pointless* journey, and you're *pregnant?*"

"It is *not* pointless." She gazed at him with sharp eyes. "We both prayed about it and knew it was the right thing to do."

"Well, I didn't *know* you were pregnant."

"God knew," she said firmly.

"And you?" he countered. "Did *you* know?"

The guilt in her eyes returned. "I suspected."

"You believed you were pregnant and you didn't tell me?"

"I was afraid you wouldn't agree to do this."

"Well, you're right about that. Maybe we should just turn around and go home."

"No!"

"Do you recall how ill you got the last time you were pregnant? You couldn't get out of bed for weeks. What am I supposed to do if it hits you that hard and we're out in the middle of nowhere?"

"I'll be fine. We need to make this journey, James. Please . . . have some faith and just . . . take me to Nauvoo. I need to . . . see the temple . . . and see if the Saints are still nearby. Please."

Eleanore knew he was still angry by the way he sighed. It was one of those moments when she felt more like he was her father than her husband. He *was* more than twenty years older than she, but rarely did she feel like anything less than his equal. Even now, she knew his stern attitude was a result of his concern for her. Frustration showed in his eyes, but he reluctantly muttered, "Fine. But we're taking it slower. I don't care how long it takes to get there; we're not going to jeopardize your health. You need to be honest with me about how you're feeling. Do you understand?"

"Yes, thank you," she said and wrapped her arms around him.

They were soon on their way again, and Eleanore felt sure her prayers were being heard. They made good time, and she didn't feel

nearly as ill as she knew she could have. When they finally arrived on
the outskirts of Nauvoo, she felt sick with dread. They slowed their
pace as they rode into the beautiful city that Eleanore remembered so
well. But the bustle of activity and the sounds and sights of a thriving
community were absent. It was eerily quiet, lifeless, abandoned. The
sweet spirit that had been there before was missing. Instead, they
encountered horrible men with angry eyes who demanded to know
their purpose in being there. James coolly told them they were just
passing through and wondered about the status of a city with so
many beautiful homes and businesses standing empty. They were told
briefly about the religious fanatics who had attempted to overtake the
area, and how they'd finally been driven away.

"And what is that?" James asked nonchalantly, pointing to the
magnificent limestone structure in the distance, with its domed clock
tower reaching toward the sky.

"They called it a temple," came the reply. "Now it's nothing."

Eleanore's nausea increased for reasons that had nothing to do
with pregnancy. The last time she and James had been to Nauvoo, the
temple had been far from completed. Now its magnificence took her
breath away at the same time as her stomach tightened. She was
utterly relieved to move away from these horrible men, but she and
James both felt strangely compelled to get closer to the temple. It was
being guarded by the same kind of riffraff they'd encountered earlier,
but they seemed indifferent to the travelers who simply wanted to
take a moment and look up at the glistening edifice. And then they
rode on, finding a place in the woods where they could dismount and
hold each other and cry.

Once they'd eased their grief and regained some composure, they
found their way across the river and made inquiries as to where the
people were who had left Nauvoo. They found where they'd been, but
they had all moved on. Eleanore felt devastated and wondered over
the purpose of their journey. She'd wanted to see the temple, and
they'd done that. But the heartache involved had been far worse than
she'd expected. She'd seen for herself that what Sally had told her was
true. But most of all, she'd longed to see her friends, to embrace them
and try to offer some hope or support. And they were gone to Winter
Quarters—wherever that might be; somewhere in Nebraska they'd

been told. Eleanore longed to go there but knew in her heart they needed to return home. The weather was turning colder, and her symptoms were growing worse. Throughout the journey home, she found it difficult to feel sorry for herself, however, considering the exposure and illness of those who had no homes to return to.

By the time they got home, Eleanore felt sure she would never be warm again. And she couldn't help being utterly discouraged over the apparent lack of purpose in their journey to Nauvoo. She reminded herself that God's purposes were not always evident from a human perspective, but it still felt so pointless. After a hot bath and some time with the children, she crawled into bed and succumbed to the nausea and exhaustion she'd been fighting for many days. That night when James slipped into bed beside her, she couldn't hold back tears as she held him close.

"What is it?" he murmured gently.

"You were right," she said. "It *was* a pointless journey."

He sighed but didn't answer, and she knew he agreed with her. He finally said, "The temple is very beautiful. In spite of the circumstances, I'm glad we were able to see it."

"Yes, so am I. But it breaks my heart to think of . . ." She couldn't finish.

"Perhaps we needed to see it in order to more fully appreciate their sacrifice."

"Perhaps."

"Or perhaps . . ."

"What?" she pressed when he hesitated.

"Its image is so clear in my mind, Ellie. Just thinking of it makes me feel that . . ."

"That what?"

"That nothing is more important than what it represents . . . even if that's difficult to fully comprehend." After a few moments of silence he said, "Why do you suppose they worked so hard to complete it, to make it so perfect, when they knew they were leaving?"

"I suppose it's because . . . God asked them to build it. They did it to prove their faith, their devotion, perhaps."

"It seems that's all they do . . . is prove their devotion . . . over and over. I don't understand."

"Nor do I," she said, and her tears increased. "But it's like I've said before. It's not about the hardships of this life; it's about earning the blessings of eternity."

"I believe that, Eleanore. But surely it's difficult to see that perspective when you're ill and homeless and freezing."

Eleanore sniffled loudly. "I'm so worried . . . for Sally . . . and Miriam . . . for all of them."

"Yes, so am I. But you should rest."

"James," she said a minute later, "are you happy . . . about the pregnancy?"

He leaned up on one elbow. "Of course I am. Aren't you?"

"Yes, of course. It's just that . . . they'll be little more than two years apart . . . if the pregnancy goes full term."

"Do you think it won't?"

"There's no way of knowing. It took us four pregnancies to get Jamie. And you know how ill I get. Keeping up with Jamie could be—"

"We'll all help, of course. You must take very good care of yourself."

James held her close while she drifted off to sleep, and his mind wandered, vacillating between gratitude and disbelief. He thought of their good friends, wondering if they had shelter, enough to eat. Were they healthy, safe, freezing? While winter tightened around his own safe, comfortable home, he wondered how he might feel to be facing this pregnancy if they had no home. In that moment, he didn't bother pondering why he and Eleanore continued to feel so strongly about staying where they were and remaining separated from the Saints. He only felt deeply grateful that they were.

Chapter Two
THE NEW ARRIVAL

Three days after returning from Nauvoo, Eleanore found her husband in the barn and approached him with trepidation. "I have a favor to ask."

He gave her a sideways glance and kept pitching hay into the animals' stalls.

"I want to go to Winter Quarters, to see Sally and Miriam, and to . . . take some supplies. Some food and blankets, anything we can get into the wagon and—"

"Absolutely not," he said.

"You haven't even given yourself a moment to think about it."

"I don't need to think about it," he said and stopped to lean on the pitchfork. "Do you have any idea how far the Nebraska border is from here? And winter is setting in fast. I am *not* taking you *anywhere* in potentially bad weather, with freezing temperatures, *especially* while you're pregnant and not feeling well. It's ludicrous."

"How can it be ludicrous if I feel so strongly about it? Maybe they *need* what we can bring. They've been driven from their homes, and we sit here with abundance and security all around." James sighed loudly and she added, "Would you pray about it, please? If God asks us to do this, we cannot refuse. Surely He will protect and bless us."

"The history of our people makes it evident that protection does not necessarily coincide with doing God's will, and blessings can be difficult to define."

Eleanore couldn't argue with that, but she did add, "And perhaps we are the means to bless these people with the abundance that *we* have been blessed with."

"There are thousands of them, Eleanore. We can't possibly make that much difference."

"We can do our part. That's all God asks of anyone."

James sighed again. "I want to do God's will as much as you do, my dear." He showed a wan smile. "You're just braver than I am."

"Or more foolish," she said, looking at the ground.

"You're a good woman with a good heart. I'll pray about it."

"Thank you," she said with such confidence that he feared he would get the answer to drag his pregnant wife all the way to the Nebraska border in winter weather, and see her ill or worse in the process. Still, he couldn't help but admire her conviction.

"We'll find a way to do what we can to help them," he said. "If we can't *take* something, perhaps we can *send* something."

Eleanore nodded, but that didn't feel right. She spent the next twenty-four hours praying that James would be guided to reason and see the necessity of this. He was on his way out of the house, pulling on his gloves, when he said to her, "I'll be buying supplies today to take to Winter Quarters."

"Oh!" She wrapped her arms around him. "Thank you! When do we leave?"

"You are staying here. Frederick and I will take the supplies." She stepped back, stunned and disappointed. "I asked the Lord if I should go to Winter Quarters and share my abundance with these people. I felt definite peace over the matter. I asked if my wife should make the journey, and I felt stupor of thought. Simple as that, Mrs. Barrington. The Spirit has assured me that your being left in charge of a house full of women and children in our absence is sacrifice enough for you at this point. I will leave you well stocked on everything you need, but I don't know how long we'll be gone. I've spoken with Ralph; he and his mother will stay here at the house while we're gone. He's man enough to do anything Frederick or I would do. He's more than willing to help. For that and many other reasons, we are truly blessed. Clearly, the matter is in God's hands." He touched her face with his gloved fingers. "What's wrong? I thought you'd be happy. You're getting your wish."

She looked down. "Part of it, at least. I'm very grateful to you, but . . . I would prefer to come along." She put her hand over his against her face. "I don't want to be away from you for so long."

"I don't want that either," he said, "but this is the way it needs to be. You know as well as I do that many men have been called away to serve missions—sometimes for years." He lifted her chin and pressed his lips to hers. "Remember what you always tell me, my dear. What we do is not about the hardship of this life, it's about earning the rewards of eternity. All will be well." He kissed her again. "Now, I must go. I've already spoken with Frederick. We'll be leaving at dawn tomorrow. The farther we can travel in favorable weather, the better. I'm hoping this sunshine holds out. It's cold, but at least it's dry."

Eleanore sat down and cried once her husband left for town. She was grateful for his willingness to go to Winter Quarters, and it *did* ease the urgency she felt in wanting to do something to help her friends and many others. But she longed to see her friends. And the thought of being apart from James felt dreadful; she was already counting the days until he might return, even though she had no idea how long the journey would take.

That afternoon, Eleanore felt a dazed shock while she watched James and Frederick finish loading the wagons. There was barely enough room in each of them, beneath the cover, for a man to sleep on top of the tightly packed crates, sacks, and bedding. She noticed Lizzie hovering close to Frederick throughout the process, appearing as agitated as Eleanore felt. Occasionally, Frederick would pause in his work to speak to her or give her a tender kiss. This separation would clearly be as difficult for them as it would for her and James. At least they could commiserate in their loneliness.

With everything ready to go, the evening went as usual, except that Eleanore felt a tight dread in her chest to think of her husband leaving at dawn. She had no trouble admitting she was thoroughly dependent on his company; she had been since the day they'd married. She wasn't so concerned about managing the chores in the men's absence; it would be a challenge, but certainly nothing they couldn't handle. She had two able-bodied and hard-working women in her household, and Ralph, who had grown into a strong and capable man. But Eleanore couldn't imagine getting through even one day without feeling her husband's arms around her, without being able to talk through any thought she might have. He was her lover and her dearest friend. And he was leaving. She held him close in the dark, not wanting to sleep, not wanting to waste these remaining hours with oblivion.

Out of the silence he said, "You mustn't worry. All will be well."

"I'm not worried," she said. "I just don't want to be without you."

He sighed. "I don't want that either. But we both know it needs to be done." He lightened his voice to tease her. "Might I remind you that this was your idea?"

"This was *not* how I planned it, at all," she insisted, not amused with his attempt at humor.

More seriously he said, "God's plans for us are rarely what we expect." He leaned up on one elbow and touched her face. "I can assure you that when He let me know you were the right woman to be a governess for my children, I never imagined sharing my life with you this way." He kissed her brow. "He has blessed me far more than my own imagination could have ever wished."

"I would echo that," she said and lifted her lips to his. Trying to distract herself from his leaving, she said, "I wish I could have foreseen the future. I would have loved to see the look on your face when you interviewed me to be a governess if I'd told you I intended to become your wife and the mother of your children."

He chuckled. "And ordering me to do your bidding, day in and day out."

"I don't have to order you to do anything," she said and pressed her face to his chest. "You're so very good to me that there's no need." She wrapped her arms tightly around him. "I don't want you to go."

"Don't speak of that now," he said and kissed her, again and again, escorting her into the most blissful and magnificent aspect of their marriage. His tenderness and sincerity had grown through the years they had shared, and she felt most blessed among women to be this man's wife.

In spite of her resistance, Eleanore slept, wrapped securely in James's arms. She woke in the dark to hear him whisper, "I must go soon." He kissed her warmly, then got dressed and finished packing his bag for the journey.

The sun was barely emitting rays over the east horizon when Eleanore and Lizzie were left standing on the porch to watch their husbands move the horse-driven wagons toward the bridge, then slowly out of sight. The women went inside and sat together to share a good cry before they began the day with some faith and courage, reminding each other frequently of all they had to be thankful for, and how much worse it could be.

Eleanore managed getting through the days rather well, but at night she cried in her empty bed while she prayed fervently for James's health and safe return. She prayed, as always, for Sally and Miriam and their families, and for all of the Saints who were suffering and struggling while she kept warm in her lovely home, stocked with more than ample to eat. Daily she fought away guilt for being so richly blessed while others endured great hardship, and instead counted her blessings and simply wondered why she would be spared. She'd been told in more than one priesthood blessing that her path was different, and she believed her life had a specific purpose. But what? Of course, even now, they were in a position to offer some help and support. She had to be grateful for that. If they had been living in Nauvoo, they likely would have had to leave everything behind, and they would have nothing now to share with others in need. But her waiting and wondering seemed like so little sacrifice, even as desperately as she missed her husband.

On a brighter note, she enjoyed having Amanda and Ralph living under her roof all the time. Ralph had a delightful sense of humor and often had them all laughing while they'd gather in the parlor in the evenings. She got to know both him and his mother in a way she never had before. And one evening after the children had gone to bed, he talked for a long while with Eleanore and his mother about his feelings for Lu Bailey, the young woman he'd met at church. His interest in Lu had come up before, but never with such sincerity. Eleanore had noticed him talking to a lovely girl with brown hair, but she hadn't noticed much beyond an impression that the girl was very poor, and that she had timid eyes. Ralph was thoroughly taken with her, but apparently the uncle and aunt she lived with did not like Ralph coming around at all.

"Is it *you* they don't like," Eleanore asked, "or any male interest toward Lu in general?"

"I'm not certain," Ralph said. He went on to say that Lu's parents had both died of a fever when she was very young. Her aunt and uncle had never had children and were excessively guarded. Her aunt was quiet and seemed unhappy, while the uncle came across as gruff and unkind. Ralph sensed that the situation in Lu's home was far from ideal, although she'd never said anything to that effect.

"Why don't we invite her to dinner," Eleanore suggested. "I could speak with her uncle at church."

Ralph beamed. "Oh, that would be grand."

"I'll talk to him on Sunday, then."

The following Sunday it snowed so badly that they were unable to attend church. The Sunday after that, Eleanore spotted Lu with her aunt and uncle before the usual meeting began, but it wasn't until afterward that she was able to approach them.

"Hello, Mr. Bailey," she said brightly, holding Jamie on her hip while Iris stood nearby. The man peered at her with skeptical eyes, and she hurried to add, "My name is Eleanore Barrington, and—"

"You got a husband?" he demanded, with the silent implication that he disapproved of a woman approaching him for any reason.

"My husband is out of state on business for some weeks. I wanted the opportunity to meet you and your good wife." She held her hand out toward Lu's aunt. "Your name would be . . ."

"Mrs. Bailey," the woman's husband answered for her, and Eleanore had to drop her hand when no effort was made to take it.

Mrs. Bailey turned away, her eyes embarrassed, her countenance starkly uncomfortable. Eleanore pushed aside her concerns over the possible reasons for such a reaction and stuck to her purpose.

"It's a pleasure to meet both of you. Actually, I have a favor to ask. I believe you're acquainted with young Ralph Leichty. He is—"

"He's come around wanting to visit with our LuEllen," Mr. Bailey said, folding his arms stiffly.

"Yes, I believe he has. He's—"

"What's he got to do with you, Mrs. Barrington?"

Eleanore felt as if she were on trial, but fought to keep her wits about her. "He and his mother have both worked for our household for many years. While my husband is away they're staying at our home in order to help in his absence. Ralph is quite fond of your niece, and we would all like the opportunity to get to know her better. I wonder if we might invite her to come home with us from church and have dinner and visit. Ralph can bring her home later, and I will come along to chaperone. I can assure you that they will be attended continually." Impulsively she added, "Or if you prefer, both of you may come to dinner as well."

Eleanore saw in Mrs. Bailey's eyes that she very much liked that idea, and she wondered if this woman had any social contacts whatsoever. She was prone to think not when her husband added quickly, "Thank you, but no. We won't be wasting our time with idle chitchat. I suppose Lu may come over." He said it as if having the girl out of the way would be a blessing. Then he pointed a harsh finger at Eleanore, "But if she gets into any trouble, I'll be holding you responsible."

"We'll take very good care of her," Eleanore said, forcing back her frustration toward this man in order to sound polite. "And we'll have her home by eight." She began to walk away, then added as an afterthought, "Unless, of course, it storms." It was standard procedure in the community to avoid any travel at all during snowstorms for the sake of health and safety, and it was a common occurrence for people to end up staying at one another's homes when the weather made it necessary. "In that case, we'll get her home as soon as it's feasible. And I assure you, as I said, she'll be carefully chaperoned." Mr. Bailey simply made a disgruntled noise and walked away, taking his wife by the arm.

"That certainly went well," Eleanore said with sarcasm.

"What a disagreeable man," Iris commented. "Makes me grateful for the father I've got."

"Indeed," Eleanore said. "Remember that the next time your father is in a foul mood."

Iris chuckled, and they went to tell Ralph that Lu would be coming home with them. They were near the chapel doors chatting, and both young people lit up at the news. Lu sat close to Ralph on the trip home while he drove the buggy. At home, Eleanore was impressed with the way Lu easily took to helping in the kitchen. Her interaction with the family was comfortable, albeit she was a bit shy and quiet—not unlike her aunt. Eleanore suspected it likely had more to do with the home she'd been raised in as opposed to her personality. In the middle of the afternoon while the dinner dishes were being washed, Ralph pulled Eleanore aside and whispered, "It's Sunday. We'll be having our usual worship service."

"That's right," she said.

"But Lu is here."

Eleanore had taken for granted that the young woman knew Ralph well enough to know this aspect of his life. "Have you told her nothing?"

"Nothing," he said. "Aren't we supposed to keep the matter to ourselves?"

"Yes, but . . . I just assumed . . . well, I got the impression that you'd become good friends, and—"

"I've not said anything to her about my beliefs."

"Do you trust her?" Eleanore asked, wishing James was here to consult on such a decision. She simply had to do what she felt was best in his absence.

"I do; yes. But I don't want to do anything to bring any problems to your household or—"

"If you trust her and you feel good about it, then you should tell her. Simply make it clear that she mustn't tell anyone. We know all too well what the results can be if the wrong people know there are Mormons underfoot."

"Of course," Ralph said, and as soon as the kitchen was in order, Eleanore noticed him taking Lu down the hall to the library. The door remained open, but she left them to talk privately. A short while later, Lu joined them for the usual private worship service that took place in the parlor. They sang some simple hymns that Iris played on the piano. She'd done well with her minimal training, and she'd learned to play enough to give them a melody to follow. Ralph blessed and passed the sacrament, then they discussed a chapter from the Book of Mormon before closing with prayer. Mary Jane sat contentedly throughout the service, playing with some rag dolls. But Jamie was wiggly and noisy and made it difficult for Eleanore to relax. She was grateful for how the others helped with him, especially since she didn't feel well due to the symptoms of her pregnancy. Once they were finished Eleanore eagerly accepted Lizzie's offer to watch out for Jamie while she rested. When Eleanore got up a couple of hours later, everyone else was gathered in the kitchen, eating cake that Amanda had made, and talking and laughing. Lu seemed to be having a marvelous time, and Ralph was holding her hand. They were both clearly pleased to announce that it was snowing hard and Lu would have to spend the night. She ended up staying in the little house with Lizzie, sharing Mary Jane's room. Eleanore enjoyed having her around and hoped that her uncle would not be angry over the situation.

The following day, Eleanore felt especially ill and was grateful for Iris watching over Jamie. Eleanore mostly stayed in bed and was pleasantly surprised when Lu came to ask if there was anything she could do. They visited for nearly an hour while snow continued to fall, and Lu spent another night in Mary Jane's room. The following morning, Eleanore still felt compelled to stick close to her bed, overcome with nausea and exhaustion. Right after breakfast Lu came to say goodbye and to thank her.

"You've been so kind," Lu said. "I hope to come back soon."

"You're welcome any time," Eleanore told her.

Amanda rode with Ralph to take the girl home, and they returned to report that Mr. and Mrs. Bailey hadn't seemed at all ruffled over Lu being gone for so long. In fact, they seemed almost indifferent over the matter. It occurred to Eleanore that Mr. Bailey's overprotective nature stemmed more out of pride than any genuine concern for the girl.

Eleanore's worry over her husband settled in more deeply when more winter storms began to howl. One storm after another left her deeply troubled over James's and Frederick's welfare. Her blind courage in wanting to make the journey herself fell into perspective when it became a challenge, in the face of the wind and snow, just to get to the barn to gather the eggs. And with the symptoms of her pregnancy leaving her sick to her stomach and exhausted, she couldn't deny her own naiveté in believing she could have made the journey without risking her own health. However, this very thought deepened her concern for the thousands of women and children who had been driven from their homes with no choice but to make the journey to Winter Quarters.

Eleanore was grateful for Lizzie's help and companionship, but even more so for her perfect empathy as they speculated and prayed together over their husbands' welfare. Lizzie and Mary Jane moved temporarily into the big house, for company as well as convenience when the snow became deep and cumbersome. And Eleanore was grateful to have Amanda and Ralph there as well. They went home only on occasion when there was a break in the weather, just to make certain all was in order there. Eleanore found their company, as well as their help, priceless and high on her list of blessings. Without Ralph hauling wood, feeding the animals, and milking the cows, the absence of the men would be much more challenging. And he also did well at entertaining the children through long, cold winter days.

Lu began coming over nearly every Sunday. She became completely comfortable with the family as quickly as she came to know the truth of the gospel. But she knew her uncle would never allow her to be baptized, much less be actively involved. In fact, she felt certain if he even suspected she was having anything at all to do with another religion, the results would be disastrous. Eleanore didn't want to ask what exactly she might mean by that. The more she got to know of Mr. Bailey, the more she disliked him. It was not for her to judge him or his actions, but she could certainly keep herself at a safe distance. And she agreed wholeheartedly that nothing should ever be said to such a man regarding the presence of Mormons in the area. So, Lu read and studied while she was in their home, and Eleanore suspected that she and Ralph were quietly making plans to one day be married. Although neither of them had ever said anything to her, she could see it in their eyes. They'd grown to love each other very much. But they were young, and Ralph had very little put away that he could use to start a new life for his own family.

Eleanore felt blessed as she realized that while she'd not stopped missing her husband, she had found comfort and strength in his absence. The days merged into weeks until she honestly lost track of how long he'd been gone. She had hoped, as had everyone else, that the men would return before Christmas, but the holiday came and went without them. She missed James so badly that it hurt while they went about their usual traditions and celebrations, but she wondered what the holiday might be like for those who had so little and were surely suffering. And again she couldn't feel too sorry for herself.

As the new year arrived, Eleanore allowed herself to speak a thought she'd hardly dared even ponder. "Do you think," she said to Lizzie in a hushed voice, "that it's possible something's happened to them, that they won't be coming back?"

Lizzie didn't move her concentration from the bread she was kneading vehemently. "I'll not even consider it," she said, but her lack of surprise made it evident the idea wasn't new to her. "I have felt the Spirit's comfort in response to my prayers that they'll return safely. We must have faith that God will keep them well."

"Of course," Eleanore said and changed the subject.

The following morning, Eleanore woke before dawn and realized that she'd begun spotting blood. She felt sure she was losing the baby; however, she felt less panic than sorrow. She'd already lost three babies and knew well how to endure the process. But the thought of going through the loss—both physically and emotionally—without her husband felt like more than she could bear. She cried into her pillow and prayed with all the fervency of her soul that this baby would be spared, and that her husband would come home safely. Gradually, her prayers merged into an acceptance of God's will on both counts, whatever that might entail. Instead, she prayed for the strength and courage to endure whatever might be required of her. When she began cramping, she went carefully across the hall to where Lizzie and Amanda were sharing a room. She woke them and insisted that while there was no need to send for the doctor, she did need some help.

Eleanore went back to bed to wait out the process, aching for her husband to be with her, grieving for the loss of this baby she'd already grown to love, and praying for peace and fortitude. Later, she was surprised to wake up, which meant she had been sleeping. Never had she been able to sleep through the painful process of losing a baby. Once the bleeding and cramping had started, it had always worsened steadily. Lizzie moved from a chair to sit on the edge of the bed and brush Eleanore's hair back from her face. "How are you, darling? You've been sleeping for hours."

"Hours?" she echoed, her surprise increasing as she realized she felt no pain. A quick check made it evident the bleeding had completely stopped.

"Could it be possible?" Eleanore murmured, holding tightly to Lizzie, feeling herself tremble. "Could it be a false alarm?" She sobbed softly. "Has God answered my prayers and saved this child?"

"Anything is possible," Lizzie replied, "so long as it is His will."

They cried together, then knelt and prayed, holding hands. Together they expressed gratitude for all they had been blessed with, and together they pleaded for the safe return of their husbands, and for the safety and well-being of all who shared their beliefs.

Although a new series of storms set in the following week, Eleanore had no further symptoms to indicate there was any problem with her pregnancy. But she did become plagued with a deep worry for her husband, and even as she fought to conceal it, she prayed harder than she ever had in her life that James and Frederick would come home safely, and soon. The weeks were beginning to take their toll. Coupled with her worry for the men was worry for Sally and Miriam and their families, and others who were enduring this winter under such difficult circumstances. She cried daily over the matter and continually wondered about God's purposes.

On a cold afternoon that was deceptively sunny, Eleanore was stoking the fire in the kitchen while Amanda mixed a cake batter and Lizzie scrubbed a dirty pot. Mary Jane and Jamie were both napping. Ralph was doing chores in the barn, and Eleanore had just sent Iris out to see if he needed any help, mostly because her chattering was wearing on her mother's nerves.

Eleanore's heart raced at the sound of Iris shouting from outside. She couldn't understand what she was saying and wondered if the child was hurt. She hurried toward the door just as it flew open and Iris shouted, "Wagons are coming, Mama. They're just over the bridge. I think it's Papa!"

Eleanore grabbed her cloak as Amanda muttered with glee, "I'll listen for the little ones. You two run along."

She stepped onto the side porch with Lizzie at her shoulder. "It *is* them," Lizzie murmured, and they both started to cry amidst a burst of laughter, hugging each other tightly as Iris ran across the yard, laughing and shouting. Eleanore's heart leapt as the lead wagon came to a halt and she heard James's laughter across the distance. He helped Iris onto the seat beside him and hugged her tightly, then drove on. Before the wagons were stopped beside the house, Eleanore and Lizzie ran out into snow that was much deeper than the shoes that barely covered their ankles. James jumped down and took Eleanore into his arms with a desperation that matched her own. She held to him tightly then took his face into her hands, fingering the beard he'd grown and the hair hanging down over his neck. He touched her face as well and kissed her over and over, murmuring her name.

"Good heavens, you're freezing," she said, once she had assured herself that he was really here and that his love for her had not waned.

He chuckled. *"That* would be a true statement, Mrs. Barrington. I haven't been warm since I left here. Well," he shrugged, "I think I was warm a couple of times in Mark and Sally's house, once we got it built, but that was only a few minutes here and there. It was far too crowded to stay long."

"You saw them, then?"

"Oh, yes."

"And Andy and Miriam?"

"Yes, of course. We helped finish their house as well—if you could call it a house. It's shelter and it's adequate." He kissed her again. "Oh, how I missed you!"

"And I missed you!" She kissed him back. "Are you well?"

"I'm fine," he said and kissed her again. After hugging her tightly once more, he laughed and glanced down, putting a hand to her rounded belly. "You're blossoming, my dear."

"Yes, I believe I am," she said, unable to hold back new tears.

"What is it?" he asked, touching her chin.

She shook her head. "Everything's fine. You must tell me everything!"

"All in good time. There's something important that needs to be taken care of first." He stepped back and found Ralph beside him, as if waiting for orders, or at least a greeting. The boy looked up to James like a father, even though they met eye to eye. James laughed and gave the boy a quick hug, then said, "Could you help Frederick care for the horses? We can unload the wagons later."

"Yes, sir," Ralph said eagerly as James helped Iris down. Then Ralph jumped onto the seat to move the wagon into the barn.

"Hold up there," James said. "Let me get something first."

Eleanore noted Frederick and Lizzie holding each other close while James walked to the back of the wagon he'd been driving and moved aside the cover, exposing the opening. She expected him to bring out his bag. She gasped to see a young boy wrap his arms around James's neck. He was bundled too tightly in a blanket and ragged clothing for her to even see his coloring or get a good look at his face before he buried it against James's shoulder, but he was smaller than Iris. Eleanore saw James meet her eyes with a silent, penetrating question. She was reminded of years ago when the children had found Jack, the dog that was still a part of the family. She could almost imagine James saying, "May we keep him?" Instead he said, "This is Benjamin. He's going to be staying with us." He looked at the child as if he meant to make more introductions, but the boy only buried his face more deeply into James's coat. James said to Eleanore, "I'll explain everything later." He moved toward the door. "Right now we need to get him warm. Iris, tell Amanda to heat some water for a bath." Iris ran ahead, and James added, "He's long over the symptoms of the fever, but it's left him weak. He's not been doing well. Perhaps he could make good use of David's clothes once he's cleaned up."

"Of course," Eleanore said. "I know right where they are."

She followed her husband up the stairs, then grew suddenly weak as an unexpected warmth rushed through her, and her heart quickened. Earthly time stood still while a ray of heavenly light seemed to descend there on the stairwell. She couldn't see it literally, but she could feel it, illuminating her husband and the child in his arms as he stopped and turned to look at her. "Are you all right?" he asked.

"I'm marvelous," she said, and he smiled. "It's just so good to have you home."

"It's good to *be* home," he said and hurried on. He went into the room that had once been David's. It had been unused since the boy's death, but it had been kept clean and in order. His clothes and most of his personal things had been long packed away, but some of his toys remained. Eleanore had offered to let Ralph sleep here when he was staying at the house, but he insisted that he preferred the long sofa in James's office. James sat on the bed, keeping Benjamin on his lap while he removed worn shoes and ragged socks, talking softly to him as he did, assuring him that everything was going to be all right now. Once James had removed the tattered piece of gray wool wrapped around the boy's head and neck, Eleanore got a good look at him. His coloring was fair, not unlike David's. His eyes were sad and timid, and he looked weak and weary to the point of almost being despondent. Eleanore knelt beside him and put a hand to his little face. He looked at her with questioning eyes, then at James, who said, "This is Mrs. Barrington. She's going to help me take care of you from now on."

Again James gave her a searching gaze, silently asking for approval. She smiled and nodded slightly before she said to Benjamin, "That's right. Everything will be fine now." She didn't know what had happened to leave the child alone and in this condition, but it was as if her heart felt what her mind didn't know, and it took all her willpower not to burst into heaving sobs on his behalf.

Amanda came into the room with Ralph right behind her, carrying two buckets of heated water. "I had water on the stove," she said, "so it's already hot; there'll be more in a few minutes." She took Benjamin's hand while she said to James, "Why don't you let me get him cleaned up while you do the same. I know how to take care of little boys."

James introduced Ralph and Amanda to Benjamin and offered some brief explanations and assurances, then they left the child in Amanda's care. Eleanore took her husband's hand and led him to the bedroom where she closed the door, pulled him into her arms, and lifted her lips to his while she unbuttoned his coat.

"Eleanore," he murmured and kissed her again in a way that he would never do in front of other people, "I'm so grimy and—"

"I don't care," she said and pushed his coat to the floor, kissing him again.

"We heated water and tried to clean up when we could but—"

"I don't care," she said again.

The passion they shared was brief, but it filled Eleanore with the security and strength of his presence that she had so deeply missed. Afterward he held her close in silence, finally admitting, "There's so much I want to say, want to ask you . . . I don't know where to begin."

"There will be plenty of time to catch up," she said. "Tell me about Benjamin." She firmly added what she already knew in her heart, "He's meant to stay with us, isn't he—permanently."

James lifted his head to look at her. Tears glistened in his eyes. "How I prayed you would know that for yourself!"

"I *do* know." She smiled and touched his face. "Tell me about him."

Eleanore saw many emotions pass through James's eyes before he pressed his face to her shoulder and wept. He cried like a lost child, sobbing like she'd not heard since David had died. She wondered about the source of his grief and cried silent, unheeded tears herself without knowing why. When his tears finally quieted, he said with a cracking voice, "I helped bury his parents. They died within hours of each other. Ben was the only one left in his family. He lost a sister in Kirtland, another in Far West, two brothers in Independence, and a brother in Nauvoo."

"Good heavens." Eleanore drew in her breath and leaned up to look at him, as if seeing his eyes could assure her it was true. "How?"

New tears showed there. "A fire started by the mob took one. The others . . . exposure, fever." He shook his head as his expression became tormented. "All a result of being driven from their homes in the winter."

Eleanore cried with him. "How can they bear such things?"

"I don't know," he said and closed his eyes. Tears leaked from the corners of his eyes into his hair. "I've never seen . . . never imagined . . . anything so horrible. Never."

Eleanore allowed a moment for that to sink in. "Not even . . . losing David?"

"No." He shook his head again and sobbed. "I watched my son die . . . in a warm bed . . . with plenty available to feed him. I buried him in a proper grave." He sobbed again and took hold of her with some kind of desperation. "Oh, Eleanore," he breathed. "The sickness, the hunger. They were freezing, dying. And yet . . ." His tone changed. He sighed and rolled his head back on the pillow to look at her. Again he shook his head, disbelieving and doubtful while his eyes took on an unearthly glow. "I've never witnessed anything so . . . incredible. The peace and hope among these people is unparalleled, Eleanore. God is with them in their afflictions."

Eleanore took in his transformation of countenance in a matter of moments. And he *had* changed since she'd seen him last. There was a conviction in his eyes that she'd only seen glimmers of in the past. She wanted to talk to him for hours, but the sound of children in the distance reminded them they would be missed. "We'll talk later," he said. "Just . . . tell me . . . I was right to bring Benjamin home with me."

"Were you worried?" she asked lightly. "Did you think I would tell you to take him back?"

"No, of course not. I just need to hear it. I'm not accustomed to making life-altering decisions without my wife concurring. But I knew it was right. There were many families willing to take him in, but they're all living in crowded conditions and barely surviving. Brother Brigham agreed that he was meant to come with me."

Eleanore sat up. "Brigham Young?"

"Yes."

"You spoke with the prophet?"

"A number of times, actually." He sat beside her and took her hand. "He told me to give you a message." He intensified his gaze and tightened his hold on her fingers. "He said that a time would come when our being in this place would give great aid to the Saints." She took a sharp breath and held it as he added, "And he said that you would be greatly blessed for your commitment to living the gospel."

"He really said that?" she asked on an exhale.

"He really did. And you'd best believe him. He *is* a prophet, Eleanore. It was the same sure feeling I had when we met Brother Joseph. He's an extraordinary man." He kissed her quickly. "I'll tell you more later. I don't want to leave Benjamin too long; he's naturally traumatized. And I haven't even seen little Jamie yet." He kissed her again. "Oh, how I missed you!"

She smiled and touched his face. "I'll sit with Benjamin while you get cleaned up. You can tell us everything over supper."

Eleanore left him with one more kiss, amazed but not surprised at how just having him home made everything better—everything! She found Amanda sitting with Benjamin, who was clean and wearing one of David's nightshirts. The child was sound asleep in David's bed. Combined with thoughts of all this boy had suffered, Eleanore felt stunned at the irony of seeing him there in David's place.

"It would seem we have a new member of the family," Amanda whispered, coming to her feet.

"Yes, we do," Eleanore said. "Thank you. I'll sit with him now."

"Iris is watching out for little Jamie," she said. "I'll check on them and get supper cooking."

"Thank you," Eleanore repeated.

While James was bathing, Ralph brought his things into the house, and Eleanore sat with Benjamin, who continued to sleep. She prayed in silence, thanking God for her husband's safe return, and for the gift of this sweet child in her home. Just watching him in slumber generated a warm sensation around her heart. Her maternal instincts took hold fully. She'd not exchanged a word with him but knew beyond any doubt that God wanted her to be a mother to this boy.

Eleanore heard a sound and looked up to see James standing in the open doorway, buttoning the cuffs of a clean shirt, his face newly shaven. "I remember you," she whispered, not wanting to disturb the child.

He smiled and came toward her, bending to kiss her. "Oh, it's so good to be home," he murmured and kissed her again.

"Amen," she said.

He sat on the edge of the bed and gently pushed Benjamin's hair back off his face, as if he'd done it a thousand times. She wondered how many weeks he'd been caring for the boy. He glanced around the room and said to Eleanore, "It feels right, doesn't it, to have him here."

"Yes, it does."

"Perhaps David is watching out for his new brother."

"I'm certain of it," Eleanore said. "Will we be adopting him officially, then?"

"Yes. I have everything we need to start the process." He turned to look at her. "But our stewardship will only be for this life. He will be with his family for eternity." Eleanore felt warmth from this statement even before he added, "They're all together now, except for this one." He touched the boy's hair again. "Apparently he has something important to do in this world before he joins his family. In the meantime, we will be his family."

"How old is he?"

"Ten."

"Small for his age," she said.

"He's been ill a great deal. Apparently he got the malaria right after they arrived in Nauvoo, and he's never been the same. His parents kept expecting to lose him, but he's held on. He became ill again after leaving Nauvoo, although he's doing much better." James let out a weighted sigh. "But I don't know that he would have survived the winter had he remained. It's the sick and the weak who are dying."

Eleanore took in the depth of such a statement and couldn't hold back more tears. She asked quietly, "And what of Sally and Mark? And Miriam and Andy? And the children? Are they well?"

"Yes, actually," he said. "It took us a while to find them. There are several settlements, several thousand people all together. Sally was so happy to see me she cried for ten minutes. They were in the process of building a little block house to get them through the winter. We helped them finish it. The place is so tiny it's a wonder they can even get any sleep. But they were grateful and happy to be there. Their family has had some illness, but not so serious as others. The same goes for Miriam and Andy and their family. When we left they were all rather well and in good spirits. Most of the people were in good spirits." His eyes grew distant. "There's a song they sing. It was written recently by one of the Saints. It's spread through the camps; they sing it often. Its words go round and round in my head."

"Sing it to me," she said, knowing he had a fine voice and that he always did well at singing the hymns they shared on Sundays.

He gave her a dubious glance. "Later; I'm not sure I'm suited to a solo. I need Frederick's voice to make mine tolerable. But Benjamin can outdo both of us. He kept us singing it on the journey home, over and over. I think it helped us keep going, especially through the storms. Sometimes we just had to camp and wait it out. And we'd all sleep in one of the wagons, with Benjamin between us to keep him warm."

Eleanore tried to block out the image of how difficult the journey had been for them. She said, "Tell me the words, then."

"There are many verses."

"Your favorite then."

"It's all beautiful."

"Tell me the words that go round and round the most," she said, sensing the song meant a great deal more to him than his minimal explanation indicated.

He looked at her firmly and said with a crack in his voice, *"Why should we mourn or think our lot is hard? 'Tis not so; all is right.*

Why should we think to earn a great reward if we now shun the fight? Gird up your loins; fresh courage take. Our God will never us forsake."
He closed his eyes, and tears trickled out as he continued, "*We'll find the place which God for us prepared, far away in the west; where none shall come to hurt or make afraid. There the Saints will be blessed. We'll make the air with music ring, shout praises to our God and King. Above the rest these words we'll tell — All is well! All is well!*"

"Oh, that *is* beautiful," Eleanore said when he'd finished.

"You didn't tell her the best part," Benjamin said and opened his eyes, bringing them to the realization that he was awake.

"No." James gave him a sad smile and wiped his shirtsleeve over his face, "I didn't tell her your favorite part. Why don't you tell her? She's going to be your mother now."

Benjamin turned to look at Eleanore, and she went to her knees beside the bed, taking his hand into hers. "Hello, Benjamin," she said, touching his face with her other hand. "I'm so glad that you came to live with us. Our family just hasn't seemed right since . . ."

"Since David died?" Benjamin asked.

"That's right. I think we needed you to be here; we just didn't know it yet."

"This was David's room," James said. "Now it's yours, although you might have to share it with your new brother when he gets a little older." He took the child's other hand. "Are you getting warm yet?" The child nodded, then silence fell.

Eleanore said, "Why don't you tell me your favorite part of the song?"

"Sing it for her," James urged. "You sing it so well."

Benjamin's eyes turned timid. "Will you sing it with me?"

"Of course," James said, and Benjamin immediately started to sing, with James joining him in a voice that quickly became strained with emotion.

"*And should we die before our journey's through, happy day! All is well! We then are free from toil and sorrow, too. With the just we shall dwell!*"

Eleanore's heart burned in her chest as the lyrics—and their meaning for this child and the family he'd lost—permeated her being. Benjamin didn't cry as he sang, but *she* did. And so did James. Again she thought that she'd not seen him cry so much since David's death.

"But if our lives are spared again to see the Saints their rest obtain, oh how we'll make this chorus swell—All is well! All is well!"

When they were finished, Eleanore could only take the child in her arms and hold him close, relieved to feel him return her embrace tightly. And then he started to cry. Eleanore looked at James over the top of Benjamin's head, then James wrapped his arms around both of them.

A few minutes later Iris brought Jamie into the room. James was so happy to see them he couldn't stop laughing. Then he introduced the children to Benjamin, who said little and kept close to James, but he seemed comfortable and content, and he was certainly polite.

When supper was ready, James carried Benjamin down to the dining room and sat him on a chair. The child ate voraciously. James and Frederick both commented numerous times how good everything tasted, and how weary they'd become of what they could manage to cook over an open fire in poor weather.

At the table, James told the story, with Frederick filling in the pieces, of their journey to the Nebraska border and what they'd encountered when they'd arrived. "It took us a while to find our friends," he said. "When we found them they were living in tents, trying to finish building block houses and—"

"What's a block house, Papa?" Iris asked.

"A very small cabin," he said, "made of square wood beams with mud pressed between them to keep the weather out. We helped them finish their homes, which were so small there was barely room for all of them to sleep close together and move about enough to make their meals. But they were so grateful to have them."

"Much better than a tent or covered wagon at keeping the wind and snow out," Frederick said.

They talked of their friends and others, and of their appreciation for the supplies they'd brought, and how they'd felt guided as to who to disperse them to. They'd helped build some other block houses during their stay, had attended church services, and had helped bury the dead. While much of what they reported was difficult to hear, both men spoke of the peace and joy among most of the people in spite of their dire circumstances. And when they spoke of encountering Brigham Young, there was a light in their eyes. He'd taken a personal interest in the illness and deaths of Benjamin's parents, considering the great losses the family had already suffered. The Jensens and Plummers had all been well acquainted with Benjamin's family, and they had also been in the final group to leave Nauvoo. James asked Benjamin if he would tell everyone about that. Eleanore saw the boy overcome a degree of his timidity as he talked rather maturely about those final days in Nauvoo, the cannon fire that was terrifying to a child, and their leaving nearly everything behind. He spoke matter-of-factly about being cold and hungry, and how a flock of quail had miraculously flown into camp. "A gift from God," he called it. Then rescue parties had arrived from Winter Quarters, sent by Brigham Young to bring them to join the Saints. And there he and his parents had all become ill; his parents never recovered.

Silence, broken only by some sniffles, followed Benjamin's story. James lightened the mood by saying how grateful he was to have Benjamin in their home, and that they'd all returned safely to find that everyone had been well in their absence.

Before bed they all knelt together to pray, as they always did. James carried Benjamin back up the stairs to his new room. He had no trouble walking but was too weak to go up and down the stairs. James and Eleanore left him there while they spent a few minutes with Iris, who was glad to have her father home to tuck her into bed. James carried Jamie with him while they checked on Benjamin and made certain he had all he needed.

"Now, our room is right across the hall," James told him. "If you need anything at all, just knock on the door. There's a lamp and matches right here on the table by the bed."

"I'll be all right," Benjamin said firmly. "It's nice to be warm."

"Yes, it is," James agreed heartily and kissed the boy's brow. "We'll see you in the morning."

Eleanore kissed him as well, and James followed her to their bedroom with Jamie in his arms. He played with the baby for a few minutes before Eleanore sat to rock him to sleep. James sat on the edge of the bed to remove his boots, then he lay back with an exhausted sigh. Eleanore considered the events of the day and all she'd learned of what her husband had been doing these many long weeks while she and her children had been safe and warm in their lovely home. She thought of those who were suffering, and of James's efforts on their behalf. She thought of how much she'd missed him, and how glad she was to have him safely back with her.

"I love you, James Barrington," she said.

He rolled onto his side and tucked his arm beneath his head. "I love you too," he said, as if it were the first time he'd uttered the words. "You're an amazing woman, Eleanore. I want you to know how grateful I am that you were so firm about the need to take supplies. I *needed* to do this. It was the hardest thing I've ever done. But it changed me, Ellie."

"I can see that," she said. "And as soon as you put your son to bed, I want you to tell me how."

James stood and took the sleeping Jamie from her arms. "He's grown so much just since I've been gone."

"He's nearly twenty months now," she said and followed James into the nursery where he laid the baby in the crib and pressed a hand over his thick, dark hair. He turned and pulled Eleanore into his arms and just held her for a long moment before they went together back to their bedroom. He stoked the fire while she undressed for bed, then they lay close together beneath the covers. He told her how nice it was to be warm, and to be with her, and he talked more of his experiences during their time apart, sharing feelings that were too tender to share with everyone, and recounting images too traumatic to voice freely.

"There was this moment . . ." he muttered. "I was standing there with a shovel in my hand, more cold and exhausted than I'd ever been in my life, throwing dirt into the grave where Benjamin's parents were buried together. There were no caskets available. The bodies were wrapped in blankets. I stopped what I was doing and . . . out of nowhere . . . I remembered this man I used to be. Lord of the manor with a house full of servants. And I wondered what I'd done to get myself into this position. I looked around at the people there, and it was like I felt their lives pass before my eyes, felt their convictions go into my heart like a bullet. And I had to thank God for leading me away from that life. I would never want to go back, Eleanore. To be so oblivious to the plight of humankind, to be without cause or purpose, to have so little meaning in my life beyond a simple concern for the well-being and happiness of my children. I felt so grateful for the path that had brought me to such an utterly miserable and overwhelmingly incredible moment. And I realized it was *you* who put me on this path, every step of the way. My love and my gratitude for you blossomed in that moment, Eleanore." He chuckled without humor. "I still wonder how I could have felt such profound gratitude and peace in such a moment, but I did. I knew Benjamin's parents were together and free from pain and sorrow. And I knew that one day you and I would be together the same way. I can't explain it; I only know I'm forever changed. And when I realized that Benjamin was meant to be in our home, it was as if some door to heaven had opened for me. He's filled a hole in my heart, Ellie. He's such a sweet boy, so much like David. It's like God spared him as a gift for us. And I wonder why we would be so blessed. I will never again take for granted the simple bounties that surround us: our peace and security, the abundance we enjoy each and every day." He tightened his arms around her. "I don't know what our purpose is in this place, my dear, but I know we have one. And with time we will come to understand."

Eleanore absorbed the faith glowing in his expression and silently thanked God for giving her such a husband as this, and for bringing him safely home to her.

Chapter Three
H A U N T E D

In spite of exhaustion, James didn't want to sleep. He preferred to just bask in the nearness of his sweet wife and the warmth and comfort of his surroundings. In the glow of a pleasant fire he pressed a hand over her swollen belly and uttered, "How have you been while I was away, my darling? I worried for you."

"I'm fine," she said after a moment's hesitation, and with a subtle tremor in her voice. "Everything's fine."

He looked into her face. "Why do you say it like that? Did something happen?"

"Only that . . . I thought I was losing the baby. I had all the symptoms, just like before. Then it stopped. But I was so afraid. I didn't know how I would endure such a thing without you. But I prayed for strength and knew somehow I would get through. Then the symptoms stopped. It was a miracle, James."

He pressed a hand into her hair. "It would seem both our prayers were heard, my dear. I prayed constantly that you would be strong and protected in my absence. Many times I felt comforted."

Eleanore wrapped her arms tightly around him. "We are truly blessed."

"Indeed we are," he said and kissed her.

They talked for a while longer, mostly of what the children had been doing while James had been gone, and the trivialities of the household that he normally would have been involved with. They finally slept with the promise to catch up more as time allowed.

Eleanore rose early and let James sleep, sensing his exhaustion. Iris and Jamie were both still asleep as well. She peered into the open door of Benjamin's room to find that he'd stoked the fire and was sitting in front of it, wrapped in a blanket.

"May I join you?" she asked, and he looked up.

He nodded and repeated what he'd said the night before. "It's nice to be warm." Eleanore sat down beside him and he added, "I don't know why I get to live here with you while so many people are cold and hungry."

"I've wondered many times myself why God would guide us to stay in this place when others have gathered together and have suffered so much. I don't know the answers, Benjamin. I only count my blessings and try to remain willing to do whatever God might ask of me."

His eyes showed understanding, and he said, "You can call me Ben. My old family called me Ben."

"If you prefer, that would be fine."

"What should I call you?" he asked with further evidence of a maturity beyond his years. Surely all that he'd endured had forced him to grow up too quickly; but he'd done it well. There was no sign of bitterness or anger in him.

"I'm going to be your mother now," she said, "but if you don't feel ready to call me that, it's all right. You may call me Eleanore or—"

"I want to call you Mother," he said. "You remind me of my mother. You don't look like her, but you're kind like her. And you talk about God as if you know each other; she did that too."

"I would have liked to know her," she said and Ben looked into the fire. A minute later she added, "I hope you don't mind using David's clothes until we can have some made for you. He was a little older than you when he died, but I'd saved some that he'd grown out of with the hope that we might have another boy who could wear them someday."

"Won't it make you sad to have me wear David's clothes?" he asked.

"Not at all," she said. "We know David is in a better place, just like your family is."

"But you must miss him. My mother always missed my brothers and sisters, even though she knew they were in a better place."

"Of course I miss him," she said. "I love him very much. But I think he would be happy to see you make good use of things he doesn't need any more."

Eleanore felt compelled to put her arm around him and was pleased when he snuggled up close to her. He asked in a timid voice, "Are you sure it's all right if I call you Mother?"

"Of course it is. I'd be very happy if you would."

"Even though you're not my real mother?" While Eleanore was considering the irony, he added, "Do you think it will be all right with Iris if I call you Mother?"

"I'm certain it will be. She told us last night that she was glad you've come to live with us. But I want to ask you something. What do you suppose is the most important thing that a parent gives to a child?"

Ben looked thoughtful. James's voice came from behind them. "It's love, of course." He walked toward them and sat on the other side of Ben. "Love is the magic that binds people together, and it's more important than sharing the same blood." He leaned closer to the boy and said, "I'm going to tell you a secret about our family; a magical secret. Eleanore is David and Iris's mother, but she did *not* give birth to them." Ben's eyes widened. He looked at Eleanore, then at James again as he added, "David and Iris's mother died a long time ago, but even before I married Eleanore, she loved them so much that the magic of her love made her a true mother to them. You will be with your own mother and father again someday, but while we are here on this earth, we will be your parents. And you will never be any less important to us than David, or Iris, or Jamie, or any other children who might be born into our family."

James hugged Ben tightly while he took Eleanore's hand, saying, "Good morning, my dear."

"Good morning," she replied then heard Jamie from the other room and left Ben in her husband's care. Throughout the day, Eleanore felt a whole spectrum of emotions with having James back home, along with the new addition to their family he'd brought with him. Her gratitude felt as deep as her sorrow as she considered all that Ben had been through in his young life, and she likewise pondered the sacrifices of so many others. Her heart swelled with admiration for both her husband and Frederick, for all they'd done to help their friends, along with many other Saints, in Winter Quarters. And her heart ached for those who were suffering and struggling with memories of their beautiful city left abandoned.

Eleanore was delighted to see how quickly Ben felt at home. After breakfast he stuck close to James while chores were done, then he joined Iris for the usual school lessons at the kitchen table. It was evident that Ben hadn't had much education, but he was eager to learn and caught on quickly. Eleanore looked forward to seeing him progress. After lunch Iris invited him to spend some time with her. They read together and played with some old toys of David's that surely held little interest for her, but she seemed eager to help Ben feel comfortable. Eleanore took a nap while Jamie did, then helped put supper on, delighted to simply have her husband around the house in his usual way. Each time their paths crossed he would stop to squeeze her hand or give her a kiss, and she wondered what she had ever done without him. She never wanted to be apart from him again.

At the supper table James said to Ralph, "So, my boy, I've heard from everyone but you about the happenings in my absence. What have you been up to?"

"Oh, not much," Ralph said with a comfortable smile.

James chuckled. "That's not what I hear. Rumor has it that a certain young lady has spent many Sundays here while I've been gone."

"Yes, that's true," Ralph said with a sheepish smile.

"And how is Lu Bailey?" James asked.

"She's well as far as I know," Ralph said. "Other than Sundays I hardly see her. Mr. Bailey isn't real keen on my visiting. I've met her in town a few times, but it's hard for her to get away."

James leaned back in his chair, "Do you think Mr. Bailey has something against you, or is it male suitors in general that he wants to keep away from his niece?"

"Likely both," Ralph said.

"How is that possible?" Lizzie asked. "I don't understand how anyone can not like such a fine young man."

"Well." Ralph looked down with an embarrassed chuckle. "He did catch me knocking on Lu's bedroom window one evening."

"Ralph!" Amanda said with astonishment.

"I just needed to talk to her for a minute," he said directly to his mother. "I'd gone to the front door, but he wouldn't let me see her, and I didn't want her to think I hadn't come when I'd told her I would. If the man were even remotely reasonable, this situation would sure be a lot easier. He is absolutely the most cantankerous, miserable human being I've ever met."

"You mustn't speak ill of others, son," Amanda said.

"I'm just stating a fact," he said without apology. "Lu tells me that living there is like being in prison. And her aunt feels the same way. She's just too afraid to speak up."

"Does Mr. Bailey hurt them?" Eleanore asked. She'd always wondered but had never found the appropriate moment to ask.

"Only if he gets *really* upset," Ralph said. "They've both learned not to upset him."

"That's terrible!" Eleanore gasped.

"Yes, it is," James said, "but it's not any of our business."

"Well, it's *my* business," Ralph declared. "Once I marry Lu, she'll be my responsibility, not his." Everyone but his mother was surprised.

"So," James chuckled, "I guess I don't need to ask my second question, which was: how serious is this?"

Ralph smiled. "I figured it was coming, so I just thought I'd let you know where I stand. After all, we're family. And now you know. I love her, and I'm going to marry her. I've already asked her, but of course we don't want anyone else to know for obvious reasons."

"Of course," Eleanore said.

"I'm saving every penny I can, and once I have enough to be able to care for her properly, I'll be marrying her."

"What he really means," Amanda said, "is that he needs enough money to *run away* with her to get married. He's certain Mr. Bailey will not let Lu go without a fight, and they feel this is best. Of course, there's plenty of room at the house, and it will be Ralph's eventually anyway, so that's not a problem. We all feel it would be best if we give the matter a little time."

"That sounds wise," James said. "If time passes and you're certain this is the right decision, we'll do anything we can to help you—so long as it's legal," he finished with a smirk. They all knew that Ralph was a fine young man with strong integrity and high moral principles. He lived the gospel in every aspect of his life. Eleanore couldn't help but think that Lu was a very lucky young woman—at least she would be when Ralph got her out from under her uncle's roof.

"Thank you," Ralph said, smiling as well. "I promise I'll make every effort to keep it legal." He looked mildly panicked and added, "Eloping *isn't* illegal, is it?"

"Of course not." James chuckled. "Lu is plenty old enough to be married if she chooses."

"Then it's all good," Ralph said. "So, I'd like to hear more about Winter Quarters. I miss the Plummers. It's never seemed right around here without them."

"It certainly hasn't," Eleanore agreed, and the others echoed the sentiment.

"You say they're all well, then?" Ralph asked.

"They were, yes. We can hope and pray it stays that way. There was much illness. But there are plans to start moving west once the weather clears and preparations can be made. Brother Brigham plans to head out with a vanguard company and blaze the trail for others to follow."

"Do you think they can go far enough into the wilderness to never be bothered again?" Ralph asked.

"We can hope and pray for that, as well," James said. "They believe God has prepared a place especially for His people."

"Yes, but Moses wandered in the wilderness for forty years with the people of Israel," Lizzie said. "I do worry for them."

"God willing, it won't take our people that long," James said, and Eleanore felt warmed to hear him claim the Saints as his own people. "And with any luck it won't be too many years before God allows us to join them—preferably in a place where they are safe and secure."

"Amen," the adults at the table all said at once.

After supper was over and cleaned up, Ralph and Amanda went home for the night, and the rest of the family gathered in the parlor to read together until it was time for bed. James carried Ben up the stairs and personally tucked all of the children in for the night. Eleanore tagged along and was pleased to hear Ben say that he liked living here. And Iris said that she liked having Ben for a brother. She declared that while having Ben there made her think more of David, it made her miss him less.

"I feel exactly the same way," James said and doused the lamp.

Once Jamie was down as well, James and Eleanore talked late into the night, still trying to catch up on their many weeks apart. Eleanore was glad to be able to fall asleep in his arms, then she woke in the darkness to the sound of a child crying—too old to be Jamie, and certainly not Iris. The very moment that she figured it out, she heard James say, "It's Ben. I'll take care of it." He rushed toward the door, pulling on a robe. "You need your rest."

Ben's crying stopped only a minute later, but James didn't come back. Eleanore lay in the dark debating whether she should intrude, while her concern kept her from relaxing. She didn't realize she'd dozed off until she felt James slip back into bed.

"Is he all right?"

"Relatively speaking," he muttered and held her close with a hint of desperation in his embrace. "He's having nightmares again."

"Again?"

"He was having them almost every night after his parents died. About halfway through the journey home they stopped, and I'd hoped it was in the past. Apparently not."

"What *kind* of nightmares?" she asked, deeply concerned for the child.

James hesitated and let out a weighty exhale. "Memories," he said. "Things that no child should ever have to endure."

"Has he told you . . . has he talked about . . . what happened?"

"He *won't* talk about it, except when he's been dreaming and he's upset. Then it just kind of . . . spills out. Perhaps if he *did* talk about it, he wouldn't be plagued with it so deeply."

Eleanore pondered the silence that followed and suggested, "Perhaps *you* should talk about it."

"I won't burden you with those images, Eleanore; I won't. I only thank God that we didn't have to live through it." He rolled over and added, "Get some sleep. You need to take care of yourself and that baby."

Throughout the following days Eleanore's concern for Ben grew in proportion to her concern for James. He spoke often of the strength and peace he'd witnessed among the Saints, and how he'd been inspired by their convictions. But there was a troubled look in his eyes. Nearly every night Ben would have an episode of nightmares, and James would sit with him until he went back to sleep, singing softly and praying with him to calm him down. Eleanore offered only once to sit with the child. James almost snapped at her when he insisted that she didn't need to hear the details of Ben's troubled memories. Eleanore could only pray for both of them and hope that time would heal their wounded spirits.

* * * * *

More than two weeks after his return from Winter Quarters, James was awakened once again by Ben's crying. He hurried into the child's room to follow the well-practiced routine of first lighting a lamp, and then gently shaking the boy until he woke up from his tormented slumber. And then the nightmare for James would begin as Ben cried and spewed the contents of his dreams. Only in his exhausted, half-asleep state would Ben utter the details of horrific persecution he'd witnessed—unspeakable atrocities against his people, and the ongoing mass exodus as they were driven from place to place, usually in horrible weather and freezing temperatures. The ones who had died were the lucky ones, apparently. Those who lived were ravaged and tortured, driven like cattle. And this child had seen much of it. What he hadn't witnessed personally, he'd been told about, or he had overheard the stories from those who had been most affected. He spoke of women and children walking through the snow, leaving a trail of blood from their exposed and frozen feet. He repeated incidents of violence and atrocities that exceeded James's imagination. He never would have imagined that people could be so cruel to other people. And for what? Differing views on religion? Wasn't that what it boiled down to? Night after night James would hold the boy close and encourage him to spill his thoughts and memories, hoping that he might finally be free of them. But as the images of Ben's stories crept into James's mind, a smoldering sickness escalated inside of him. The injustice and abominations that had been perpetrated by evildoers were more horrifically abominable than he'd even begun to comprehend.

Eleanore suggested that James give Ben a priesthood blessing to help him find comfort and strength in light of the atrocities he'd witnessed in his young life. James thought it was a good idea, but he'd never become fully comfortable with using the power of the priesthood that had been conferred upon him following his baptism. He knew in his heart that the power was real; he'd felt and seen much evidence of that. But he often felt inadequate to be trusted with such power. He worried about not saying the right thing, or perhaps putting his own interpretation or wishes upon the circumstances surrounding the need for a blessing. He'd discussed his feelings with Eleanore, and she'd told him more than once that as long as his life was in order and he approached his use of the priesthood humbly and with an appropriate attitude, surely God would not guide words to his mind unless they were fitting and suitable. She felt sure that he would be appropriately inspired, and he had to concede that she was probably right. Her faith in him couldn't help but encourage more faith in himself to use what he'd been given for righteous purposes.

James asked Frederick to help him give the blessing. Before bedtime the family gathered in the parlor and knelt together for a prayer before the men put their hands on Benjamin's head to begin. James initially felt as if his mind had gone completely blank. There was an awkward silence while he couldn't think of a single thing to say. Then words flowed into his mind with clarity and precision. From his own mouth came the message that Benjamin's spirit would be comforted and he would find peace concerning the trials he'd endured in his young life. He was promised peace as he prayed and lived for that blessing; not temporary or surface peace, but deep, genuine peace. He was told to give the burden to the Savior, who had already suffered all things, and it would surely be lifted. He was also told that a careful accounting of the suffering of the Saints was being kept in heaven, and that in God's time, justice would be met on all counts. James heard himself saying that the tribulations of now would give strength to generations to come, and that their present tribulations would give strength to generations to come, and that there was purpose in all these things. He uttered that no righteous life was lost in vain, and that those who laid down their lives or suffered for the sake of defending God's kingdom on the earth would reap great rewards in the life to come. Ben was also told that his family was together and watching over him, and that he had been spared to be part of a great work in Zion.

James felt drained once the amen had been spoken. And he couldn't help noting a change, however subtle, in Ben's countenance. That night the child had no nightmares, but James couldn't sleep, as if he'd been tuned to wait for Ben to wake up. And while he stared into the darkness, images of the tales he'd been told marched through his head. He fought to take the same advice that Ben had been given in his blessing, to give the burden to the Savior and be free of it. But something cold and frightening continued to hover inside of him, making the darkness around him almost tangible.

Days passed into weeks while Ben came back to life, physically as well as in spirit. His nightmares ended completely, and he blended naturally into the family. Eleanore worked with him every day on school lessons, and he was given chores to complete as he became stronger. He started keeping a journal, a tradition in the family since Eleanore had started David and Iris doing it back in England. As his writing skills gradually improved, Eleanore encouraged him to write down his experiences so that they would be preserved and perhaps have value to his children and grandchildren one day. James felt concerned that writing about the issues would bring them too close to the surface once again, but it seemed to have the opposite effect. Ben continued to heal, while James only became more disconcerted with all that he'd witnessed, combined with the accounts he had heard of the persecution of the Saints. He told Eleanore more than once that Ben was handling all of this much better than he was, and he admitted to being deeply troubled. She encouraged him to keep praying, and suggested that perhaps he should have Frederick and Ralph give him a blessing. He couldn't dispute that it was a good idea, but he avoided doing anything about it, not wanting to bring attention to his personal struggle over the issue. Eleanore also suggested that perhaps he should write about it, the way that Benjamin was. James owned a journal, but he wrote in it rarely, and he really didn't want to commit such thoughts to paper, for reasons he didn't care to analyze.

Spring came with refreshing warmth, and James found that he felt better being able to get outdoors more without being cold, which always made him think of his weeks among the Saints, when he'd never been able to get warm. As always, he enjoyed working in the garden, and it was a delight to have Ben, as well as Iris and Ralph, helping him.

Eleanore loved the spring weather, especially when the long row of irises bloomed along the side porch. She loved to sit there with her feet up and inhale their fragrance while she watched James and the children work in the garden. He'd become nearly fanatic about keeping it free of weeds, but she knew that part of his motive was an excuse to give the children work to do. And working with them gave him the opportunity to talk and laugh with them while the other adults were busy elsewhere keeping everything else under control. Eleanore normally would have worked in the garden with them, dividing her time between keeping the house in order and helping Amanda in the kitchen. But James had been stubbornly insistent that she rest and keep her feet up; he didn't want to risk anything happening to jeopardize the pregnancy. And she couldn't argue with him, given her past of history of losing babies. So she sat on the porch, often with a good book, and enjoyed the scene in the garden as well as the beauty around her.

Eleanore was thrilled when letters came from both Sally and Miriam, profusely thanking James and Frederick for all they had brought to Winter Quarters, and for the time they'd spent there offering great help and support. They reported that even though their opportunity to write was minimal, all was well beyond some ongoing struggle with illness in their families. They each wrote vaguely of illness and challenges among the Saints, but they both had great hope invested in the prophet's plan to take the people west. Eleanore shared that hope with all her soul. And she also hoped that once the Saints were gathered in some new location where they could live in peace, that God might answer her prayers and give her the approval of the Spirit to live among them. For now she remained content with her cozy surroundings and the life she'd been blessed to live, and she kept a constant prayer in her heart for her friends in Winter Quarters.

Ralph continued seeing Lu, mostly on Sundays when she came for dinner and took part in their private worship service. She made the decision to be baptized and simply not tell her aunt or uncle about it. She declared firmly that she'd prayed over the matter for quite some time and felt that it was the right thing to do. Once the weather became warm enough so that the river wasn't unbearably cold, Ralph had the privilege of baptizing her there. It was a beautiful event, especially with the obvious love that Ralph and Lu had for each other. Eleanore looked forward to the day when they could be married. Ralph had told her that he could feasibly afford to care for a wife, but Lu didn't feel quite ready. He was willing to give her the time she needed, but he did wonder if her reluctance was based more on fear of her uncle's reaction than anything else.

The longer days of summer brought the garden to life with a variety of green bursting out of the soil, and Eleanore became increasingly uncomfortable with her pregnancy as the time for delivery drew closer. She marveled at the miracle when she considered that they had lost three babies before having Jamie, and now they would have another. The anguish of those losses became less significant with the reality that they were about to have a second baby. And in the same respect, Ben's presence in their family had eased the sting of David's death. Eleanore prayed that they would all stay strong and healthy, and especially that she would encounter no difficulties through the remainder of the pregnancy and in bringing this child into the world.

Beyond the anticipation of giving birth, Eleanore could find no reason for concern in her household except for the occasional hint that James was troubled over something. He always met her questions with vague answers, but she suspected that he was worried for their friends, and troubled by what he knew of the Saints' suffering. More than once she encouraged him to find a way to be free of such burdens. He said that he was trying, but would say nothing more. She finally left the subject alone, certain he would come to terms with the matter in time.

A bit of an upset occurred when Lu showed up late one afternoon, distraught and looking for Ralph. Her uncle had gotten angry with her, and the argument had escalated until he'd slapped her hard and she'd run out, taking one of the horses. The argument had started because Lu's aunt was ill, and Lu had been expected to take over all of her duties. Lu didn't mind, but her uncle was fussy about his meals, and he'd declared that she was a terrible cook. He'd thrown his food on the floor, expecting Lu to clean it up and cook something else. Ralph was initially so angry over the report that James had to get stern to talk him out of going back to Lu's home to confront her uncle. When he convinced Ralph that he had no rights concerning Lu until he married her, Ralph shifted his energy into trying to convince Lu that they should just leave now and get married. But she wouldn't have it, and Ralph grew more and more frustrated. When they heard a knock on the door, they weren't surprised to see Mr. Bailey, but they *were* surprised to see that he'd come with the sheriff to get Lu. Mr. Bailey treated the matter as if Ralph had done something wrong and should be punished, but Sheriff Willis was a kind man who was apparently just trying to appease Mr. Bailey and keep the peace. He simply told Lu that she needed to come home with her uncle, but he made Mr. Bailey promise to mind his temper.

For an hour after Lu left with Mr. Bailey and the sheriff, Ralph paced and ranted about his concern for the woman he loved, wondering how he was ever going to get her away from the situation when she was so utterly terrified of her uncle. James, Eleanore, and Amanda all talked with him about appropriately discussing his feelings with Lu and biding his time. James pointed out that if he didn't calm down he was going to end up behaving like Mr. Bailey and only make matters worse. The very idea was clearly sobering for Ralph. He apologized for getting upset and said that he *did* need to learn to mind his temper and be patient, if only to be sure that Lu never had to deal with a man who was out of control ever again.

That night when Eleanore climbed into bed next to her husband, she commented on what a fine young man Ralph was.

"He is indeed," James said. "I've truly come to feel like he's my own son. I pray that this can work out without causing more trouble. Lu's a sweet young woman. She certainly deserves what Ralph can offer her."

"Yes, she does."

"How are you feeling?" he asked, snuggling close to her.

"I feel pregnant," she said. "Only a few weeks left."

"I'll be glad when it's over," he admitted.

"No more than I will," she said, and he chuckled. "How are *you?*"

"I'm fine. Why wouldn't I be?"

Eleanore wondered if she should just keep her thoughts to herself, but she felt compelled to say, "I sense that something is troubling you, James. Every once in a while, you just seem . . ."

"What?" he demanded, mildly defensive.

"Angry, perhaps. Or afraid. Maybe both."

"With good cause, I'd say."

"James." Eleanore sat up and took his hand. "You can't let these feelings have a place in you. There's nothing that can be done except to let it go and give it to God."

"I've tried, Eleanore; truly I have. Maybe I'm doing something wrong, but . . . every time I think about it . . . I feel haunted. And then I feel angry."

"Angry with what . . . who? What can you possibly do? You need to follow Ben's example. He's at peace. He's happy. I'm certain the memories can be disturbing for him; he talks about it now and then. But he's not angry or bitter. It happened to *him,* not you. If *he* can find peace with it, you must too."

"It's not just Ben," James said. "What I saw . . . and heard . . . what those people have been through."

"And yet you said yourself that they are in good spirits for the most part, that they are faithful and cheerful. Sometimes I think you would handle all of this better if you were in the middle of it, as opposed to being apart from the situation and stewing over it."

James was silent a long moment and Eleanore wondered if the concept might be sinking in. He finally said, "I suppose I just can't help wondering . . . what if it had happened to us, Eleanore?"

"If *what* had happened to us?"

"Any of it. I'm not certain I could withstand such a test of my faith."

"I think your faith is much stronger than you think it is . . . but you can't give in to your anger, James. You must find peace over it. You must. You are the head of this household. It's your responsibility to set an example of forgiveness, not hatred."

James listened to her words reverberate in his mind. He knew she was right, but the feelings inside of him felt too overwhelming to simply command them to leave. He *did* feel afraid; afraid that this season of peace and security was only temporary. And when he contemplated his fear, he felt helplessly angry on behalf of those who had already suffered so much. Eleanore said nothing more before she drifted off to sleep, and she said nothing more the following day. But he knew she was on to him. He just didn't know what to say to reassure her when he felt so troubled. He could hardly look at Ben without recalling the child's nightmares and their source. How *could* he be at peace over it? How *could* the Saints be so content to leave behind everything they'd worked so hard for and live in such meager circumstances? He began praying harder that he could let go of ill feelings, and he paused often to take account of all that he had to be grateful for. Still, these unsavory feelings hovered inside him. He couldn't discern whether they were getting better, or if he had just buried them deeper. He told himself that time would help, and that was exactly what he needed to give the matter—time.

Chapter Four

THE PLIGHT OF
WINTER QUARTERS

A week passed with James and Eleanore saying nothing more on the topic of his uneasy feelings. Each day, Eleanore became more uncomfortable with her pregnancy. She looked as if her belly might explode at any second, and she could hardly move from one part of the house to another. She would go down the stairs in the morning and stay there until it was time to slowly make her way back up to go to bed, although she slept very little. She often sat in the kitchen and helped with the meals by doing tasks that could be done at the table. Or she lounged in the library or on the side porch while James did his usual chores and worked in the garden. James noticed her sitting there with her feet up and the dog curled up near her chair when Ralph returned from town in the wagon, which was loaded with feed for the animals and some items from the general store, according to the list Eleanore had given him. He knew that Jamie was down for a nap and that she was enjoying the reprieve. Jamie was a typical two-year-old boy, with a great deal of energy, continually making everyone laugh over his antics. Even with others helping, the child preferred his mother and often wanted to try to sit on what little lap she had, or he would cling to her skirts when she'd walk if he was the least bit unhappy. Jamie was a great light in their lives and had fulfilled their longtime wish to have a child of their own, and everyone loved him dearly. James found it ironic, however, that after years of Eleanore not being able to have a baby, she was now ready to give birth a second time in little more than two years. He could see the exhaustion in her eyes, but he could also see her joy, and it reminded him of his own. Still, nap time was appreciated.

James brushed the dirt off his hands and left the garden to help Ralph unload the wagon once it was parked in front of the barn. Ralph jumped down and handed the mail to James, since he'd stopped to pick it up while he was in town. James thumbed through it and noticed a letter from Sally. He took it to Eleanore and wasn't surprised by her smile as he handed it to her.

Eleanore looked up at her husband as the letter exchanged hands, and she was struck suddenly with a wave of gratitude. In the space of a few seconds she felt the full spectrum of all he had done for her, and she wondered what she would do without him. She held the letter in one hand and reached out the other hand for him. He took it and squeezed gently while he bent to kiss her.

"I love you, James Barrington," she said, then pressed his hand over her belly while the sensation lingered with her.

"I love you too," he said and kissed her again before he walked away to help Ralph unload the wagon.

Eleanore turned her attention to the letter, wanting to savor it. Since her friends had left Nauvoo, the letters had been much more sparse, both in frequency and in content, and she had treasured every little connection. She missed both Sally and Miriam, and hourly wondered how they were and what they were doing. While she had become very close to Sally through letters, it was Miriam who had once lived nearby. They had visited often and had done projects together. Their families had shared meals and had worshiped together. Eleanore had given Miriam a copy of the Book of Mormon and had told her of the joy the gospel had given her. The entire Plummer family had joined the Church as a result and Eleanore had been blessed by having someone with whom to share her beliefs. Then the Plummers had left for Nauvoo, and Eleanore had never stopped missing them. She missed Sally as well, in a strange sort of way, even though they'd only met face-to-face on one occasion. Now, any word from either of these women was deeply appreciated.

Eleanore hesitated as she opened the envelope. She recalled how it had felt when Sally had written of their evacuation from Nauvoo, and how it had felt a couple of years earlier when she had written of the

Prophet's death. A chill rushed over her at the memories, then she hesitated, wondering if the feeling was some kind of premonition.

"Oh, please . . . not more bad news," she muttered aloud and pulled out the letter.

James was barely in the bed of the wagon, pulling on his gloves, when he heard Eleanore scream and call his name. He rushed toward her, his heart throbbing, his stomach twisted. He stopped abruptly when she came into view. She was on her knees, her arms wrapped around herself, heaving for breath. The letter lay discarded beside her, and the dog was watching her, apparently alarmed. Was her reaction from bad news, or was this some kind of physical pain related to the pregnancy? Either way, he felt terrified and had to force himself to her side where he knelt to face her.

"Eleanore," he murmured, taking hold of her shoulders. "What is it? What's wrong?" She looked up at him, her eyes expressing palpable anguish. "What is it?" he repeated, his voice gruff. "Are you in pain? What?"

"The letter," she muttered, barely audible, clutching onto him. She pressed her face to his chest and he could barely understand her as she squeaked out the answer to his question. "Andy is dead."

James drew a painful breath and pulled back abruptly to look into her eyes, unwilling to believe it. In a matter of seconds his memories reminded him of how much he cared for this man. They were friends. They'd shared a thousand little events and a few big ones through the years when they'd been neighbors. He couldn't believe it. It couldn't be true. Even the horror in Eleanore's eyes would not convince him. He let go of her to snatch up the letter, scanning it frantically with his eyes until the words jumped into his brain. *Suddenly ill . . . overtook him quickly . . . gone before we hardly knew what was happening.*

"No," James muttered and sat down hard on the porch, barely aware of Eleanore sobbing with her face in her hands. Sounds penetrated his clouded mind, and he looked up to see the others standing there, drawn by Eleanore's scream, looking as horrified as he felt. Lizzie and Frederick, Amanda and Ralph, and the children had all gathered. They all looked frightened, silently questioning him over the reason for the outburst.

"What's happened?" Frederick demanded quietly on behalf of the group.

"Andy is dead," James reported, and the news was greeted by a chorus of gasps and moans. Iris ran and threw herself into his arms, but he felt only a small measure of comfort from his daughter. He held her tightly, as if her faith and youthful strength could sustain him.

"How?" he heard Amanda ask, her voice trembling. She'd known the Plummer family long before James and Eleanore had moved here.

"Illness apparently," James said and held out the letter. Ralph took it and moved unsteadily to a chair, where he read Sally's words aloud. The others listened, visibly shocked and upset. Hearing the words spoken forced the news to sink in a little further, and James felt his chest tighten while his throat became hot. A bleak silence followed Ralph's conclusion of the letter. Even Eleanore's crying had stopped. They all exchanged glances of disbelief, while no one knew what to say. He noted Frederick and Lizzie holding each other close, both crying silent tears. Feeling his own grief threaten to explode, James took advantage of Eleanore's condition as an excuse to be away from the others.

"Come along," he said, helping her to her feet. "I think you need to rest. Would you look after the children?" he asked of no one in particular.

"Of course," Lizzie said with a quavering voice at the same time as Amanda said, "Yes." Between them, James knew the children would be well cared for as he walked into the house with Eleanore leaning heavily against him. He helped Eleanore toward the stairs while they clung to each other, consumed with silent shock. He wondered if her thoughts were wandering into the same territory as his, but he didn't want to ask. As horrible as it was to learn of the death of a dear friend, it was made doubly alarming because of their personal relationship with the Plummer family and with the plight of the Saints. It was like standing at the edge of a street and seeing someone hit by a runaway coach, knowing that you were only a few seconds shy of stepping in front of it yourself. And James felt barely able to breathe while the message pounded through his head that it could have been him. It could have been *him* that died of the illness that was running rampant in Winter Quarters, most of it a direct result of exposure and poor living conditions. It could have been *his* family left on their own, *his* children left without a father, *his* wife left to survive in deplorable circumstances with an inevitable, long journey and more tribulation before her, solely responsible for the family. The plight of Winter Quarters felt suddenly very close to home.

James was startled from his thoughts when Eleanore stopped partway up the stairs and groaned.

"What's wrong?" he demanded with an unnatural sharpness. She only groaned again and doubled over, going to her knees on the step. "Eleanore?" He shouted and took hold of her shoulders. "Is it the baby?"

Eleanore nodded and held to him tightly. "I think it's labor, but . . . it didn't start this way last time." She began heaving for breath until he feared she would pass out.

"Calm down, Ellie. Do you hear me?" She paid him no mind, and he shook her gently. "Eleanore! Calm down and breathe." She focused her eyes on him. "Just take a deep breath." She attempted to do so, and he breathed with her, although it took a full minute to get her breathing almost normally. "Come along," he said, helping her carefully to her feet. "Let's get you to bed, and I'll send Ralph for the doctor."

Once Eleanore was lying down, her focus shifted fully from the news of Andy's death to the pain in her abdomen. James was glad to know that Ralph was riding a fast horse into town to get the doctor, especially when Eleanore concluded, "I don't think it's labor, James. The pain is constant. It's different; and it's not letting up."

In the space of a second, James felt unfathomable panic then talked himself out of it with the need to remain levelheaded. He'd always trusted Eleanore's instincts, so he simply asked, "What do you think it is? Are you worried?"

His heart thudded, but he kept a calm countenance while he watched her think about it. "No," she said and seemed to mean it. "I'm sure everything is fine."

James sat close beside her on the bed and held her while they waited for the doctor. He could tell she was uncomfortable, but no longer consumed by unbearable pain. And then she reminded him of the very thing he was trying to avoid thinking about. "I can't believe Andy's dead."

"I can't either."

"It could have been us, James." She looked up at him and her lip quivered.

"I know," he muttered.

"I'm the one who introduced them to the gospel. Maybe I should have just—"

"Eleanore," James took her hand firmly, "you knew it was the right thing to do; neither of us can dispute that. The gospel brought great joy into their lives. It was the answer to their prayers. They said it many times. And they knew beyond any doubt that going to Nauvoo was right."

"Then they ended up being driven from their home, left freezing and desolate. And now this. They didn't know it would come to this."

"No, but they did what they knew in their hearts God wanted them to do, Ellie. You cannot blame yourself for this. The very idea is ludicrous."

She nodded and choked on a sob. "But . . . what if it had been us? What if God had told *us* to go to Nauvoo? What if *we* had been driven out, forced to leave everything behind? What if *we* were stuck in Winter Quarters, and . . . it was . . . it was . . . you . . . who had . . ." She became too emotional to speak.

"But it *wasn't* me."

"It could have been, and . . . I would never survive it, James. I cannot live without you."

James swallowed his own fears, certain he could never live without *her*. Again he fought for the presence of mind he needed to remain calm and try to soothe her. Now was not the time to express his own sense of panic. "You *could*, Eleanore. But you won't have to."

"How can you say that? We don't know what will happen, where we'll end up. You can't promise me that I won't be left to live a significant portion of my life without you."

"No, I can't, Eleanore. But I *can* promise you that I will do everything in my power to stay safe and healthy. And we will keep doing what we've always done. We will live close to the Spirit and do whatever God requires of us, because we both know that . . ." his voice broke with thoughts of Andy, ". . . that it is the blessings of the next life that matter more than the hardships of this one."

Eleanore tried to ignore the pain in her belly and nodded again, wrapping her arms around him. While she held him close she prayed with all the fervency of her soul that God would not take her husband prematurely. They'd survived the death of a child, but she wasn't sure she could survive losing James. He was thoroughly good to her, and she had come to rely on him in so many ways. He was her best friend, the father of her children, her soul mate; the best thing that had ever happened to her. And she needed him. Just thinking of the many weeks he'd been gone on his visit to Winter Quarters, she knew she wanted never to be without him again. Never!

Eleanore didn't realize how worried James was until the doctor arrived; then he became visibly upset before he left the room to let the doctor examine her. After James returned, the doctor reported that it was likely some kind of muscle spasm that would relent on its own, and there was no apparent need for concern. A short while after he left it *did* relent, and by suppertime she felt no pain at all. But after removing her attention from the physical distress, she couldn't help but be consumed by grief on behalf of her friends. She couldn't imagine what Miriam might be going through—and the children. Mark and Sally and their children had all been close to Andy and Miriam, and this was surely hard for all of them.

A pall hung over the household for days as each person had to contend individually with the loss of a friend. They had all known Andy and Miriam well, and their relationships had all been varied. But they found strength in sharing their grief. Long conversations over their meals and in the parlor helped sort out complicated emotions. And one conclusion stood out boldly and unanimously. Not one of them had lost faith to any degree. They all agreed that the gospel was true. They could not deny it, and they were wholly united in living it—whatever the cost. Eleanore prayed with all her being that the price would never require giving up her husband or anyone else in her family.

Eleanore hadn't yet gotten up the courage to write letters to Sally and Miriam when Ben found her on the side porch and held out an envelope that was ready to mail. "It's for Sister Plummer," he said.

"I can see that."

"Can Papa mail it when he goes into town?"

"I'm certain he can," Eleanore said, feeling guilty that she'd not overcome her own sorrow enough to reach out to her friend. It wasn't the first time Ben's attitude had been an example to her. "It was very kind of you to think of writing to Sister Plummer."

"Do you want to know what I wrote?" he asked, and she realized he had ulterior motives in bringing the letter to her, as opposed to taking it directly to James.

"I would love to know what you wrote, but only if you want to tell me."

"I told her what Brother Joseph told me when my brother died in Nauvoo."

Eleanore caught her breath. She hadn't realized that Ben had actually had contact with the Prophet prior to his martyrdom. And she knew that by the time Ben's brother had died in Nauvoo, he'd already lost four other siblings.

"What *did* Brother Joseph tell you?" she pressed gently when he hesitated.

"He told me that the blessings of eternity were more glorious than we could possibly imagine for those who endured such loss for the sake of building the kingdom." Ben said it so maturely; it was one of those moments when his childlike face was contradicted by eyes that had lived three lifetimes. Eleanore wrapped him in her arms and murmured, "Oh, thank you for sharing that with me, Ben. And thank you for writing Sister Plummer to share it with her, as well. I'm certain it will give her great comfort."

Ben returned the hug then said, "I felt better after I wrote to her. Maybe you will too."

It wasn't the first time Ben's perception had taken her aback. She touched his face and said, "I'm certain you're right. I'll go and do that now and send my letter along with yours."

Ben seemed pleased and ran off to play, as if he'd accomplished what he'd set out to do. It took some serious effort for Eleanore to get out of the chair and walk into the house. Instead of going straight to the office to write a letter, she felt compelled to find Iris, but she knew it would take far too much effort to make it up the stairs. She stood in the hall and called her name, expecting to hear her call back from her room. But Iris answered from behind and startled her. Eleanore turned to see her peeking her head out of the library.

"Did you need me?" Iris asked.

"No, I was just wondering if you're all right."

Iris looked at the floor and leaned against the door jamb. "Why wouldn't I be?"

"I don't know. Is there a reason I might sense that something's wrong?" Iris tucked her head down further, and Eleanore realized she was hiding tears. "What is it, my darling?" Eleanore asked, taking the child in her arms.

Iris held tightly to her and said, "It's no different than what everyone else is feeling. I just feel so badly for them. I want to stop thinking about it, but I can't."

"Yes, I know what you mean." She let her cry for a minute, then added, "Ben has written a letter to Miriam, and I thought I should do the same; it's long overdue. He thinks it will make me feel better, and maybe it will. Would you like to join me? We could both write her a letter, and maybe we'll both feel better."

Iris nodded and forced a smile while Eleanore wiped her tears. They went together to the office and sat on opposite sides of the big desk with the inkwell between them. Eleanore found that she *did* feel better as she opened her feelings on Miriam's behalf and poured them out freely, with genuine concern and compassion. She didn't know what Iris was writing, but she was busily engaged and using a second page.

The following day the letters were mailed to Winter Quarters. That evening Eleanore felt especially tired but hardly got any sleep during the night. Just after breakfast her labor started. She told James they didn't need to send for the doctor yet, but he didn't feel good about waiting and sent Ralph after him anyway. Eleanore was glad that he had when the pain quickly became difficult to contend with.

James left Lizzie with Eleanore while he checked on the children. He left Jamie in Iris's care while Amanda was busy in the kitchen. Ben was put in charge of doing the chores in the barn that James would otherwise be doing. He went eagerly to do as he'd been asked, and James felt grateful for being blessed with such good children. He returned to the bedroom to find Eleanore in more pain than when he'd left just a few minutes earlier. He sat beside her and tried to sort out his feelings. He didn't remember it being this bad before, and while he was trying to convince himself that the comparison was distorted due to the present distress, Eleanore gripped his hand tightly and whimpered, "It wasn't like this before. Something's not right." She groaned and writhed. "I need a blessing . . . before the doctor gets here."

James tried to accept her meaning into his mind through a clouded jumble of fears and memories. He forced logic and reason to override all else and answered, barely firm, "Of course. I'll get Frederick."

James had forgotten Lizzie was in the room until she said, "I'll get him. You stay with her."

The blessing gave James a vague sense of comfort and the feeling that everything would be all right. But he wondered what path might have to be taken to get to that point. While Eleanore's labor progressed, the sky darkened and the summer breeze turned to an angry wind. Rain pummeled the windows violently, and Eleanore's pain steadily increased. Images appeared in James's mind of what this moment might be like if their only available shelter from the storm was a tent or a covered wagon. He wondered how many Mormon women had given birth in such circumstances, with their health doubly at risk when physical complications were coupled with exposure to the elements. He recalled all too clearly the winter storms he had endured through his journey to Winter Quarters and back, and the times when there had been no choice but to huddle inside the wagon's cover and wait it out. The canvas had done little to hold back the bite of the wind, and he'd been so cold that he'd feared he would never recover. But he'd been strong and healthy at the time, and Eleanore had been safe at home.

More than once throughout the course of her labor, James left Eleanore to check on the children and offer comfort that made him feel like he was lying. Iris and Ben were both concerned, but they expressed faith and said they were praying for their mother. Little Jamie was in a temperamental mood, as if he sensed the distress of his mother, or perhaps he just wanted to be in her presence and felt displaced because she wasn't available. Amanda and Ralph went home, as usual, once supper was over and cleaned up, but she insisted that Ben come to get them if they were needed. When bedtime came, James had prayer with the family then put Jamie to bed himself, rocking him while he wiggled and squirmed until he finally relaxed and drifted off to sleep. He checked once more on Ben and Iris, making certain they were tucked in and that all was well. Frederick took Mary Jane home to put her to bed, but Lizzie stayed with Eleanore and declared that she wasn't going anywhere until the ordeal was over. For the millionth time in his life, James wondered what he would do without Frederick and Lizzie. They were surely two of the kindest, most giving people in the world, and their friendship was utterly priceless.

James returned to the bedroom to find Lizzie holding Eleanore's hand and trying to offer encouragement. But Eleanore writhed and groaned and was apparently oblivious to anything but the pain. James took Lizzie's place, not unaware of the tears in her eyes. The storm continued along with the pain, and around midnight the doctor declared that it was getting close and he would soon be able to deliver the baby. He divulged that the reason for the excess pain and longer labor was due to the baby being turned the wrong direction. When he asked James to hold Eleanore's shoulders to the bed while he turned the baby in order to deliver it safely, James wanted to tell him that he'd rather die than watch this. But he nodded stoutly and did as he was told, knowing he would go through anything to spare Eleanore more suffering. If only he *could* spare her suffering. The trauma of having the baby turned facedown instead of faceup, followed by the actual delivery, was absolutely the most horrible thing that James had personally witnessed. He loved this woman beyond his own comprehension, and seeing her suffer so unspeakably seemed more than he could bear. Then suddenly it was over. The baby's cry provoked a burst of unexpected laughter from Eleanore. The doctor declared him to be a perfectly healthy boy as Lizzie wrapped him up to keep him warm, weeping as she laid him in Eleanore's arms.

Eleanore examined him closely and cried as well, while James simply immersed himself in the relief that it was over, and in the wonder of a new life born into the world. With each passing event of their lives, he loved Eleanore more. When she looked up at him, he couldn't even speak. Instead he kissed her and pressed his brow to hers, hoping she could feel all he was feeling.

"What will you call him?" the doctor asked.

"Isaac?" Eleanore said to James. "As we discussed?"

"Isaac is perfect," James said, his voice catching.

"And a middle name?" Lizzie asked, every bit as emotional as James.

Eleanore looked at the baby, then again at James. "I was thinking Andrew . . . which was Andy's given name. What do you think?"

"I think it's perfect," James said and kissed her again. "I love you so much, my darling."

"I love you too," she said, then became distracted as the doctor warned her that the delivery of the placenta was about to occur. James took the baby. Lizzie held Eleanore's hand, and it was quickly accomplished.

As soon as the ordeal was over, the rain stopped and the wind settled, as if little Isaac's entrance into the world had allowed the elements to stop lamenting over his mother's struggle to deliver him safely. Eleanore slept with the aid of something the doctor gave her for the pain, and thankfully the baby slept as well, which allowed James and Lizzie to do the same. By morning, all signs of the storm had passed, and James brought the children in to see the new baby. Jamie cried, wanting to be with his mother. He laid beside her for only a minute before he began to wiggle and cause her pain, and Amanda took him from the room, wailing. She'd arrived early and James was grateful, as always, for her expertise and composure in handling difficult situations. Iris and Ben were thrilled over the baby and beamed as they took turns holding him, but they were both old enough and sharp enough to see how bad off their mother was. James finally told them they needed to go and let her rest, and they assured him that they would see to the chores and watch out for Jamie, even without his asking.

Alone again with Eleanore and the baby, James found himself unable to avoid his turbulent emotions. It didn't take many hours for the summer sun to quickly bring on humid heat, and the windows were opened wide. But that didn't keep sweat from adding a glisten to Eleanore's skin that had developed a sickly pallor. Even in sleep there was a subtle grimace in her expression, and she would whimper when she shifted even slightly. Although the ordeal had been significant and she'd lost a lot of blood, James had been assured by the doctor that she would be all right with time. And the blessing Frederick had given her echoed that assurance. But "all right" was relative. In that moment, it was difficult to imagine her ever returning to her normal, vibrant self. And would she ever be able to have more children without complications? Even if she could, was it wise to do so? With speculations about the future came the fear that perhaps next time she gave birth, she very well *could* be without proper shelter and medical care. Ever since James had been lowered into the waters of baptism, he'd known in his spirit that he had to be prepared to do whatever God required of him. He and Eleanore had prayed then—not for the first time—to inquire whether they should go to Nauvoo and be among the Saints. The answer had clearly been no. But James knew that it was only a matter of time before they would be making the move. He wondered if it would be a well-planned departure, and if the journey would take them to a place where the Saints truly had found security and peace. Or would they be forced to leave hastily in poor weather? Would they confront illness and exposure as others had done? He felt as if he were stuck in the middle of reading a traumatic novel, constantly wondering how it was going to end, but unable to finish the book for reasons beyond his own control.

With his thoughts churning and his emotions roiling, James finally had to leave Eleanore in Lizzie's care. Once beyond the bedroom his eyes began to sting, and his chest burned. He rushed from the house, fearing he would explode in front of the children and then be forced to explain his outburst. As soon as he was outside, he ran, sobbing as he did so, not surprised to end up at David's grave even though he'd not consciously premeditated going there. He dropped to his knees and groaned, wrapping his arms around his middle. He wept without restraint and prayed with all the energy of his soul, begging God to spare Eleanore's life. "Not just now," he prayed aloud, "but next year, and the one after that. Please let her be healthy and strong and safe. And let me be the same for her. Don't take me from her when we need each other so much. Let us grow old together, Father, I pray. I will go wherever you want me to go. I will give up all that I have if it will keep my family safe and strong. *Please.*"

James prayed and cried until his voice was hoarse and his head hurt more than his knees. He finally rolled onto his back, finding the ground beneath him dry in spite of the recent downpour. He realized how hot it was when he became conscious of his clothes sticking to him with sweat. His fingers reached habitually into his pocket, and he pulled out a piece of worn hair ribbon. He pressed it to his nose and closed his eyes, inhaling the sweet scent of Eleanore. He'd kept her supplied with the perfume since before their marriage, even though it had to be ordered from back east. And many times he'd replaced the piece of ribbon that he kept sprayed with her scent. She'd called him a romantic fool for doing so, but she'd also said that it was one of many reasons that she knew he loved her. He *did* love her. He loved her with all his soul. Thinking of her prodded him to his feet as he tucked the ribbon safely away and hurried back to the house, feeling the need to check on her.

James found Eleanore awake and trying to feed the baby with Lizzie's help. She was so weak that she couldn't hold the baby on her own. Lizzie had helped prop him up with pillows, but it wasn't going very well. James sat beside Eleanore and took her hand, pressing a kiss to her brow. He noted that she looked miserable in spite of her effort to show him a smile. Observing her closely, he noted that her desire was to focus on the baby and take in the joy and miracle of his presence. But she was distracted by her own pain and weakness. Throughout the course of the day, the ritual was repeated a number of times without success, while Isaac became increasingly fussy. Amanda told James that sometimes it took a day or two for the mother's milk to come in, but if the baby needed something in the meantime, goat's milk would be better than cow's milk. James immediately sent Ralph to find and purchase a goat that was giving milk. He was grateful for Amanda and Lizzie's help—with Eleanore *and* the baby—since he had no idea what to do in either case. There had been no such problems last time. Eleanore had been happy and vibrant in spite of having given birth, and she'd been able to feed the baby on her own without giving James cause to even consider the possibility that a mother might not be able to do so. When Caroline, his first wife, had given birth to David and Iris, she had chosen not to nurse the babies and had gone through some painful days of letting her milk dry up. He had hired wet nurses and nannies, while Caroline avoided caring for her children as much as possible. But for Eleanore, being unable to give Isaac what he needed was breaking her heart. His crying often caused her to cry as well. The pain she was in, and the weakness that made it impossible to do anything at all without help, surely contributed to her sensitive emotions. The baby was given some cow's milk and slept soundly, and before he woke again, Ralph had returned with a new addition to the small menagerie that resided in the barn. Iris immediately took to the goat as a pet and named it Gretchen, and Jamie loved to pester it, giggling each time it would bleat. James declared that since Iris loved this goat so much, she could protect the poor thing from her little brother.

The goat's milk worked well at keeping Isaac content, and Amanda soon guided Eleanore into a routine, with Lizzie's help. When the baby was hungry Eleanore would nurse him sufficiently to try to stimulate her milk coming in, and then he would be fed goat's milk until he was full. And often while he slept he was put close to Eleanore's side so that she could enjoy him and they could share what Amanda called important bonding. James observed the entire process with concern and a lingering sense of fear. He was grateful for Isaac and already loved the child dearly. But he didn't want Eleanore to ever get pregnant again. He didn't want to lose her, *couldn't* lose her. And seeing her in the condition she was in kept merging into his mind with the scenario of how it might have been if they were living in Winter Quarters, or on the trail somewhere, confronted with the elements. What if they'd not had the luxury of a doctor, a soft bed, plenty of clean water? He prayed hard and admitted humbly that he was grateful for all they *did* have, and to know that in time, all would be well. But the uncertainty of the future left him feeling uneasy.

Attempting to appreciate the good, James was naturally drawn to little Isaac. He had dark hair, similar to Jamie's, which had started out dark and remained that way. But Isaac looked nothing like his brother in features. In fact, James could see a very clear resemblance to Eleanore in his little face. He marveled at the miracle of loving a woman so much, and of seeing her in the face of this beautiful, perfect infant. Jamie loved his little brother and always wanted to be near him. It was a challenge to keep the balance in allowing Jamie time with his mother and the baby, while allowing them to get the rest they needed. While Eleanore and Isaac slept, James took charge of Jamie and kept him occupied with picture books, toys, and long walks. Iris and Ben were both wonderful about helping with Jamie, and James let them know how much he appreciated all they did. But Jamie needed at least one parent to be an active part of his days. Ben and Iris too were smitten with little Isaac and loved to hold him. They both quickly learned how to change his diapers and to feed him the goat's milk, and they found pleasure in being able to do such important tasks in the baby's care. Iris took to mothering so well that James felt certain she would make a wonderful mother someday. Observing Ben as he fit so naturally into the family, it was difficult to imagine him not being there. In so short a time he'd become completely comfortable, and he was a great asset to their family. There were moments when James would look at him and remember all he'd been through, and then it was difficult to control his feelings. At other times, he would get a glimpse of the child's faith and feel a deep sense of awe. Occasionally he would think of David and wonder how one boy could be living and breathing within a family, and two years later, another could be sleeping in the same bed, wearing the same clothes, and everything could feel as if it had been this way all along.

A month after Isaac's birth, Eleanore was still pale and weak, but she was getting out of bed some and starting to see to her own care for the most part. The doctor had encouraged her to start moving around more to build up her strength, but as of yet she'd not been brave enough to tackle going down the stairs. James had carried her up and down a few times so that she could be involved with the family, but on her own she never ventured very far. She'd never been able to nurse Isaac enough to sustain him, but she continued to do so anyway, even though every feeding required an increasing amount of goat's milk to fill him up.

As always, James wondered what he'd do without Frederick and Lizzie, who lived so close that they were always there to help. Often, before James could even think what he might ask them to do, they were already doing it. Their little daughter, Mary Jane, meshed naturally with the other children, and she especially enjoyed following Ben around while he did his chores. James also felt sure he could never get by without Amanda and Ralph. He joked about building them a house on the property as well, since they always went home late and arrived early each day. Although neither of them were employed on Sunday, they all went to church together, then shared Sunday dinner and their private worship service in the afternoon. It had gotten so that the household felt a little empty during the increasingly rare times when Amanda and Ralph were not around. Occasionally they even spent the night, especially more recently when Eleanore and the baby had needed extra care. Ralph often stayed in the attic room above Frederick and Lizzie's home. It had an outside entrance from stairs that went up the side of the house, and had been added into the construction at the suggestion of the builder. It had proven a good idea when Ralph and Amanda stayed over. Amanda preferred the extra bed in Jamie's room, but Ralph preferred the attic apartment unless it was dreadfully hot, and then he took the couch in James's office.

Ralph started bringing Lu home with him more and more, mostly on Sundays. It became normal for her to come home from church with them and stay until late when Ralph and Amanda would take her home before going to their own house for the night. Everyone in the family had grown to love Lu and to enjoy her company. She was helpful in the kitchen and with the children, and had a sweet temperament, even though she didn't say much. James felt certain it wouldn't be much longer before Ralph stole her away and married her. He just hoped it wouldn't stir up too much trouble when it happened. And he hoped that Ralph and his bride could continue to be a part of their household indefinitely.

At Sunday dinner on a rainy summer day, James took hold of Eleanore's hand across the corner of the table and noted that she was finally starting to show a little color. He glanced at Isaac, asleep in the crook of his arm, then he looked down the long dining table, smiling to consider how crowded it felt. He thought of the grand dining room he'd left behind in England. It would have dwarfed even this group. But he preferred the coziness of this room, and the way the table barely seemed to give everyone the elbow room they needed in order to eat. He loved the pleasant chatter and laughter that was taking place while everyone ate and shared their thoughts. Technically, there were three families present. Frederick, Lizzie, and Mary Jane. Amanda, Ralph, and Lu. And his own wife and children. But to him they all felt like one. And he loved them all. He paused a moment to observe each of his children and their uniqueness. Iris was beautiful; she always had been. But she was sweet, too—unlike the woman who had given birth to her, the woman Iris looked like more and more. Ben was growing well and was full of energy; nothing like the barely living child he'd taken from Winter Quarters. Jamie had so much energy it was exhausting just to watch him. But everyone worked together to keep him safe and somewhat obedient. And he was always the cause of much laughter. He'd been dubbed the family clown, and he lived up to his label well. James looked again at the baby sleeping in his arm, then at Eleanore as she squeezed his hand, passing him an inquisitive gaze, as if she sensed his thoughts wandering.

"You're not eating," she said.

"I'm just trying to appreciate what I've got while I've got it," he said. She furrowed her brow in confusion. He smiled and added, "We have a beautiful family, Mrs. Barrington."

"Yes, we do," she said. He kissed her hand, then ate his dinner.

Chapter Five

SANCTUARY WEST

When Isaac was three months old, Eleanore was finally moving around the house more and helping some with household tasks. She could actually carry the baby, as opposed to having someone give him to her while she was sitting or lying down. But she rarely put any effort into getting dressed, and instead mostly stayed upstairs in a nightgown, only putting on a robe when she occasionally came downstairs where she might encounter Ralph or Frederick. James stuck to his usual routine of working in the garden and seeing to other necessities around the house and yard, but he didn't go long without finding her, just to make certain she was well and that she wasn't overdoing it. She'd always been so strong and vibrant, and now she seemed so fragile that he hardly dared hug her tight for fear of breaking her.

James was preoccupied with this ongoing concern while he mindlessly pulled weeds, and a familiar layer of sweat held his clothing close to his back and chest. He caught movement from the edge of his vision and turned to see an image that forced the air out of his lungs. He sucked it back as he stood and took in the view more fully. It was like a painting, a moment captured in brilliant colors that compelled the viewer to step out of life and consider thoughts deeper than ever before. And if it were a painting, he would have titled it *Everything I've Ever Wanted.* There stood Eleanore, his sweet wife, looking toward him eagerly with a countenance that betrayed her love for him. She wore a dark skirt and white blouse that made her look less pale than she had in some time. Or perhaps it was the sun on her face. Her hair was pinned up more neatly than it had been in months. In her arms was Isaac, wearing a little white hat. And clinging to her skirts was Jamie, holding unnaturally still. Behind Eleanore at a perfect angle was the home they lived in, with trees and prairie stretching out beside it, occasionally dotted with the color of flowers. And sitting on the porch to Eleanore's left were Iris and Ben, their heads bent together as if telling secrets. James forced the image more deeply into his mind, uttering a prayer that some miraculous event might occur to permanently emblazon it there so that he might recall it vividly at any given moment in the future. He found it ironic that a clear memory of seeing the temple in Nauvoo came to mind, as if to remind him that it represented the means to keep eternally all that he'd been blessed with that truly mattered. He was grateful in the moment to have seen the temple, in spite of its abandoned state. He knew in his heart that eventually the Saints would build another temple, and he would have the opportunity to be with his family forever. With that idea impressed firmly into his spirit, he once again took in the image before him. For a long moment he remained frozen, wanting everything around him to stay the same, just so he could soak it in to its fullest extent. Then suddenly, he needed to be in the picture. He brushed the dirt off his hands and stepped carefully out of the garden to stand before his wife. She smiled with perfect happiness as he approached, and he didn't have to think about kissing her. He just did it.

"I'm out," she said, as proudly as a child who had just read her first word.

"I can see that." He kissed her again. "The sun becomes you, my dear." He took Isaac from her and chuckled at the silly expression on the baby's face as he squinted against summer light. With the baby in one arm he put the other around Eleanore and kissed her once more. "I love you," he murmured.

"I know," she said and kissed him again with a hint of passion that he'd not felt from her in months. "I love you too, James Barrington."

Jamie tugged on his father's pant leg and insisted that he be picked up as well. James easily lifted him into one arm. "Look at these fine boys," he said, holding them both. He offered a little bounce that made Jamie giggle. Isaac was still apparently taking in what it felt like to be out of the house for the first time. Eleanore took the baby back when he made a little fuss. James motioned with his arm and called to Iris and Ben, "Come here." They ran with no hesitation, as if they instinctively sensed the tender moment taking place and wanted to be a part of it. With no urging, they all wrapped their arms around each other in some semblance of a tight circle. Eleanore laughed, and James paused once again to imprint the moment fully into his memory. *Everything I've ever wanted.*

That evening after the children were all asleep, James slipped into the bedroom to find Eleanore sitting at her dressing table, taking down her hair. He peered into the bassinet to see Isaac sleeping, and he pressed a gentle hand over his wispy dark hair. He sat down to pull off his boots then got undressed for bed while Eleanore told him about a visit she'd had that afternoon from a woman she knew in the congregation that they attended on Sundays. Mrs. Rollins had stopped by to simply see how Eleanore was coming along, seeing that she'd not been to church since the birth of the baby. Eleanore had enjoyed the visit, even though Mrs. Rollins had run on and on talking of things and people that Eleanore didn't care for or knew nothing about.

James and Eleanore knelt together to pray, then he turned down the wick on the lamp, and they both crawled into bed. While he held her in his arms, she put her lips to his with a kiss that was warm and passionate. James held her closer but murmured, "We must be careful."

She drew back slightly. "Why?"

James hesitated, not wanting to admit how he really felt. But they had an agreement of complete honesty, and he knew that he had to. "I don't want you to get pregnant."

"Not too soon, of course, but . . ." She sat up abruptly, as if that might help her perceive his implication more clearly. "Do you mean now, or ever?"

Again he hesitated. "I fear for your health, Eleanore. I don't want to lose you."

She chuckled with no hint of humor. "There was never any danger of losing me, James. It was painful and difficult, but my life was not in peril."

"I'm not certain I believe that," he admitted. "And what if next time we don't have a doctor, or even adequate shelter, or—"

"Do you truly believe that we could be living among the Saints before our next child comes?" While he pondered the question, Eleanore felt some gratification to think that gathering with the Mormons had come to mean something to him. But she didn't like the implication of his concern.

James answered readily. "We know that eventually it will happen, and we may not have much warning. I'm willing to go wherever the Lord would have us go, Eleanore, but I don't want to put your health at risk by having you give birth in some kind of beastly circumstances."

"So, what are you saying, James?" She lit the lamp again, then turned to face him. "That we shouldn't have any more children because we might have to leave suddenly and the situation could be unpredictable?"

"That's exactly what I'm saying. If we—"

"James." She put a hand on his arm. "Whatever happens, I will be fine."

"How can you say that?" he asked, hearing himself echo words she had asked him not so long ago, following the news of Andy's death. "You can't promise me that something won't happen to you, and having children certainly raises those risks considerably."

"My life was not at risk, James. You can ask the doctor if you like."

"I just might do that."

She took his hand. "Do you remember what you told me after Andy died?"

James sighed and shook his head. He hated it when she turned his words back on him.

"You told me," she said, "that you would do everything in your power to stay safe and healthy. And I will do the same. You said that we would keep doing what we've always done; that we will live close to the Spirit and do whatever God requires of us, because we both know that it is the blessings of the next life that matter more than the hardships of this one."

James heaved a ragged breath. "In principle it all sounds very nice, doesn't it? But the reality of losing you is not something I believe I could survive."

"I feel the same way, James; I do. But we must not worry over such things. Besides, we have been given the greatest possible promise in regard to the very thing you're concerned about."

"We have?" He tightened his gaze on her.

"A prophet of God told us that I would bear and raise many fine children who will settle in Zion and carry forth God's kingdom on the earth. I wouldn't say two is many. But I'm certain the Lord will preserve me long enough to see such a promise fulfilled. We must trust Him and press forward."

James took in her words—and her faith. He touched one side of her face and kissed the other. "Yes, I'm sure you're right." He kissed her lips. "You keep reminding me."

"Of course," she said and kissed him again. And again.

* * * * *

The following Sunday, Eleanore went to church, where many people expressed how delighted they were to see her again, and especially looking so healthy. James eagerly agreed. Little Isaac got a lot of attention and many comments about how he looked a great deal like his mother. His hair had remained thick and dark, much as Jamie's had. But it had a little auburn tint to it, just like Eleanore's.

Ralph was distressed during the meeting due to Lu's absence. Her aunt and uncle weren't there either, and he whispered to James that he couldn't help wondering if something was wrong. James noted Ralph fidgeting restlessly through the sermon and the hymns, and the moment the service was over he bolted outside, stopping only long enough to ask if his mother could ride home with them.

Ralph returned to the house just as they were all sitting down to dinner. Once the food had been blessed, Ralph reported that Lu's aunt was ill, and not only had Lu been given the responsibility to care for her aunt, but also to take over every household chore that her aunt was unable to do.

"She doesn't mind," Ralph said, "and she never complains, but it would be nice if her uncle might lift a finger to help carry the extra load, or at least show a little appreciation."

"Do they know what's wrong with her aunt?" Eleanore asked. "And do you know the woman's name? I think I'd like to stop calling her 'Lu's aunt.'"

"It's May, and Lu's uncle—whose name I do not know and I would prefer not to—won't call on the doctor. He's certain it will pass and May will be right as rain and up cooking in no time. He much prefers May's cooking over Lu's, and makes no hesitation about saying so. But whatever it is May's suffering from keeps coming back and getting worse."

Amanda said, "Ralph tells me that she has trouble breathing, and sometimes coughs and coughs. But it doesn't sound like a cold or the flu. She has no fever or other symptoms."

"That doesn't sound good at all," Lizzie said.

"Is there something we can do to help?" Eleanore asked.

"Oh, we wouldn't dare!" Ralph comically shuddered in terror. "Old Man Bailey would shoot someone before he'd accept charity of any kind. I slip Lu a little money here and there, and it helps get some food and medicine, but she has to be careful about how she goes about it."

Eleanore made a noise of disgust. "The entire situation is maddening."

"Yes, it is," James agreed, "but we need to keep our distance. We can support and encourage Lu, but otherwise we need to bide our time. We'll pray for them. If the Lord wants us to do something, the inspiration will come."

"I tell myself that every day," Ralph said. "I just wish Lu would get inspired to get out of there and marry me."

"Perhaps the time's not right because her aunt needs her," Lizzie suggested.

"I tell myself that too," Ralph said with chagrin. "It's probably true, but I wonder when—or if—that will ever change."

Weeks passed into months and May's condition only worsened. Lu practically became a slave in her household, and Ralph became relatively grumpy about the entire matter. Lu hadn't been to church, or to their home, in a ridiculously long time. Ralph reported that May wasn't so bad off that Lu couldn't leave her, but her uncle would get angry, mostly because he didn't want to help his wife at all. Ralph went to see Lu nearly every day. Usually he got lucky and could go there when Old Man Bailey, as he called him, was far out in the fields working, or in town. If he ever did cross the uncle's path, both he and Lu would certainly hear about it.

One autumn afternoon Lu showed up to see Ralph, saying that her aunt had insisted that she would take responsibility for her leaving once her uncle came home. But Lu hadn't been there an hour when Mr. Bailey showed up at the door with the sheriff. Again the sheriff was kind and gracious, but Ralph felt furious. He did well at keeping his temper under control, but James and Eleanore both hoped that something might change soon, or the situation could get out of hand.

Letters came from Miriam and Sally, posted together in the same envelope, that brought exciting but poignant news. Eleanore quickly read them through, then she gathered the household and read them aloud so that everyone would know of the great events that had occurred. Word had returned to Winter Quarters that Brigham Young and the company that had set out with him had found the place where God had intended for the Saints to settle. There was great joy over the prophecies of Brigham Young in regard to the Salt Lake Valley, located somewhere in the Rocky Mountains. The prophet had stated boldly that this place would flourish and blossom, and that the people would never be driven from there.

Eleanore stopped reading as everyone expressed their pleasure over such a prospect and how much that meant in regard to the prior history of the Saints. Eleanore went on to read Sally's words. "Knowing that we will never have to move again for the sake of peace and safety, the journey of a thousand miles seems—"

"A thousand miles?" James echoed. "Did you read that right?"

"Yes, it says a thousand miles."

"Good heavens," James said. "They *have* gone far into the wilderness this time."

"Perhaps that's the only way they can find peace," Frederick commented.

"Go on." James motioned with his hand, and Eleanore continued to read. Sally reported with obvious glee that the journey of a thousand miles didn't seem so bad with the possibility of worshiping in peace, and it had been reported that the prophet had decided on a place to build the temple only days after his arrival.

Eleanore's excitement waned somewhat then turned to tears as she read that their friends had already left Winter Quarters for the Salt Lake Valley, and they didn't know when they would be able to send mail, but promised to do so at the first opportunity. Miriam's letter spoke of the companies that would be going back and forth between the two places until all the Saints could be gathered in the west for sanctuary.

"Why are you crying?" James asked, taking his wife's hand while she paused in her reading to wipe her tears.

"They'll be so far away."

"And one day we will join them," James said, "when the time is right."

"Maybe the time *is* right," Ralph suggested.

James took in his words along with the expressions of everyone else in the room, silently seeming to plead that they all travel west. He'd come to accept his role as the head of this household, not only in regard to his own family but for those that worked for him as well. He knew there was only one thing he could say. "We'll certainly make that a matter of prayer. Even if it is time for us to head west, we won't be going until spring. I've had enough travel in winter to last me a lifetime."

"Hear, hear," Frederick said at the same moment that Ben said, "Amen to that."

"Read the rest," Iris urged, and Eleanore went on to finish Miriam's letter. She reported that she and the children were doing well in spite of Andy's death, and she expressed much gratitude for all she'd been blessed with, and her confidence that they would all be with Andy again one day. Again Eleanore cried to read of such faith. Miriam reported that Sally had taken her in as a sister, and that Sally's husband, Mark, had officially taken on the care of her and her children.

Once the letters had been read, the family spent more than an hour sharing their feelings over the matter and their hope to join the Saints before too much time passed. They all knelt together and prayed on behalf of their friends and others who were traveling so far to be free from persecution.

That night, Eleanore lay in the dark, staring upward, unable to sleep as memories of their traveling by wagons to Iowa City merged with images of her friends making a thousand-mile journey. Those miles across the prairies of America had seemed eternal to Eleanore, and it had positively been one of the worst experiences of her life. But the destination had proved worth every miserable minute, and she felt certain the same would be the case for those traveling to the Salt Lake

Valley. Still, it was, as James had defined, in the wilderness. There would be no fine homes already built and waiting for them. The Saints would surely have to work very hard even upon arriving, simply to meet their most basic needs of food and shelter. She thought of once living in the manor house in England, and tried to comprehend the contrast between that life and this one. Even with the prospect of traveling so far one day, and having to work hard to start over, she would gladly choose this life over that one.

"What are you thinking about?" James asked from the darkness.

"I thought you were asleep."

"No, you didn't. You tell me I breathe differently when I'm asleep."

"That's true. But I wasn't paying attention. Sometimes you snore."

"Well, sometimes *you* snore too, Mrs. Barrington. And *you* certainly breathe differently when you're asleep. So, what are you thinking about?"

"I was thinking that I'd much prefer life in Salt Lake City than life in the manor house in England."

"And why is that?" he asked, rolling toward her.

"I would say that starting a new life in the wilderness with you sounds much more exciting than spending my life a spinster, working for the lord of the manor."

"A spinster? You?"

She laughed softly. "Someone once told me," she lowered her voice to mimic, "'What do you think the likelihood might be of a woman in your position to receive *any* proposal of marriage, let alone one based on *love*? How many eligible men do you come in contact with, Miss Layne?'"

James groaned as he realized she was mimicking *him.* "Did I really say that?"

"You really did." She laughed again. "You also said, 'I can assure you that in spite of your charm and beauty, Miss Layne, you will *not* receive any such offer again.'"

James groaned once more, then chuckled. "I must have been terrified that you would turn me down. I was surely lying to you for the sake of—"

"You've never lied to me."

"Not intentionally, no." He chuckled again.

"I'm certain you were right. There were no eligible men in my life, at least none that would have been worth even considering for marriage." She giggled. "There was Mr. Crocker." James laughed to recall a toothless farmer in his sixties. He'd been dirt poor and too lazy to work very hard. "And Mr. Piggot."

"I never knew a Mr. Piggot."

"He sold flowers on the high street. He would flirt with me sometimes if I ever bothered to get near him."

"And why not marry Mr. Piggot?"

"His selling flowers barely managed to conceal his self-neglect, and he was rumored to like liquor more than women."

"No, you couldn't have married Mr. Piggot."

"No, I couldn't have, because I was destined to marry James Edward Barrington, the wealthiest, most handsome man in the county."

"I dispute most handsome."

She laughed. "But you don't dispute wealthiest?"

"No, I can't dispute that."

"Well, I'm absolutely certain you were the most handsome. But perhaps Mr. Piggot took over that position when you moved away."

"Perhaps," James said and kissed her while they both laughed. "We should get some sleep," he added just before Isaac made a noise to indicate he was waking up to be fed. "Or perhaps we should just stay awake a little longer and feed the baby."

"Excellent idea," she said, and he got out of bed to get the baby's milk, according to their typical routine. It was much easier to just get some warm milk straight from the goat than it was to heat it to the right temperature in the middle of the night.

ßEleanore opened her eyes and smiled at him from where she was resting in bed. "Funny how a blessing comes out of every trial, somehow."

"Yes, it seems that way," he said and watched the baby drift off to sleep while Eleanore did the same.

* * * * *

Winter settled in while Eleanore thought a great deal about her friends, hoping they had arrived safely in the Salt Lake Valley without having to face any harsh weather. She felt frustrated by not being able to send them letters, but she wrote to them often anyway, tucking the pages away until a time when they could be mailed.

Some significantly foul weather marked the one-year anniversary of Benjamin's joining their family. They celebrated with a party, and everyone heartily agreed they were grateful to be safe in a warm home and not making the journey that Ben had made with James and Frederick a year earlier. Their celebration ended with a family prayer on behalf of those who were still at Winter Quarters, and those who were starting over in the Rocky Mountains.

In February Eleanore discovered she was pregnant. She felt more concerned about her health than she let on. And she knew that James shared that concern, but he too assumed a hopeful attitude and said nothing negative. She told him she appreciated his faith and support, and they didn't bother discussing speculations over the outcome. Their prayers about moving west had continued to receive the same answer—that they needed to remain where they were. But they both knew that the answer could change overnight, and they needed to be prepared. They talked about what they would take with them, and what they'd leave behind—which was practically everything. They even started buying some supplies and keeping them in the barn, things that could easily be loaded into the two wagons they owned.

Two weeks after the discovery of Eleanore's pregnancy, Lu's Aunt May finally passed away. The entire Barrington household attended the funeral service, but Old Man Bailey didn't even acknowledge their presence or their attempt to offer condolences. In the few minutes that Lu was able to be alone with Ralph, she'd told him that May's death was a relief. Lu had watched her suffer intolerably with her illness, and she was glad to know that this sweet woman was in a better place. But in the weeks following the funeral, Ralph's hope that the situation would improve for Lu was shattered by the evidence that it had only worsened. Now Lu's uncle was drinking too much on top of expecting Lu to completely take care of the house and meals and laundry. Ralph's repeated efforts to get Lu to marry him and leave her uncle's care were continually avoided and turned down. Ralph discussed the situation many times with James and Eleanore, reiterating that he absolutely knew she loved him and wanted to be with him, but that she was afraid of her uncle's reaction, that even if she were Ralph's wife, her uncle would know where to find her, and he might even do her harm.

James suggested they speak to the sheriff concerning the matter, since Ralph genuinely feared for Lu's safety. Her uncle had only struck her a few times, but his drunkenness was worsening. Sheriff Willis was kind and agreed that Mr. Bailey's attitude was ridiculous and inappropriate, but according to the law he could not intervene in the matter. He gently expressed to Ralph his confidence that the young man could find a viable solution, and James thanked him for his time. Ralph continued to be patient and prayerful, but James feared the situation would eventually become too difficult to ignore.

In late March, Eleanore miscarried the baby with no complications or trauma. It was over in a short time and with minimal pain in contrast to the childbirth she'd endured. James marveled at how well she came through it, both physically and emotionally. Her faith and strength had certainly grown during the years they'd shared. Her grief was obvious, and the loss was certainly difficult, but it was evident that she'd come to more fully trust in the Lord to give them another baby when the time was right.

With spring came the arrival of five letters all at once from Salt Lake City. The Saints were earnestly settling in there, and the city was growing. Miriam and Sally both wrote of many challenges but also of great hope among the Saints. If they had turned the swamps of Nauvoo into a beautiful city, they could certainly make the desert thrive. And they spoke again of the hope they'd found in the prophecies given by Brigham Young that from this place the Saints would never be driven.

News of Zion provoked James and Eleanore once again to prayer over the matter of joining the Saints, but again the answer was clearly no. They needed to wait. James reminded himself and Eleanore that Brigham Young had personally told him that their being in Iowa would serve some purpose. So James stopped asking what he should be waiting for, or how long the wait would be. He just enjoyed the life they were living and ignored any unrest over the fact that his household was living their religion in secret and alone.

* * * * *

A short while after supper on the first warm evening of the year, Eleanore left Iris looking after Jamie and Isaac while they were playing. She found James in the library and sat down beside him.

"What are you reading?" she asked, and he offered an explanation about the topic of American politics he was studying, which held little interest for her. She listened for a few minutes, then he chuckled and set the book aside.

"Why don't you just admit that you're bored instead of letting me ramble?"

"I'll get even, I'm sure. I'll be needing to reread my Jane Austen novels one of these days."

He chuckled again and kissed her. They heard some distant commotion and the stairs to the attic being lowered. The attic was a place where Ben and Iris had spent many hours playing, or just reading and talking. But in the winter it was too cold up there and they'd not even pulled the stairs down for months.

"I wonder what Ben is up to. It had better be Ben; I left Iris watching the boys."

They heard the attic stairs snap into place; then there was silence. James commented, "Maybe Ben was just looking for something." Their conversation returned to the topic of favorite books they'd read, a common ground they'd shared right from the start. A pounding at the front door startled them both.

"Who on earth?" James murmured and went to answer it. Eleanore stayed close beside him, sensing urgency in the repeated knocking at the door.

On the porch they found Mr. Bailey with the sheriff and a man they'd never seen before who was apparently a deputy.

"Have you seen that niece of mine?" Mr. Bailey bellowed without any greeting.

"No, we haven't," James said with genuine innocence, while Eleanore discreetly took hold of her husband's hand.

"Well, I've a mind not t' believe ya," Mr. Bailey snarled. "That Leichty boy has been—"

"Mr. Barrington," the sheriff interrupted, behaving more seemly, "Miss Bailey has apparently run off, and it's important that we find her."

"Of course," James said, "but we haven't seen her for days. Did you check at the Leichty home or—"

"Mrs. Leichty ain't seen neither o' them," Mr. Bailey snarled. "She said her boy might be here; he's here an awful lot."

"He is indeed," James said, "but we've not seen him this evening."

"I'm not sure I believe ya," Mr. Bailey snapped.

"My husband is an honest man!" Eleanore defended.

"I'm sure he is," the sheriff said, "but I'd feel a lot better if we could take a look around."

Eleanore noted her husband hesitating, and she wondered if he was concerned that the sheriff might find something suspicious. He then stepped back and motioned with his arm. "Feel free," he said with easy nonchalance. "I only ask that you not alarm the children."

Eleanore felt decidedly uneasy as the three visitors entered the house and moved in different directions. James motioned for Eleanore to follow the sheriff who was heading down the hall of the main floor, and James went with Mr. Bailey and the deputy who headed up the stairs. Eleanore felt hesitant to be separated from her husband under the circumstances, but she understood the need for keeping track of what these men were doing. And she preferred being with the sheriff as opposed to the cantankerous Mr. Bailey.

James hovered with these men as they looked into each room, checking behind draperies and under beds. The children were playing in Iris's room and were not happy about the invasion. James assured them there was no cause for concern, but Iris didn't appear convinced.

When the men found nothing, they stood in the hall where Mr. Bailey made an exasperated noise, then cursed his niece for causing him so much trouble. Then he glanced at the rope hanging from the ceiling and asked, "What's that?"

"It goes to the attic," James said and immediately stepped forward and pulled the rope down, not wanting these men to think he was trying to hide anything. Considering what he knew of Ralph and the things he'd told them about Lu and her life at home with her uncle, he prayed they *weren't* hiding something.

James led the way up to the attic, with Mr. Bailey right on his heels. He found a lamp burning and Ben leaning up against a trunk, immersed in a book and looking startled by the intrusion, then alarmed when he saw Mr. Bailey.

"What's going on?" Ben asked, jumping to his feet.

"Lu is missing," James said.

"Well, she obviously isn't here," Ben said, but Mr. Bailey wandered through the attic, looking in every corner before he let out a disgruntled noise and huffed back down the ladder.

"Sorry to bother you, son," the deputy said and followed Mr. Bailey. James patted Ben on the shoulder and went down in time to see Mr. Bailey heading toward the stairs. James followed him down to find the sheriff and Eleanore just coming out of the kitchen.

"That's it except the office," Eleanore said, motioning the men toward the closed door.

James opened it, and light shed into the room to illuminate a sleepy Ralph who squinted and muttered, "Is this a party or what?"

Mr. Bailey took him by the collar and dragged him to his feet, making him suddenly alert, although his eyes still looked bleary. "Where is she? What have you done with her?"

"What on earth are you talking about?" Ralph muttered, terrified.

"There's no need to get rough," the sheriff said, putting a hand on Mr. Bailey's arm.

Bailey reluctantly let go and backed away. The sheriff said, "Lu's gone missing, and—"

"Missing?" Ralph echoed, astonished and overtly afraid. "What's that supposed to mean? We need to find her and—"

"That's what we're trying to do," the sheriff said. "Can you tell us anything that might help?"

"No!" Ralph shot frightened eyes to James, then Eleanore, then back to the sheriff. "I haven't seen her since church yesterday. We talked for a minute after. That's all."

"Did she say anything that might make you think she had plans of running off or—"

"No, nothing. I said goodbye to her, since I'm going west to settle."

"Are ya now?" Mr. Bailey snarled.

"That's right. I'm leaving tomorrow. I've been planning this for weeks. You can ask anyone who knows me."

Eleanore forced a straight expression as the three men turned to look at her and James, who said with perfect ease, "He talks of little else. Supplies and wagon are waiting in the barn."

Eleanore never imagined her husband could be such a good liar. Neither of them had ever heard anything beyond a someday speculation of joining the Saints. Her heart pounded while she wondered what Ralph might be up to. He went on to say, "Lu's known for a long time that I was leaving. She wanted nothing to do with going west. I told her I'd seen the last of her. I don't understand what would make her run off."

"Is there anything else you know that might help us?" the sheriff asked.

"No, nothing," Ralph said again.

"All right then," the sheriff said.

James offered with confidence, "Did you want to check the barn or—"

"We already checked before we came to the door," the sheriff said and James felt a little unnerved at the thought.

"Thank you for your time," the sheriff said. Mr. Bailey made another disagreeable noise and huffed out the front door.

Chapter Six

ELEANORE'S FORTÉ

James, Eleanore, and Ralph all stood in stunned silence in the hallway while the sound of horses galloped away.

"I wonder where she could be," Eleanore said. "I hope she's not—"

"Lock the doors," Ralph said and rushed toward the front door. James shot Eleanore a skeptical glance but hurried to lock the back door. They saw Ralph run up the stairs and went after him, coming into the hall just as he pulled down the rope to drop the ladder from the attic.

"Ralph, what have you done?" Eleanore demanded.

They followed him into the attic and found him helping Lu out of the trunk that Ben had been leaning against. Eleanore halted her temptation to scold them for their dishonesty when she saw the bruises and tears on Lu's face.

"What's happened?" Eleanore asked, moving between Ralph and Lu to assess the damage.

"I couldn't take it any more," Lu cried, "and I told him so. I think I'd rather have him kill me than live like that any more. I can't go back there."

"No, you *mustn't* go back there!" Eleanore insisted. "We'll just—"

"That's why we're leaving before sunup." Ralph put his arm around Lu and she held to him and cried. He looked directly at James and said, "We can't cause you any trouble over this. We just need to go. I know it sounds impulsive, but it's not. I've been praying about this for weeks; I knew it would come to this. I think the Spirit has been preparing me. Maybe I should have said something, but . . . I didn't want to get anyone else in trouble with Old Man Bailey, especially you."

"We can find a way for you and Lu to be married, Ralph," James said. "And we can handle him. Don't leave just because you're concerned for us. You're family to us, and—"

"I know that," Ralph said, "I do. And I'm grateful. But I know this is right. I have some money saved. I'm hoping you'll let me buy one of the wagons and some supplies so we can be packed tonight and—"

"No, I won't," James said, and Eleanore looked at him sharply. "I'm not taking your money. You're like a son to me. You take the wagon and anything you need. We'll help you pack."

Ralph sighed deeply but said, "I can't take it for nothing. I—"

"You take it!" James said in a nearly harsh voice that he rarely used. "I won't accept any other answer. You save your money. You're going to need it."

Lu calmed down somewhat, and Ralph wiped at her tears. Eleanore felt too aghast to speak. James asked in a voice that was more quiet, "Do you have a plan? Or are you just going to—"

"We're going to Winter Quarters. I'm certain there's someone there with the proper authority to marry us. And then we'll head west with one of the wagon companies. We have friends in Salt Lake City. I'm certain we'll be fine."

"I'm certain you will," James said. Taut silence made the difficulty of the moment evident. James broke it by saying, "Ben, would you go and get Frederick. Tell him I need his help."

"Yes, Papa," Ben said and hurried down the attic stairs.

"Come along," Eleanore said to Lu. "Let's get some salve on those bruises and see that you have what you need for this journey while the men get everything packed."

Eleanore guided Lu down the stairs and to her bedroom while the men went the other direction to leave the house. She left Lu with a cold compress on her face and went to put the children to bed with Iris's help. Once the boys were down, Eleanore quietly told Iris what was happening. She insisted on seeing Lu before she went to bed, knowing they would be gone before morning. Iris cried when she saw Lu's discolored face, and she cried harder when Lu told her how much she was going to miss her. Eleanore left Lu resting and walked with Iris out to the barn so that Iris could tell Ralph goodbye as well. Again she cried as she hugged him, then she ran to her room to be alone. Eleanore suggested that Ben also tell Ralph and Lu goodbye and go to bed, but he insisted that he would stay up and help them pack. He promised to do his chores the following morning and James told him the help would be appreciated.

While James and Frederick made an accounting of supplies that would be needed, and loaded them carefully, Ralph rode home to pack his personal things, and Eleanore returned to be with Lu. She assessed that there was no damage beyond the results of some brutally hard slaps to Lu's face, then she helped the girl put salve on the bruises, while Lu cried and told the story of her uncle's drunken rages that had blown out of control since May's death. Eleanore listened and tried to soothe her with hope for the future, knowing in her heart that the best possible course would be exactly what Ralph had decided. But the thought of them leaving broke her heart.

Eleanore pulled out a couple of nightgowns and some clothes that she wouldn't miss and packed them in a bag for Lu. The young woman was slightly smaller and shorter than Eleanore, but they would be sufficient. She also gave her an extra hairbrush and some miscellaneous sundries that she might need, things that Eleanore could certainly replace.

"You've always been so kind to me," Lu said as they put the things carefully into a bag. "I don't know what to say."

"You just stay safe and have a good life, and one day we'll see you again—hopefully before too long."

Lu nodded and choked on more tears. They were interrupted by a man's footsteps in the hall, then James peered into the room and said, "Eleanore, I need you to come downstairs. Lu, you should rest."

"I'm fine," Lu insisted.

"Ralph is out in the barn," James said and Eleanore heard an indication that he didn't want Lu to go wherever they were going.

Once they reached the bottom of the stairs, Lu went out the back door, and James guided Eleanore toward the kitchen. "Amanda wants to speak with us."

"She's here?" Eleanore asked and entered the room to see Amanda sitting at the table, overcome by tears.

Eleanore couldn't imagine how difficult this must be for Amanda to let her son go. But Eleanore felt like a fool for not seeing the obvious when Amanda said firmly, "I must go with my son."

Eleanore sank into a chair, grateful to feel James take her hand. It took her a long moment to absorb the shock. Ralph and Amanda had been a part of their household since they'd first arrived here from England. Eleanore would miss Ralph, of course. But Amanda was a woman she had worked with, side by side, day in and day out. The woman had helped her through losing babies, through David's death; she'd helped her learn how to be a mother to her babies. She'd been there with her quiet strength and wisdom, hour by hour. And now she was leaving. But what could Eleanore say? If she were in Amanda's position, she would do the very same thing.

The tightening silence prompted Eleanore to say, "Of course you must." She was unable to say anything else without tempting her sudden grief to the surface.

"It breaks my heart to leave here," Amanda said, wiping at tears. "I mean . . . we've talked of being with the Saints, but I always thought we would go together . . . all of us. I can't imagine what I'll do without you . . . all of you."

"I can't imagine that either," Eleanore said, her voice shaky and cracked.

"But my son needs me. I'm certain he could manage well enough, but . . . Lu needs me too. She needs a mother, and . . ." She laughed softly, "I suppose they need a chaperone until they can be married. I just pray that it won't be long before the rest of you will be following us. I'll miss you so very much."

"Yes," Eleanore said. "It . . . will never be the same without you."

More silence was spattered with many sniffles while the women cried and James just sat beside his wife, looking grim and distressed.

Eleanore tried to think of something productive to say. "So . . . can I help you pack or—"

"No, it's done."

"Already?" Eleanore asked.

"There isn't much we'll be needing. We've taken what's sentimental and what will get us by. The rest doesn't matter much. We've not spent a lot of time in that house anyway, since you came." She looked more at James. "I wonder if you would sell it for us; perhaps you could send us the money when—"

"That would be fine," James said and left the room abruptly. Eleanore wondered if he was struggling with his emotions.

"I can't thank you enough for all you've done for us," Amanda said.

"It's the other way around," Eleanore insisted.

Amanda chuckled uncomfortably. "Tomorrow I'll think of a thousand things I should have said right now, but . . ."

"It's all right. It doesn't matter. We'll write of course, and we'll see you soon . . . hopefully soon."

"Of course."

James came back in the room and handed Amanda a thick envelope.

"What is this?" she asked and opened it. Eleanore caught a glimpse of a large amount of cash. She knew James kept money in a safe, as well as in some accounts at the bank. "Good heavens!" Amanda gasped. "What on earth is—"

"For the house," he said. "I think that's a fair price from what I know at the moment. I have the money, so it's not a problem. Better that I give it to you now, so you'll have what you need. Who knows if sending it would get it there safely."

"Thank you," Amanda said and stood to hug him. "Thank you for everything."

James said nothing. Eleanore knew this was difficult for him. Amanda hugged her as well, then she hurried out of the room, perhaps fearing she might fall apart again if she didn't. Eleanore moved into her husband's arms and wept, aware that he was doing the same.

Before dawn, final goodbyes were said as the contents of the wagon were checked once more. Everyone but Lizzie, Iris, and the younger children had been up all night helping make sure that everything needed for the journey was in place. Frederick had cleverly situated the contents of the wagon so that Lu could get into a concealed space and hide should they be stopped and searched before getting out of the area. Eleanore sent Ben to wake Iris and Lizzie so that they could say goodbye to Amanda and the others. Lizzie hadn't even known the situation, since she'd gone back to sleep after Frederick had been summoned to help. Eleanore could barely keep herself from completely crumbling as she observed the tender farewells between Lizzie and Amanda. Lizzie had worked even more closely with

Amanda than Eleanore had. It was common to find them laughing together in the kitchen, or absorbed in deep conversation. It was clear to see that Lizzie's tender heart was breaking. Frederick kept an arm around his wife except for when he hugged Amanda himself, a rare glisten of tears showing in his eyes.

Lizzie and Iris cried the most when the wagon pulled away. James held his daughter close while she wept without restraint, and Frederick kept Lizzie in a tight embrace while she did the same. Eleanore had spent most of her tears already. But as she went up to bed to try to get a little rest before the boys needed her, she cried again. And she fell asleep praying that Ralph, Lu, and Amanda would be protected and healthy, and that all would be well.

The first day with Ralph and Amanda gone brought back memories of losing a family member to death. Eleanore kept reminding herself, and her loved ones, that their friends were alive and well and they would see them again someday. But someday felt as abstract and difficult to grasp as knowing that David was on the other side of the veil. They were all out of reach, and none of them had any idea when they might be reunited.

The work that Ralph had normally done was divided among James, Frederick, and Ben. They managed well enough, and James commented more than once that with Ben's efforts to make up the difference, he was left doing hardly anything extra at all. It was evident that Ben missed Ralph a great deal, and one more loss couldn't be easy on him. But as with everything, Ben handled it bravely and without complaint. And this with practically no sleep the night before.

Amanda's work in the kitchen was not so easily substituted. Lizzie and Eleanore both felt awkward attempting to do all that Amanda had done so effortlessly, and the quality of their meals decreased dramatically.

Eleanore woke up the day after her friends had left and didn't even want to get out of bed. Following a simple breakfast of oatmeal, toast, and fresh milk, Eleanore asked the children to help her clear the table, then she sent them off to do their other chores while she and Lizzie cleaned the dishes. But neither of them had much to say. They were barely finished when James came into the kitchen with an expression that indicated he wanted to talk to his wife. Lizzie had become familiar with that look and discreetly left the room. He announced with no preface, "I'm going to advertise today for someone to replace Amanda and Ralph so that we—"

"We do not need to hire someone to replace them," Eleanore insisted. "No one could ever replace them, and I'm not in the mood to adjust to having strangers working in my house."

"They won't be strangers for long. I wouldn't hire someone if I didn't believe they could fit in well and—"

"Amanda and Ralph were like family. It could never be the same."

"I'm not disputing that, Ellie. I'm not, but—"

"Before you hired Amanda I wasn't terribly keen on hiring anyone at all." She looked at him directly and with firm resolve in her eyes. "I felt good about it because I believed they needed us at least as much as we needed them. I'm not disputing what a blessing they've been in our lives, and they've certainly made many things easier. But we have Frederick and Lizzie, and the children are getting older and more capable of helping. Most families don't have a choice. They could never afford to hire extra help. We can manage just fine. Sometimes I wonder if we're far too spoiled."

"I could never spoil you; you're unspoilable. But what happens when you get pregnant again and can't get out of bed for weeks?"

"We'll manage. I don't want you hiring anyone."

"And who will do all of the cooking? It's no small task to put on three meals a day."

"*I* will. Lizzie will help me." She heard him sigh loudly, and she added, "I'm well aware that my skills are nowhere near that of Amanda's, but I've worked with her for years. It's time I learned to cook for my family. I'll learn."

"I'm not worried about that."

"What *are* you worried about?"

Again he sighed and said, "It's hard to say. I'm just worried."

"Well, don't be," she said and rushed out of the room, grateful that he didn't follow her.

Eleanore kept busy with washing some laundry and enlisted Iris's help in hanging it in the yard to dry. She couldn't help thinking that they'd managed the previous day to put on lunch and supper with some soup Amanda had made the previous day, but that was gone now. Lizzie put out cold roast beef and sliced bread for sandwiches, which made a fine lunch. But once again, Eleanore couldn't help thinking that Amanda had baked this bread, and it would soon be gone. She'd watched Amanda make bread dozens of times, and she'd tried to pay attention, but she doubted she could ever duplicate the results of Amanda's years of experience, and her special knack in the kitchen. She would just have to learn.

Soon after lunch Lizzie admitted that she had a nasty headache, and Eleanore insisted that she go lie down. For the first time ever, Eleanore set to work completely alone in a kitchen. In England she'd helped in the kitchen here and there, but it was always under the supervision of the cooks, and it had been easy to simply do the task assigned to her. Since coming to America, Amanda had been in their home even before they'd gotten settled in. And Lizzie had always helped as well, although she readily admitted that her cooking knowledge was equivalent to Eleanore's.

While she prepared fried chicken, mashed potatoes and gravy, and carrots, Eleanore kept praying and telling herself that she could do this. But the carrots ended up too soft, the potatoes were lumpy, and the gravy was atrocious. She was about to dump it out when James caught her and stopped her. "It's horrible," she insisted. "We'd do better with butter on our potatoes, I can assure you."

"It will be fine," he said and set the gravy on the table.

As they were being seated, all except Lizzie who was still resting, Eleanore warned everyone about the gravy, and she chose to avoid it herself. The children also avoided it, but James and Frederick both ate it as if nothing in the world were wrong. She couldn't help appreciating their diplomacy, but in a way it made her angry—even if she couldn't articulate the reasons.

In the absence of Amanda and Ralph, there was an unusual lack of the normal pleasant conversation at the supper table, made worse by Eleanore's realization that the food they were eating was a much poorer quality than what they'd become accustomed to. She knew the others would be too polite to say anything critical of her cooking, but it made Amanda's absence all the more evident. Overcome by a wave of unexpected tears, Eleanore excused herself and hurried out of the room. The library seemed more convenient than her bedroom, which was upstairs. She rushed inside and closed the door, praying that James would just eat his supper and leave her in peace until she had a good cry. Perhaps with her gone, the others could discuss the inferior quality of the meal and get it over with.

Eleanore almost cursed under her breath when she heard a knock at the door. It had a particular strength and rhythm to it that she knew all too well. It was her husband.

"I want to be alone," she called, but he opened the door.

"I told you when I married you that your tears were my responsibility. I'm not going to leave you alone crying unless I know the reason for it."

"It's obvious, isn't it?"

"You miss Amanda and Ralph?" he asked, closing the door.

New emotion tightened her chest and made her voice quaver. "So badly it hurts," she said. She sobbed quietly. "I want to go with them, James. I want to be where they are. I want to be with Sally and Miriam. I don't want to live more than a thousand miles from my friends. I want to go to church on Sundays and hear words I can believe coming over the pulpit. I want to sing our most precious hymns with a congregation and walk the streets with people who share my beliefs, instead of living in fear that my neighbors will find out and persecute us for them."

"I want all of that too, Ellie," he said, leaning against the door. "And you know as well as I do that God wants us to stay here—for the time being. Eventually we will gather with the Saints; we know that, too."

"But when?"

"The matter is in God's hands. We'll know when the time is right. We must be patient."

"Well, I don't *feel* patient," Eleanore insisted, willfully swallowing her tears.

Silence left her hoping that he'd leave the room and allow her to indulge in her grieving privately, but he moved behind her and put his hands on her shoulders. "What else is wrong?" he asked. She wanted to tell him that it was nothing, but he immediately added, "And don't tell me nothing, because I would know that you're lying."

Eleanore knew better than to beat around the bush. He would persist until he got an honest answer. And it wasn't as if he didn't already know. She took a deep breath and blurted out the truth. "I'm a terrible cook."

"You are not!"

"You're just being diplomatic. You know very well that my cooking could never measure up to Amanda's." She turned to face him. "Don't lie to me, James. You have to admit that it's true."

"I fail to see where your abilities in the kitchen have anything to do with—"

"My *lack* of abilities in the kitchen," she corrected.

"You do just fine!" he insisted.

"Compared to what?"

"Why does there have to be a comparison?"

"How can there not be when Amanda has done such a fine job all these years and—"

"I offered to hire someone."

"So you *do* agree that I'm a terrible cook?"

"I did *not* say that. Don't put words in my mouth, Mrs. Barrington."

"But you'd prefer to hire someone as opposed to having *me* cook or—"

"That has *nothing* to do with my reasons for—"

"Admit it, James. Tell me the truth. I can deal with the truth, but don't patronize me."

James sighed and looked down. "Eleanore, truthfully . . . Amanda was gifted in the kitchen, and she had a great deal of experience. I will *not* patronize you; I never have. There are many things that *you* are gifted at. You can't be good at everything. There were things Amanda could never do that you do brilliantly. Comparing is ridiculous. And just because cooking isn't your greatest forte, that does not make you a *terrible* cook. If you *want* to cook, then clearly practice will help. And no one is going to starve or be miserable over eating what you provide. You do just fine. If you would prefer not to cook, then I'll hire someone. If we couldn't afford it, then we would manage. But we can, which leaves the choice up to you."

Eleanore sighed and sat down. She couldn't dispute what he was saying. He wasn't the kind of man to patronize anyone—especially her. And he hadn't lied to her. But he was kind and had a good heart.

"If you weren't a wealthy man, you would have been putting up with my cooking all along."

"And look at all the practice you would have gotten by now," he said, attempting to lighten the mood. But her scowl only deepened. He sighed and sat beside her, taking her hand. "Eleanore, you are a remarkable and gifted woman. You don't need to prove anything in the kitchen."

"Gifted how?" she demanded, as if he might be lying.

Eleanore expected him to stammer or struggle to come up with an answer, but he stated with firm resolve, "I never had anyone working in my household who would stand up to me the way you did, and yet you did it so gracefully. You never got angry or left me with any cause to feel put off or defensive. But you could always manage to say what I needed to hear. And you had such wisdom beyond your years, as if you'd come to this world with a spirit more mature than the average human being. You're still that way; you always have been. It's one of a million reasons why I love you."

"But . . . surely that is not . . . a gift, or—"

"It most certainly is. You are rare among women for that aspect of your character. And that makes you gifted in that respect. You are also gifted with the children. When I first hired you I admit that I was impressed by our interview, but it was mostly instinct that led me to choose you. Within days I was stunned by your ability to keep the children disciplined and yet so happy and comfortable. They were completely at ease with you and had no qualms about minding what you told them to do. Again, it's still that way. I am in awe of how you can handle anything that comes up with the children. You have taught them as well as any school teacher ever could. Not only are their reading skills excellent, but you have also instilled in them a passion for reading. And you've also given them a love for keeping a journal, something that's a great blessing to all of us. You're not just a good mother, Eleanore, you are a *great* mother. It's a part of your deepest instincts; it's who you are. In my opinion, such things make your abilities in the kitchen completely irrelevant. When our children are grown, they will remember the love and wisdom and guidance you gave them far more than the quality of food on the table. And it's not only the children who will remember your gifts. You are generous and charitable to others in need. You never make any fuss over it, but

I've seen how many times you've gone to visit women we go to church with who are struggling. You are sensitive to things others would miss, and you've soothed many ailments—emotional as well as physical."

Eleanore took in his words, realizing that if he would admit she couldn't cook nearly as well as Amanda, then he would not lie to her about anything else. Still, she had to clarify. "You really mean that, don't you?"

"I really do."

"You're very good to me."

"Being good to you has never been hard, Eleanore. You are easy to love, and easy to please. I couldn't ask for a finer wife. You have made this house a home, and you have filled it with a warm spirit and much good. I don't care whether or not you can make gravy."

"So, you admit that the gravy was deplorable."

"Yes," he chuckled, "the gravy was deplorable."

"I was trying to dump it out, if you'll recall."

"Then it's my own fault for eating it," he said.

"So, next time just . . . let me dump out what isn't suitable for the table, and I'll just . . . keep practicing."

"Fair enough. Now, why don't you come and eat your supper? I'll help you reheat it."

"I'm not sure I'm very hungry," she admitted.

"You need to eat anyway." He took her arm and guided her toward the door. "Are you sure you don't want me to hire someone?"

"I don't know," she said, and they hesitated before opening the door. "I feel like I *should* spend more time in the kitchen."

"But do you *want* to? Lizzie readily admits that she'd prefer not to and that she's not very good at it, but you know she'll do anything you ask of her."

"I know."

"So, why can Lizzie admit it and not feel upset over it?"

"I suppose because Lizzie is not the mistress of this house."

"If we lived in England you wouldn't even question whether or not you should work in the kitchen, because it was well established that the mistress of the house would not."

"But this is a different culture here, James, a different society."

"That depends on how you look at it," he said. "We have socialized among different classes of people here. Those snobbish people we were going to parties with for a while? I bet those women don't ever bother to cook or even set foot in the kitchen."

"But I don't *want* to be among the snobbish."

"And you never could be. I prefer that we fit in more among the farmers and people who live simple lives. And we do . . . we did, even with Amanda working in the kitchen. I'm not disputing that hard work is good for us, and I didn't do nearly enough of it in England. But I would rather have you working with me and the children in the garden, and giving the children their lessons, than toiling in the kitchen when you hate it. And unless you consider yourself done having children—"

"Of course I don't!"

"Well then," he said, "you have to be realistic enough to accept that during pregnancy you are not going to be up to cooking for a household. And Lizzie has plenty to keep her busy. Just think about it. I'll do whatever you wish."

"Very well. I'll think about it."

"Good. In the meantime, let's eat."

Eleanore wrapped her arms around him before he could open the door. "I love you, James. Thank you for not leaving me alone even though I wanted to be. You always talk sense into me."

"And vice versa."

When they returned to the dining room, everyone else had finished eating and had cleared their places and left. James helped Eleanore reheat their food, and he dumped out the gravy. After they'd eaten, he helped her clean the dishes while they talked and laughed, and later she apologized to Frederick for the horrible gravy. He laughed and told her it wasn't so bad, and reminded her that she'd warned him. He also hugged her and told her she was doing just fine. He then added, much to her surprise, "You've come a long way from the child who scrubbed pots and polished furniture, saving all your money to buy books."

Eleanore felt taken aback by the memory of being that girl, and even more so by recalling that Frederick Higgins had been one of the few people in a very large household who had been genuinely interested in her and her life. They had shared many conversations in the kitchen over meals that were purposely planned to avoid the rest of the servants. Lizzie had often been there as well, along with a few other servants who had been more friendly than concerned with backbiting and gossip. Eleanore never would have dreamed during those conversations that they would all end up this way together. But she was glad for it. She'd far rather be cooking mediocre meals in her lovely Iowa home, than living as lady of the manor with dozens of servants available. And she knew that Frederick and Lizzie far preferred this life to that one. They'd come far, and they'd been through much together. Surely they could all survive Eleanore's cooking. And that meant they could survive adjusting to the absence of Amanda and Ralph. They would be missed, and it would never be the same. But Eleanore knew that one day the Spirit would guide them to know when it was the right time to leave this place, and they would join their friends in Salt Lake City.

That evening Eleanore offered a lengthy silent prayer as usual, on her knees beside the bed. But tonight she devoted extra time to pondering the situation of the household in Amanda's absence, and her own place there. She asked her Father in Heaven for guidance on the matter, then went to sleep with the issue uppermost in her mind. She knew that James and Frederick could handle much of what Ralph would have been doing, especially since Ben was getting older and more capable of helping. In fact, he seemed eager to do so. It was apparent he'd grown up accustomed to working hard and he seemed to feel more out of sorts when there wasn't enough to keep him busy. And he loved working alongside his father. For that reason, Ralph's absence almost seemed a blessing in regard to Ben's situation. This could likely be the very opportunity the boy needed to feel like a more integral part of the household and to keep busy.

Eleanore woke up with the situation still on her mind. While she was braiding her hair for the day, she spoke with James about her thoughts regarding Ben. He heartily agreed and gave her a genuine compliment on her insight. She realized then that he'd frequently mentioned her wisdom and intuition, which left her certain he wasn't simply trying to prove something related to yesterday's conversation. In fact, she felt certain that James wasn't thinking about it at all. Eleanore had never considered her insight something special, but now she had to wonder if perhaps it was. And if it truly was a gift from her Father in Heaven, it would be well for her to acknowledge and appreciate it, and to use it on His behalf. And that's when the answer to her dilemma appeared in her mind with subtle clarity. She recalled how her reluctance to hire help had been alleviated when she'd realized how much Amanda needed the job, and how both she and her son had been in need of a family to become connected to following the death of her husband. Eleanore felt certain in that moment that there was someone who needed the work James could afford to pay for more than Eleanore needed help in the kitchen. But Eleanore also realized that it was all right for her to feel confident in accepting that cooking was not one of her gifts and that she simply didn't like to do it. She was capable, and if they had no choice, she *would* manage. But perhaps her own time would be better spent, as James had suggested, focusing on the children's lessons—as she had always done—and helping James with the things he loved to do, most especially the garden. He'd mentioned the time she spent visiting women who might be in need of some company or comfort. She'd never thought of it as being a burden or a challenge, but it might become that way if she were solely responsible for putting on three meals a day. Still, she felt that some practice in the kitchen *would* be good for her, and that the children could also use some training in that regard—especially Iris, who might eventually have to run her own home and not have the luxury of hiring help. So the conclusion was obvious.

"I've come to a decision," she said to James right after he'd bent to kiss her before going out to begin his chores. They both knew Ben was likely already out in the barn, milking the cows.

"I'm listening," he said.

"I *do* think you should hire someone."

"Really?" He chuckled with surprise. "Why?" Apparently her motives mattered to him.

"Because I think, as you suggested, that my time might be better spent elsewhere. I do want some compromise, however. I will help in the kitchen so that I can keep learning, and I want all of the children to help as well, so that if they ever need to cook, they can. The boys as well."

"How brilliant you are, Mrs. Barrington," he said.

"If you would please post an advertisement, I would like to interview any applicants myself. I want someone that I can feel comfortable with."

"Of course. I'll take care of it today."

"Thank you," she said. "And thank you . . . for all that you said yesterday. And for the way you support me, no matter what I do—even if it's making horrible gravy."

"I love you, Eleanore," he said, pressing a hand to the side of her face. "I would do anything for you."

"I know," she said, turning back to face the mirror while she pinned the long braid into a bun at the back of her head. "Which is why you need to hurry and see to the animals, because I'll be needing your help with breakfast. Until we hire someone, it wouldn't hurt *you* to learn your way around the kitchen a little yourself."

He laughed and moved toward the door. "You're a shrewd woman, Eleanore Barrington."

"Which is one of a million reasons why you love me," she said, and he laughed again.

Chapter Seven

THE SKEPTIC

The following day while James was in town he heard a rumor that made him realize he needed to visit with the sheriff. He went to the office and was told the sheriff had gone out and would return in an hour, so James took care of his other errands and then went back, but still had to wait a short while. Sheriff Willis shook James's hand and invited him into a room where they could speak privately. James told him that he was relatively certain Lu Bailey had gone west with Ralph and his mother, and there was no longer any need to consider her missing or kidnapped.

The sheriff surprised James when he said, "I thank you for the information, Mr. Barrington. We actually received a note from Miss Bailey; came with the mail carrier, addressed to me, telling me the same thing. She asked that I assure her uncle that she's fine, but she gave no indication of her whereabouts. I'm certain he'll not have the inclination to go looking for her."

"That's good, then," James said. They chatted a few more minutes, and James was glad to go home and tell Eleanore about his conversation with the sheriff.

Eleanore felt good about her husband taking the honest approach, and it was nice to hear some evidence that Lu was fine.

Late that evening, Eleanore enlisted James to join her on a secret errand. After dark they drove discreetly to the edge of Mr. Bailey's property, and quietly left some food and supplies on his porch. She told James that they certainly didn't agree with the way he'd treated May and Lu, but he was likely having a difficult adjustment to being all alone.

Three days later the family had survived Eleanore's cooking fairly well, and she *did* feel her confidence growing regarding her ability to keep the household fed. But her attempt to make bread didn't turn out so well, and she took a trip to the bakery in town so the family wouldn't be forced to eat the poor results of her bread-making efforts. For that and many other reasons, she felt anxious to turn the cooking over to someone else. Lizzie and the children helped, and she even gave James an assignment here and there. But she could admit that she really didn't *like* cooking. For that reason, she was especially grateful to have married a wealthy man. She was even more grateful when she considered that she might never have to master Amanda's ability to make bread.

Four different women applied for the job of "cooking three meals a day, six days a week, keeping the kitchen in order, and applying herself to some minimal housework when necessary." Following their interviews, Eleanore told each of them that she would need some time to think it over and that she'd get back to them. At the supper table, she discussed with the family what she felt were the strengths and weaknesses of each of the candidates. Then Eleanore commented, "You realize that if we have someone in our home so many hours a week, it will be difficult to hide our religious beliefs. It needs to be someone we can trust."

"You're right, of course," James said. "So it should be a matter of prayer . . . which goes without saying, I suppose, in any case."

"At this point I feel best about Miss Stella Carter; she prefers to be called Stella."

"She's never been married?" Lizzie asked.

"Apparently not, but she's fifty-seven. I don't think there's much chance of her running off to do so now. She was very kind, and I felt comfortable with her. She's recently come to Iowa City from back east. She said that she'd settled in New York after coming to America with her brother from Ireland more than twenty years ago. She would have preferred to stay in Ireland, she told me, but she and her brother had no other family, so she came with him. He died a few months ago. She never liked New York, so she sold most of her belongings and got on a coach without asking where it was headed. After doing that a few times, she ended up here and felt like it was the place for her to stay, but she's living at the hotel and looking for work."

James heard something in the description that warmed him. Maybe it was the way this woman had simply followed her feelings and had some confidence in trusting them. Or maybe it was simply the Spirit whispering that she was the right one. He also liked the way Eleanore had mentioned that she preferred to be called by her given name, which fit comfortably into the atmosphere of their home. For the sake of comparison, he asked Eleanore to tell them about the other applicants. She did so, but his vote stayed with Stella Carter.

"But can she cook?" Frederick asked.

"Certainly better than I can," Eleanore said lightly. "Perhaps we should invite her over for supper and let her cook it, and see what we think."

"That's not a bad idea," James said. "Why don't we?"

"One problem I see," Eleanore said, "is that Amanda and Ralph lived close by. All of these women live in the city, which makes it a significant drive each day."

"But Miss Carter doesn't have a place to live yet," Iris said. "She could get someplace close by."

"Maybe she could buy Ralph and Amanda's house," Ben suggested.

"That's a lovely idea," Eleanore said, "but I don't think Miss Carter can afford a home with land. She'll probably rent an apartment."

"Then why don't we just have her stay here?" Frederick said. "Provided you hire her, of course. Have you forgotten about the attic room in our house? We built it that way for just such a purpose. Ralph stayed there a few times, if you'll recall."

"Good heavens," Eleanore said, "I *had* forgotten." She had certainly known that there was a nice furnished room above Frederick and Lizzie's home, with stairs that went up the outside of the house so that it had a separate entrance.

"Oh, that would be ideal," Lizzie said with enthusiasm. "It's just sitting empty. It can get terribly hot up there in the summer, but it's not bad at night if you leave the windows open. And it's got an adequate heater for winter. She would likely spend most of her daytime hours in the big house anyway. If you decide to hire this woman, she could live there—if she chose to, of course. And even if you hire one of the others, they might prefer that option as well, depending on their circumstances."

"We can offer the apartment as a benefit of the job," James said. "Which means that whoever we hire truly *does* need to be someone we *all* feel comfortable with."

"And you always have the option to let her go if it doesn't work out," Frederick said.

James looked at Eleanore and said, "So invite her over, and we'll all make it a matter of prayer."

"I'll do that," Eleanore said, and the following afternoon she went to the hotel where she knew Stella Carter was staying.

The woman looked pleasantly surprised to see Eleanore when she answered the door to her room. Stella was shorter than Eleanore, with a tiny frame and a beautiful complexion that seemed to contradict her completely gray hair that she wore in a loose bun. Knowing that she might offer this woman a significant place in her household, Eleanore looked carefully into her eyes as she spoke.

"I haven't made a final decision," she said right off, "but you are top on my list of considerations."

"Oh, that's nice," Stella said.

"We would like you to come to the house this evening and have supper with us, and—"

"I hope you'll let me cook it. Surely you'll be wanting to know if my claims at being able to do so are valid."

"That was exactly my thought," Eleanore said, and Stella smiled again. "If you would like to ride home with me now, it might save your need to arrange for transportation."

"Oh, that would be very nice," Stella said, "if you don't mind."

"Of course not."

Stella was ready in just a few minutes, and they were soon headed out of town with Eleanore driving the buggy. Eleanore asked if she'd found a place to live yet, and Stella answered that she hadn't. "I didn't mention," Eleanore said, "that if you get the job, room and board is part of the deal, if you want it. The room isn't much, but it's comfortable and would give you privacy."

"Oh, that would be grand!" Stella said. "But we should wait and see if you feel that I'm right for the job."

"Of course," Eleanore said, then she asked Stella more about her upbringing and her journey to America. She then told Stella about her own background, finding her very easy to talk to.

At the house, Frederick took the buggy to unharness the horse, and Eleanore introduced him to Stella. Ben was working in the garden with Jamie trying to help him. Iris was sitting on a blanket in the shade with Isaac. Eleanore called them over to meet Stella. Lizzie heard the conversation from inside and stepped out onto the back porch to be introduced as well.

Once Lizzie had exchanged friendly greetings with Stella, and the children had gone back to what they'd been doing, Eleanore asked, "Do you know where James is?"

"In his office, I believe," Lizzie said and opened the door for them to enter the house.

"The children are delightful," Stella said to Eleanore, "but you don't look old enough to have children that age."

"Thank you," Eleanore said facetiously. "Actually, Iris is from my husband's first marriage, and Ben was adopted after his parents passed away."

"Oh, I see," Stella said. "What a lovely family. I hope I didn't sound too nosy or—"

"Of course not," Eleanore said. "We're all very open and casual around here." She opened the office door and added, "You must meet my husband."

"Oh, hello," James said and stood from behind the desk, holding out a hand toward the newcomer as the ladies entered the room. "You must be Miss Carter."

"Stella, please," she said.

"Stella, then. It's a pleasure to meet you."

"This is my husband, James," Eleanore said. "And yes, you must call him James. He loathes formality. Don't you, my darling?"

"I do, yes," he said and pressed a kiss to her cheek once he'd concluded his greeting with Stella. "We're all very open and casual around here."

Stella laughed softly. "That's *exactly* what your wife said, not a minute ago."

"Then it must be true," James said. "Eleanore, why don't you show Stella around, and I'll see both of you at supper."

"I'll do that," Eleanore said, and the ladies left the office. She gave Stella a quick tour of the house, explaining some of the habits, personalities, and situations of all who lived and worked there. And she told Stella her reasons for needing to hire someone, omitting any reference to religion or eloping. She simply said that Amanda and Ralph had felt compelled to move west and everyone missed them very much.

In the kitchen, Eleanore showed Stella where to find all that was needed, and told her what food was available in order to make a variety of options. She offered Stella an apron, which she put on eagerly, then she politely asked Eleanore to make herself busy elsewhere and leave her to her work. Eleanore said she would be in the library or the office if Stella needed anything, then she went immediately to find James, who was still working behind his desk. With the door closed behind her she said, "I really like her, James. I do hope it works out."

"So do I," James said and beckoned Eleanore to his lap where he gave her a warm kiss and hugged her tightly.

"And with any luck, she'll make excellent gravy."

"Indeed." James chuckled and kissed her again.

When supper time came, Stella admitted she was pleasantly surprised by the way the children pitched in to set the table. While everyone was taking turns at washing up to eat, they all discreetly told Eleanore that they really liked Stella and felt she would be a good choice. Eleanore could find no reason to object, as long as her cooking was tolerable. Stella was kind and appropriate, and she was downright shocked when James told her she would be eating with them.

"But I can eat in the kitchen," Stella said. "It's more—"

"We're all like family here," James told her. "And we would all appreciate the opportunity to get to know you a little better."

The meal was unquestionably superb—even the gravy. And everyone at the table, including the children, had questions for Stella. They were fascinated with her memories of Ireland and her experiences in New York City. Stella didn't seem to mind the questions at all. In fact she seemed comfortable and glad to answer anything that was asked of her. She wasn't at all shy or lacking in confidence, but neither did she talk excessively or try to dominate the conversation.

After a minute of contented silence while everyone enjoyed Stella's bread pudding, Eleanore was surprised to hear Frederick ask, "So,

Stella, do you have a particular religious affiliation?" She noticed a subtle conspiratorial glance pass between Frederick and Lizzie.

Stella didn't appear alarmed or annoyed by the question. "No, I don't," she said. "I *am* Christian, but part of my brother's motivation for leaving Ireland was the lure of America offering a variety of religion." Eleanore caught amazed glances being passed around the table, although she felt certain Stella was oblivious. "We attended a particular sect that was strong in the area where we lived in New York, but I must confess there were matters taught that I didn't entirely agree with. I hope that doesn't offend or concern you."

"No, of course not," James was quick to say, then the room became eerily silent. Eleanore met her husband's eyes and saw her own awe reflected there. She felt certain he was experiencing the same warm sensation that she was. Not only did she feel completely confident that this woman was the right person to hire and bring into their home, but in that moment she believed that there was a higher purpose to their connection. She had no qualms about being open with this woman concerning their beliefs, and perhaps, with time, if Stella chose, she would become a part of them. James took Eleanore's hand across the corner of the table and squeezed it with discreet tightness. She knew their thoughts were the same. A quick glance at Frederick, Lizzie, and the children revealed a similar, barely masked incredulity in their expressions.

"And might I ask the same of you?" Stella said, breaking the quiet that had become awkward. "If you don't mind, of course."

"Of course," James said. "We attend a particular sect on Sundays, but we all share your sentiments on a certain . . . discontentment over what we hear there. We keep that to ourselves, however. Should you stay on, we can discuss that more another time."

"Well." Stella glanced down. "I would certainly love to stay on. You're a wonderful family." She looked up, and Eleanore caught a glisten of moisture in her eyes. "But I realize the decision is up to you and—"

"The job is yours if you want it," Eleanore said. "And if you choose to take it, someone can drive you back into town this evening to collect your things . . . unless you would prefer to wait."

"Oh, it's too grand to be true!" Stella said with a delighted laugh, putting her hands to her cheeks as they became flushed. "This is more an answer to my prayers than I'd ever dreamed possible."

"Well then," James said, "that gives us all something in common."

After supper, the children cleared the table while James and Eleanore cleaned the dishes, and Frederick and Lizzie went with Stella back to the hotel so that she could pack up her belongings. The kitchen was in order when they returned, and Frederick carried Stella's only trunk up the stairs to the room above the little house. Lizzie carried a small valise and followed, and Eleanore went along to see how Stella liked the room. While Stella had been cooking supper, Lizzie had opened the windows, dusted, and put clean linens on the bed. She'd also left a little vase of fresh flowers on the dresser. Apparently she'd been confident that Stella would be staying.

"Oh, it's grand!" Stella said while she turned around in the center of the room as her luggage was deposited near the bed.

"It gets rather hot up here in the summer," Lizzie reported, "but if you leave the windows open the evening usually brings a breeze that makes it tolerable."

"I'm certain I'll be very comfortable here," Stella said. "Thank you!"

The following morning, Eleanore went down to the kitchen early and found Stella already there and busy, wearing a cheerful countenance. They chatted for a few minutes while she helped fry some bacon. Stella greeted the children warmly as they trickled into the kitchen, then the adults arrived to wash up and received equally kind hellos. They all shared a pleasant and delicious breakfast, then Lizzie offered to help Stella put the kitchen in order and watch out for the children while James and Eleanore went into town for the usual weekly errands.

"How did you know I was going along?" Eleanore asked.

"You always go with him when the weather is pleasant—and if you don't, you should. Have lunch out or something."

"What an excellent idea," James said, and they were soon off.

Through the drive into town, Eleanore told James how pleased she was with the way things were working out with Stella. "I really like her," she admitted.

"I like her too."

"I wonder how she'll get along with the children. I mean, she's been polite and kind, and I wouldn't expect anything less. But I wonder if she's the kind of woman who takes to children and enjoys being with them, or if she'd prefer not being too involved with them."

"I don't know. I guess we'll see. Since we didn't hire her to look after the children, it really doesn't matter."

"No, I was just wondering."

Eleanore enjoyed their time out but was disappointed, as usual, when no letters from her friends were included in the mail. They arrived home to find the children all up to their elbows in flour while Stella guided them through making jam tarts. James and Eleanore entered the kitchen just in time to hear Stella laughing and the children joining in. Lizzie was watching while she dried a freshly washed pot. She caught Eleanore's eye and said, "It was Stella's idea, but they've been having a marvelous time."

Eleanore heard James chuckle softly near her side, then he whispered, "I guess that answers your question."

Over the next few days, Stella settled in comfortably. She was helpful beyond her kitchen duties without being meddlesome, and she got along well with everyone in the household. The only challenge came when Eleanore found her crying in the kitchen just prior to supper on Saturday evening. She was upset because she'd overbaked the biscuits and they were too hard to eat.

"We will manage fine without biscuits," Eleanore said, then she told her the story of her dreadful gravy and got Stella laughing.

On Sunday Stella was thrilled to go to church with the family, and she admitted to James and Eleanore how wonderful it was to feel a part of their family. A few minutes later James whispered in Eleanore's ear, "We'll see how she feels once she finds out what we do on Sunday afternoons. When we swear her to secrecy she may think we belong to some sort of cult or something."

Eleanore whispered back, "Or we may be what she's been searching for without even knowing that something was missing. That's how *I* felt."

"We'll see."

Once Sunday dinner was all cleaned up, with everyone pitching in as usual, Stella was invited to join the family in the parlor. James took over the task of appropriately telling the newcomer that they had privately embraced religious beliefs that some people believed were

cause for persecution. He explained the need for secrecy in order to
protect the family. Stella looked concerned but stated firmly, "I would
never say or do anything to bring harm to your good family, Mr.
Barrington, whether I agree with it or not."

"Thank you," he said. "And it's James, please."

"Sorry," she chuckled. "It just seems so . . . improper to call my
employer by his given—"

"You'll get used to it," James said and went on to briefly tell the
history of Eleanore finding a book of scripture in England, her feelings about the truthfulness of the book, and how they'd been guided
to a missionary who had baptized her, and to a home that belonged
to people who shared their beliefs. He told a brief history of the
horrors their people had been through, and that they were now gathering 1300 miles west of Iowa City. He also explained that the Lord
had repeatedly answered their own prayers by making it clear they
needed to remain where they were. James emphasized his feelings on
the irony of the situation, since America was meant to be a land of
religious freedom. Stella vehemently agreed with him and was clearly
astonished by such atrocities.

"So," James continued, "now that you know some background
about our religion, and how we came into it, we hope you will understand why we choose to attend church in order to be a part of the
community and keep up proper appearances, and then share our
private worship service here. I'm certain I've talked long enough to
count it as our discussion for the day, but we would like to sing a
hymn, and pray, and also share a sacrament ordinance according to
the guidelines we've been taught. Of course, it would be inappropriate for you to actually partake of the sacrament when you're not
officially a member, but we would love to have you join us for these
gatherings if you are to be a part of our household. Still, that choice is
yours. We simply wanted you to know the truth about us. We have
nothing to hide. We just want to remain safe from people who would
mean us harm."

"I understand," Stella said with genuine kindness. "Go on with
whatever it is you do."

Together they sang a hymn, Ben offered a prayer, then James and
Frederick blessed and passed the sacrament. Stella bowed her head for

the prayers and seemed mildly curious about the bread and water the others were taking, but she made no comment. James told the family they'd already had a sufficient meeting, comically suggesting that the review of LDS history had been purposely intended as a gripping sermon. So they sang one more hymn, and Iris offered a closing prayer before everyone dispersed. Frederick and Lizzie took Mary Jane back to their home for some quiet family time, as they typically did on Sundays. And Iris took Isaac with her, as she often did. Jamie followed Ben in a way that was becoming more and more common. Eleanore was glad for an opportunity to be alone with James and Stella, wondering if the woman might have any questions.

"What did you say this religion is called?"

"Did I say?" James asked and immediately answered. "The official name is The Church of Jesus Christ of Latter-day Saints." She'd obviously never heard that before. Eleanore held her breath as he added, "Most commonly referred to as the Mormons."

Eleanore reached for her husband's hand when Stella's eyes grew wide with overt fear and astonishment. "Mormons?" she countered, as if just saying the word had exposed her to some kind of evil. "My brother *hated* the Mormons."

Eleanore felt James squeeze her fingers in a silent reminder to be calm, but she wondered what they'd done. Had they brought someone into their home who would actually be antagonistic toward their beliefs? Would trouble come from this in spite of her having just promised to never do anything to bring them harm? She was grateful for James's steady demeanor as he asked Stella, "And what do *you* think?" Stella hesitated to answer and James added, "Are your opinions based solely on rumor, or do they have any substance?" Again she was hesitant, but her eyes had become skeptical, almost hard. "I ask because much of the persecution our people have endured is largely based on unfounded rumor and bigotry. You seem like a levelheaded woman, Stella, and we all felt that bringing you into our home was a good thing. You have the choice to attend or not attend any worship service available, here in our home or anywhere else. We will respect your beliefs and opinions, and only ask that you do the same for us."

Eleanore held her breath and trembled inwardly. She'd come to love having Stella in her home. The thought of losing her now hurt deeply. And the very idea of losing her over this matter felt unbearable at the moment. She wanted to protest all of this but couldn't find the words.

"That would only be fair," Stella said. "And yes, I consider myself a levelheaded woman, but I have difficulty believing that a religion could be good when it attracts so much evil."

Eleanore suddenly found words in her mind and the strength to speak them clearly. "The Church does not attract evil, Stella. The truthfulness and power of Christ's restored church on the earth attracts Satan's most zealous attention when he would prefer to see it undone. There is no difference in the principle behind this and the fact that Jesus' disciples were persecuted and martyred for the cause." Stella looked taken aback by the comparison, but her eyes softened, if only slightly. Eleanore went on. "Our people have endured much that is difficult to speak of, but many remain faithful in spite of these things. If it were not true, then surely facing such persecution would quickly dissolve our numbers. But the Church flourishes and grows, and our members our gathering in the west, where they can be safe and worship freely."

A tortured silence preceded Stella's next words. "I can see that your beliefs mean a great deal to you, and I can respect that. I can also respect your privacy and assure you that my knowledge of these things will never pass my lips outside of this home. But I . . ." Her voice broke, and tears rose in her eyes, "I don't know if I should stay. I don't know that my being in your home . . . with the way I feel . . . would be best for any of us."

Help me, Father, Eleanore prayed, and once again words came to her mind with clarity. "Stella," she let go of James's hand and leaned forward to look at her more directly, "we respect your feelings, and also your integrity. It takes courage to not be a part of something if you can't support it or believe in it. However, I'm asking you with all sincerity if you would give the matter some time and not make a hasty decision. I would ask that you pray about it and ponder the issue of rumors and predetermined beliefs, as opposed to what you see and feel in our home. We are not some kind of strange cult. We believe in Christ and we strive to live by His teachings. Examine the way we live, and see if you can be happy in our home, whether you choose to endorse our beliefs or not." Stella still looked wary and Eleanore added, "Just . . . give it a week. You told me that you felt good about taking this position, and we felt good about giving it to you. I plead with you not to make a rash decision and leave us now before truly giving us a chance. A week. If you get to this time next Sunday and you truly feel you can't stay with us, we will give you more than adequate wages for your time here so that you can make a fresh start elsewhere."

Eleanore glanced at James for approval, wondering if he might have anything to add. He just nodded subtly, encouraging her to go on. She looked again at Stella, who thoughtfully said, "Very well. A week sounds fair."

"Thank you," Eleanore said. "And through the coming week I hope that you will keep your mind and spirit open, trust your instincts, and feel free to ask us anything you like. As my husband said, we have nothing to hide." Stella nodded, but Eleanore didn't stop there. She rose to pull out an extra Book of Mormon from a shelf where scriptures were kept for easy access during the many family meetings they shared in this room. Eleanore handed the book to Stella and sat down beside her, saying gently, "I also ask that you take some time during the coming week to better understand our beliefs. If you're making a life-altering decision, then make it an educated one. If you find anything in this book that is contradictory to Christianity, please let us know." Eleanore took advantage of Stella's stunned silence to speak passionately about the Book of Mormon and her deep, abiding love for it. She recounted her experience of finding it, and how it had changed her life, and she bore firm testimony of the truths contained in its pages, concepts that had given her perfect peace through many trials. She pointed out the verses in Moroni near the end and turned down the corner of the page to mark it. She read Moroni's words aloud and asked Stella to take his challenge to heart.

When Eleanore had nothing more to say, Stella was left holding the book, looking at it as if it might explode in her face. But when she glanced up at Eleanore, then James, there was no trace of cynicism in her eyes. Had she felt the sweet spirit present in the room? Had the testimonies that James and Eleanore had borne worked their way into a portion of her heart?

Stella came to her feet, and the others did the same. "I'll give it a week," she said and left the room abruptly.

Eleanore sat back down, suddenly exhausted, as if she'd just run a great distance. James sat as well and crossed his ankle over his knee. "That was very impressive, Mrs. Barrington. I wonder you don't go into politics."

She passed him a skeptical glance that made him laugh. "I didn't say anything that wasn't completely true."

"I know. But it's the way you said it that leaves me amazed. She was ready to go pack her bags. Now you've talked her into actually reading the book. I did say you were gifted."

"I just said what came to my mind. It was purely inspiration."

"Well, you're gifted enough to listen to such inspiration and act on it . . . which is one of a million reasons why I love you."

Eleanore sighed. "And what if we're back to eating my cooking in a week's time? Will you still love me when you have to eat my gravy?"

"I will *not* eat your gravy, but I will never stop loving you." He came to his feet and bent to kiss her cheek. "You mustn't worry. God brought her to this place, Ellie. The matter is in His hands."

"Do you think she'll stay, then?"

"I don't know. Whether she stays or not, perhaps we've given her something she needed."

"Perhaps."

"Either way, maybe you could get her to teach you to make gravy sometime this week."

Eleanore scowled at him again and ignored his chuckle as he left the room.

* * * * *

Throughout the week, Stella behaved as if nothing had changed and no deep conversations of religion had ever taken place. She did so fine a job in the kitchen and interacted so pleasantly with the children that Eleanore felt brokenhearted to think of her leaving. She marveled that she'd not even known of this woman's existence not so many days ago, and now she didn't want to be without her. She tallied such feelings as evidence that she needed to be more receptive to the doors that God would open in her life. And while she missed Ralph and Amanda dreadfully, she couldn't dispute the fact that if they hadn't left, Stella wouldn't be here. She just hoped and prayed that Stella would stay.

When Sunday came, Eleanore was terrified over the possibility that Stella would announce she'd given it a fair chance and had decided that she needed to leave. She wondered if they would have to wait through the entire day before her decision was announced. But over the breakfast table Stella simply said, "Oh, I'll be staying . . . indefinitely; till I die, maybe. Hope that's all right."

"More than all right," Eleanore said with a relieved chuckle. "That's wonderful news for us."

Stella just smiled and went on with eating her meal. The day proceeded as normal, and no comment was made as Stella quietly joined them for their afternoon service in the parlor. The passing weeks escorted them into summer while Stella settled in beautifully, but she never said a word about whether or not she'd read the Book of Mormon, nor did she offer any of her opinions regarding the family's beliefs and their practice of them. She continued to join them for every activity, and always seemed to be relaxed and comfortable. Eleanore stopped worrying about what Stella might think of their beliefs; instead, she simply appreciated this dear woman's presence in their home. And always she kept in her heart the prayer that one day Stella might be willing to embrace that which had given Eleanore such great joy.

Chapter Eight
TIME

James found Eleanore alone in the kitchen and asked, "Do you know where Iris is?"

"I think I heard her come in and go up the stairs. Why?"

"She snapped at me when I asked her to help me with something, then she burst into tears and ran off."

Eleanore turned to look at him and they shared silent seconds of mutual alarm before she asked, "Did you say something to make her—"

"No, nothing. I was too surprised by her talking to me like that to get a word out before she fell apart." He motioned toward the stairs. "Would you please . . ."

"Of course," Eleanore said, drying her hands on her apron. Nothing more needed to be said for her to know what he meant. It had been long established between them that some problems were better dealt with by a woman. And vice versa.

James watched her leave then forced himself to go back outside and get to work, knowing his concern for Iris would be best transferred into physical labor, as opposed to stewing and wondering what might be happening. It was more than two hours later when Eleanore entered the barn, not looking upset, but definitely looking resolved to tell him something.

"What?" he demanded, more impatient than he'd intended.

"She's fine . . . in a manner of speaking."

"What does that mean?"

"It's a feminine thing, James."

"Oh?" he said, still not grasping any connection between such matters and his daughter's temperament.

"It's common knowledge that when a young woman is . . . passing into maturity, her emotions become more . . . fragile."

"Is it?" he asked. "Common knowledge, I mean? *I* didn't know that."

Eleanore laughed softly. "And all this time I thought you knew *everything* about such matters."

"I didn't know *that.*"

"Of course you did. You're well aware that I tend to get more emotional during certain times of the month."

"Not like *that.* She was practically hysterical."

"I believe it's worse during the initial adjustment. It's a great shift to evolve from a child into a woman."

A woman? he wanted to shout, then the meaning behind the conversation sank in. "Wait a minute. Are you saying that . . . she's . . ."

Again Eleanore let out a gentle laugh, as if she found his ignorance amusing. "She's begun her monthly cycles, yes."

"But she's only . . ."

"She's fourteen, James. I've discussed it with her before, so that she'd be prepared. Many young women start before now. She simply didn't expect it to upset her emotions this way. She'll be fine."

James moved to a bale of straw and sat down. As usual, he knew that Eleanore must have sensed his distress by the way she sat beside him and took his hand. She said nothing, and he knew she was waiting for him to share his thoughts. He finally pulled them together enough to say, "Have I been blind? Have I somehow . . . missed her growing up?"

"You didn't miss it, James. You've been there for her, day in and day out. But we see her every day. Perhaps we haven't noticed the changes because they've been so gradual. But it will likely only be a couple of years before she'll have suitors vying for her attention."

"Suitors?" he echoed as if he'd never heard the word before.

"Yes, James, suitors. She's a beautiful young woman with many fine qualities. You need to prepare yourself for the fact that, even though you'll always be her father, you'll need to give her away in marriage."

"Marriage?" he repeated, even more astonished.

"Yes, marriage," Eleanore said and let out a stifled chuckle.

"Is this funny?"

"Ironic," Eleanore said. "In less than three years Iris will be the age I was when I married you." James knew his astonishment was evident by the way Eleanore added, "Apparently such things are much different from the perspective of a father than they are for a prospective husband. Do you think if my father had been alive he would have approved?"

"Not likely," James muttered and looked at the ground.

"And why wouldn't he? He would have had no reason to believe you weren't a fine match for me in every respect." James said nothing. He couldn't bring himself to admit how horribly different the perspective was for a father. Eleanore added gently, "There's no need to be alarmed. We still have some time."

"Time? Two or three years? It will go far too fast."

"Yes, it probably will. And apparently you'll need that long to prepare yourself."

James looked up at his wife and confessed his deepest wish. "I don't want her to grow up, Ellie. She's my little girl."

"She loves being your little girl. I would wager that not many fourteen-year-old young ladies still want to be tucked in at night by their father. You just have to enjoy it while it lasts and hold on to the memories." She chuckled. "I dare say her husband wouldn't be fond of you tucking her in at night."

"That's it, isn't it." James said, trying to sound facetious if only to feebly attempt to lighten his own mood. "Some other man is going to take over the job of tucking her in at night. Do you think he'll tell her a bedtime story and tickle her?"

"Maybe." Eleanore eased closer and put her head on his shoulder. "Will you tell *me* a story?"

"I'd rather tickle you."

"Sorry. I'm too old for that."

"I'm not so sure, but I'll have to spring it on you when you're not expecting it."

"I can't wait," she muttered with sarcasm. She lifted her head and looked into his eyes. "But no matter what, you can tuck me in every night for the rest of my life."

"How delightful," he said and kissed her.

"And you mustn't worry. Iris is going to be just fine. You wouldn't *really* want her to be an old maid and stay with us forever."

"No, I wouldn't want that."

"She'll find a good man, and they'll be happy together. We must simply be patient and take good care of her until it becomes someone else's responsibility. Everything will happen in God's own time, and in His own way."

James exhaled slowly. "Yes, I'm sure you're right. You usually are." He put his arm around her and pressed a kiss into her hair. "Do you think it would be all right if I go visit with my little girl?"

"Of course," Eleanore said, and he stood up. "I'll see you at supper."

James kissed her again before he went into the house. He consciously calmed his nerves and took a deep breath before he knocked lightly at Iris's bedroom door.

"Who is it?" she called in that snappy voice he'd heard earlier.

"It's your father."

He heard nothing for a few seconds and wondered if she would ignore him. He thought for a moment of the antagonistic and unpredictable nature of Iris's blood mother, and he felt briefly afraid that she might have inherited such a nature. But it only took him another moment to realize that was absurd. Even if Iris went through some difficult ups and downs associated with evolving into a woman, she'd always had far more tenderness and integrity than the woman who had given birth to her. She'd always been a sweet girl with a genuine desire to do what was right.

James's heart quickened as the door opened. And there stood his little girl. But she didn't look like a little girl at all. Had he simply chosen not to notice that she was nearly as tall as Eleanore, and that her figure was becoming curved and feminine? He wanted to apologize to her for being oblivious to changes that were taking place in her life, but he thought it best left unsaid. Before he could speak she said, "I'm sorry I snapped at you."

"It's all right," he said and chuckled with the hope of easing the tension. "Just don't make a habit of it." He opened his arms, and she rushed into them, hugging him tightly, the same way she had since she was old enough to throw her arms around his neck. While she cried softly against his shoulder, he pressed a hand over the back of her head and spoke in a gentle voice. "Your mother told me that you're growing up." He felt her become tense, and he quickly added, "It's all right. There's no need to be embarrassed or upset. I knew about such things long before you were born. And I want you to know that . . . no matter how old you get . . . or what challenges you come up against . . . I will always . . ." He hesitated as the words caught in his throat and tears moistened his eyes. He couldn't keep his voice from cracking as he finished, "I will always be your father. I will always be here for you. I want only for you to be happy, Iris. Never forget that."

She looked up at him, and he saw no hint of embarrassment, only a tender smile and a familiar sparkle in her eyes. "I love you, Papa."

"I love you too, precious," he said and touched her face.

"Do you still need some help in the garden?" she asked.

"Maybe it would be better for you to rest a while," he said.

"Oh, I'm all right," she insisted, and they walked outside together, passing the kitchen where Eleanore was back at work, helping Stella. She winked at James when their eyes met. What would he ever do without her? With Eleanore in his life, he had hope of surviving his daughter's growing up.

That night after James climbed into bed next to Eleanore, he lay staring into the darkness, pondering this transition with Iris. Eleanore's earlier words settled in, along with evidence of her wisdom. He had no choice but to accept that his little girl was on the path to becoming a woman. He wanted her to be happy and confident in whatever course she chose for her life. And whatever that might be, marriage would surely be a part of it.

James made certain Eleanore was awake before he said, "She really is growing up. I never noticed until today. I'm glad you were paying attention."

"That's what mothers are for," she said, as if it were nothing. But James couldn't help considering that while Eleanore wasn't Iris's mother in a literal sense, but she nevertheless took the role very seriously; she always had.

"Forgive me," he said, "but I have to ask . . . does she know . . . about intimate things?"

"Of course she does. I talked to her about that a while back when she began asking a lot of questions. I told her the way you told me on our wedding night." James looked at her sharply, even though it was dark and he knew she couldn't see him. Recalling their conversation the night following their marriage, he found it difficult to imagine discussing such things with his little Iris. "I certainly wouldn't want her to be as naive and frightened as I was. And before you tell me that marriage is still some years away for her, let me remind you that my mother died long before I reached marriageable age, and I was left with no one to help me be prepared."

"If you're implying that something might happen to you before—"

"I have no intention of dying, but neither did my mother. We just never know. But I felt the time was right. As I said, she was asking questions. And I believe it's important for her to understand exactly why it's so important to protect her virtue when she's already got young men paying attention to her."

"She *what?*" He sat up abruptly and wanted to accuse his wife of lying.

"How can you be that surprised? You've seen her talking with young men before and after church meetings; and it even happens when we go into town."

"Yes, of course, but . . . I thought they were just friends."

"They *are* just friends. But her friends are growing up too. Iris needs to understand *why* she feels attracted to the opposite sex, and how important it is to keep those feelings and thoughts within a righteous perspective. You *know* all of this, James."

He sighed and laid back down. "Yes, I know it all in theory. I just never bothered to connect it to my daughter." He took Eleanore's hand. "It's a good thing you were paying attention. I'll just add one more thing to that list of a million reasons why I'm grateful I married you. I shudder to think what life might have been like for Iris if she didn't have you for a mother. I would have been oblivious and helpless over such matters."

"I'm certain you would have managed just fine," Eleanore said, but he just snorted a sarcastic laugh.

* * * * *

On a hot Sunday in the middle of July, Stella announced to the family without any prior explanation that she wished to be baptized. While everyone remained in stunned silence, Stella bore a sweet and stirring testimony of her personal struggle to overcome ill feelings, not only toward Mormonism, but regarding other matters in her life that she didn't go into specifically. She spoke of her diligent study and prayer that had led to an undeniable witness that these things were true. She asked James if he would perform the baptism, and she expressed gratitude to the entire family for taking her in and for being such a good example to her. She knew in her heart that God had led her to this place. Eleanore couldn't help thinking once again that if Amanda and Ralph hadn't gone west, Stella would not have had this opportunity in her life. She felt certain that all of these matters were in God's hands.

That very day Eleanore stood on the bank of the river and watched James lower this good woman into the water, then bring her back up again. She cried tears of joy on Stella's behalf, and also for herself as she was given such sweet evidence of how richly blessed her life was. Her heart swelled to see her husband acting in his priesthood capacity, knowing there had been a time when she'd sorrowed over his resistance to embrace the gospel. And seeing Stella's happiness couldn't help but enhance the happiness of everyone in the home who had helped her come to this point by the strength of their individual testimonies.

Autumn brought Mary Jane's eighth birthday, and everyone who could remember her arrival into the world was amazed at the passing of time. She'd been born after they had settled into their Iowa home. And prior to leaving England, Mary Jane's parents, Frederick and Lizzie, had never considered the possibility of ever ending up married to each other, even though they'd worked together for many years.

Mary Jane's father baptized her in the river, and the day was spent in great celebration for this step the child had eagerly taken, and also for the milestones that every member of the household had passed during their years in America.

Soon after Mary Jane's baptism, Eleanore discovered that she was once again pregnant. She became terribly ill at first but did very well through the remainder of the pregnancy, and she had no trouble enjoying the little trip that James took her on to celebrate their tenth

wedding anniversary. As happy as she felt with the life she lived, she
found it difficult to believe how time had passed so quickly. She tried
to imagine how her life might have been if she'd not accepted James
Barrington's proposal of marriage, but quickly realized that she didn't
even want to think about it. And now ten years seemed like forever.
She couldn't comprehend her life ever having been any other way.

James was surprised to receive word that his estate in England had
sold, and the money from the sale was sent by his solicitor and arrived
via a special carrier. The original buyer, who had purchased the manor
house and accompanying property at the time James and Eleanore
had left England, had forfeited on his agreement, and James had
purchased it back from him at a later date. James had always been
deeply grateful for the financial abundance he'd been blessed with,
but he'd known that without the sale of the estate, their funds would
eventually run out. Now that it had sold again to a reputable buyer
who had committed in writing to care well for the estate and the
people employed there, he felt completely confident that he could
now indefinitely care for those for whom he was responsible. And he
now also had the freedom to help others when the opportunity and
need arose. He considered his wealth a great blessing and privilege,
and he was more than willing to do with it whatever God guided him
to do.

Joseph was born in June of 1849, as healthy and strong as his
brothers. He had the same dark hair, but his features didn't resemble
either of them strongly. Jamie bore a strong resemblance to his father,
and Isaac to his mother. Joseph had come with an intriguing combi-
nation of both that was completely unique.

Joseph immediately proved to be a more demanding baby, but
James insisted that his strong will would surely be of great use to him
some day. Everyone in the household enjoyed taking part in caring
for him, which made it easier to keep him happy since he preferred
being held, whether he was asleep or awake. Eleanore was able to feed
him on her own with no difficulty, and James felt some healing over
the trauma he'd felt related to Isaac's birth and Eleanore's long and
challenging recovery. She gradually got the baby trained to stay in his
own bed at night, but during the day he was only content if at least
one person was giving him their full attention. He was so adorable

that this didn't prove to be much of a problem. Eleanore commented often that it was a good thing Heavenly Father had sent Joseph to a home full of people. Even little Isaac, who was only two, could sit beside his baby brother on a blanket on the floor and talk to him and make silly noises, keeping the baby thoroughly enthralled. In fact, Joseph wasn't very old before it became clear that Isaac was one of his favorite people. A close second to Isaac among the baby's favorites was Jamie. He too could keep the baby entertained, and, at the age of four, he loved the responsibility of being put in charge of the baby for short periods of time while someone kept an eye on them. Jamie loved to talk, and he did it well, and Joseph loved to listen. It was Jamie who first got the baby to laugh. And all of the boys loved the dog. Jack preferred to lay on the floor near the children, keeping an eye on them as if he considered it a personal duty.

As Joseph quickly grew and changed, the other children did also, but at a slower pace. The onset of winter put Iris at fifteen and a half, and Ben was nearly thirteen. Mary Jane had passed her ninth birthday, and time settled in around the Barrington household with a comfortable serenity.

Eleanore was delightfully surprised to receive a letter from Miss Gibbs, a woman who had once served with her in the Barrington household in England. Eleanore had shared her beliefs with Miss Gibbs when she and James had returned to England briefly some years earlier. And now Miss Gibbs had written to let Eleanore know that she had joined the Church and had come to America with a significant group of Latter-day Saints who had been baptized by missionaries in England. The letter had been posted following her arrival in America, just before she had begun her journey west with a wagon company. She expressed appreciation for Eleanore bringing the gospel into her life, and the hope that they might one day see each other again when they were all gathered in Zion.

Letters from loved ones in Salt Lake City were sparse but greatly appreciated when they did come. Ralph and Lu were happily married and had a baby daughter; Amanda was thrilled to be a grandmother and to see Ralph and Lu so happy. They all missed Iowa, but they all agreed that they were where they needed to be, and life was good for the most part in Salt Lake City. Their joy in being gathered with the

Saints in this new community was clearly evidenced in letters from all their friends who were now in the Salt Lake Valley. Still, they'd all had hardships and things were not easy. Building a community up out of the desert was no small thing, and Satan's opposing forces were still evident. Yet every letter conveyed a spirit of peace and joy and evidence of firm testimony.

With every reminder of the happenings in Zion so far away, James and Eleanore felt prone to ask the Lord once again if it might be time for them to go west. And again the answer was the need to remain in Iowa. James declared to his wife that he was going to stop asking. "When the Lord wants me to leave, I'm certain He'll let me know."

Time continued to slip away as another year ended, and then winter became spring once again. Ben hit a spurt of growth that required a wardrobe adjustment, and not many weeks later, Iris did the same. At least Ben still looked more like a child than an adult; the same couldn't be said for Iris. She looked and behaved very much like a woman, a fact that James had trouble coming to grips with, but he did his best not to let his concerns show. By the time summer came, she'd turned sixteen, and her innate beauty suddenly blossomed into a strong resemblance to her birth mother. There were moments when James struggled with the ill feelings he'd had toward his first wife in contrast to the love he felt for his sweet and precious daughter. She was a continual reminder that he'd once lived another life, but discussing it with Eleanore helped him to find the perspective of gratitude in no longer living that life, as opposed to feeling any regret or bitterness. And he could readily admit that he would go through it all again just to have Iris, and to have her be the person that she was. He did jokingly tell Eleanore that it might be better if his daughter weren't quite so beautiful. He didn't even want to let her go into public without him, certain that she would turn the heads of many men. When he considered the fact that Eleanore had been this age when she'd started working as the governess—and how drawn he had felt to her—he decided that he most definitely had a different perspective as a father than he'd had as a suitor. Eleanore reminded him that he'd always been a man with honorable intentions, but they both had to agree that beauty like Iris's could draw the attention of many kinds of men. They both spoke with her gently but frankly about the importance of being discerning over her associations with the opposite sex, about heeding the guidance of the Spirit, and always standing by her values. She assured them repeatedly that she knew all of that, and that she certainly would do all these things, but James couldn't shake an ongoing uneasiness on behalf of his daughter.

On a Sunday just after Joseph's first birthday, James was surprised— perhaps alarmed—when he saw Iris talking with a young man after church and he realized it was the third week in a row that this had happened. She was often seen talking with others her age, and the boys certainly gathered around her. But this was different. She was speaking alone with this young man, and it *was* the third week in a row. They had trouble getting her to end her conversation and to get in the buggy to go home. Eleanore reminded James that she was sixteen and certainly old enough to be interested in the opposite sex, and they had taught her well. He didn't want to admit, even to Eleanore, that he had trouble thinking of Iris growing up. He truly didn't want to let her go, but he trusted Eleanore's advice in allowing nature to take its course and not to interfere beyond appropriate parental guidance.

The following Sunday at church, Eleanore suggested that they make a point to meet this young man. Once the church service ended, Iris was out the door like a rushing wind, and they found her at the corner of the building, chatting with the same boy. He appeared to be a little older than Iris, with a maturing stature but the face of a child. James approached them with Eleanore at his shoulder and held out a hand, saying with a smile, "Hello. I'm Iris's father, and this is her mother. It's a pleasure to meet you."

"Hello," the young man said, returning the handshake.

When he said nothing more, Iris cleared her throat and said with unnatural awkwardness, "This is Dillon."

"Hi," Dillon said when she offered no further introduction or explanation.

"It's so good to meet you, Dillon," Eleanore said. Then to Iris, "We'll be waiting in the buggy. Come along quickly." Again she turned to Dillon and added, "You're welcome to come and visit Iris at the house."

He looked surprised, and Iris looked annoyed. James took Eleanore's arm and guided her toward the buggy, where Ben was waiting with Joseph on his lap and Jamie and Isaac were doing some form of wrestling on the other seat. Eleanore said to James, "If they want to spend time together, better they do it on our own territory so we can keep track of them. Perhaps if we make him feel welcome, he will be a little more open with us than 'hello' and 'hi.'"

"Perhaps," James said, still feeling disconcerted over the entire thing.

That night in bed James pondered his nagging concern for Iris. He finally determined that he needed to talk to his wife. She was always so good at helping him see reason.

"I don't want to sound like a paranoid, overbearing parent," he began right after she'd climbed into the bed beside him, "but I feel uneasy over this new friend of Iris's. Is it just me and my hesitation to let her grow up? Or should I be paying attention to these feelings?"

He felt more than saw Eleanore lean up on one elbow and look toward him. "I believe such feelings are at least worth discussing and considering. Tell me what's bothering you."

"Well . . . does she seem different to you?"

"Yes, a bit. I've just credited it to her becoming more independent. I believe it's normal for young people that age to be distant to some degree."

"And nervy?"

"Perhaps. I've not allowed her to speak unkindly to me or anyone else. But now that you mention it, she's gotten so she hardly says anything at all."

"So is something wrong? Or should I just be patient and allow nature to take its course, as my wife has advised me?"

"I don't know," she admitted. "Let's give that some thought and prayer."

"Agreed," he said and tried to sleep.

Twenty-four hours later, James and Eleanore concurred that they should give more attention to the changes in Iris's behavior. After talking it through they decided not to call negative attention to the situation, but rather try to encourage more openness about it. On Sunday Eleanore invited Dillon to dinner at their home. He accepted the invitation, but while he was with the family he hardly said a word, and neither did Iris. Any effort that was made to politely inquire about Dillon in an effort to get to know him better was responded to with yes or no answers and a subtle irritation at being spoken to. Once the meal was over, Dillon and Iris slipped outside and talked nonstop once they were out of hearing range from anyone else. Eleanore kept peeking discreetly out the window to keep an eye on them almost as much as James did. Then the two of them walked into the woods holding hands. Eleanore kept James from boldly running after them, but after twenty minutes she agreed that he should check on them and not leave them unchaperoned for too long.

James walked into the woods calling his daughter's name. She came toward him with Dillon right behind her, both wearing distinct scowls.

"Can't I have a little privacy?" she grumbled and walked past her father.

"You're welcome to all the private conversation you want with Dillon, as long as I can see where you are."

"Don't you trust me?" Iris snapped, turning to face him.

James swallowed carefully and took a deep breath before he responded with forced calmness. "We can discuss trust another time. And keep in mind it's something I would be more prone to give you if you weren't quite so snippy and closed these days."

She looked mortified and even more angry as she hurried away, and Dillon followed her without a word. By the time James got back to the house, Dillon had left on the horse he'd arrived on, and, according to Eleanore, Iris had stormed up to her room and slammed the door. James repeated the incident to his wife, and they wholeheartedly agreed that they needed to have a firm talk with their daughter.

"But stay calm," Eleanore said, putting a hand on his arm as they walked up the stairs together.

"I will," he promised, but he couldn't deny his gratitude for having Eleanore with him as he considered the mood Iris's attitude had inspired in him. He knew his lingering anger was likely a disguise for his fears and concerns. But he felt angry, nevertheless.

At the door to Iris's room, Eleanore knocked, and they heard a sharp, "Who is it?"

"Your parents," Eleanore answered. "We need to talk."

"I don't want to talk," she called back. "I have nothing to say."

"Well, *we* have something to say," James said in a voice that barely hinted at his frustration. He felt almost proud of himself for his self-control, and prayed it would hold out.

Iris said nothing more. While James was wondering what to do, Eleanore knocked again, then opened the door slowly without waiting for an answer. She peered in then motioned for James to follow. They found Iris staring out the window, her arms folded stiffly. He couldn't recall ever seeing her look so stubborn, even as a young child when she'd been trying to get her way over some silly matter.

Eleanore sat on the bed, and James sat beside her. Not knowing where to begin, he was grateful when his wife said, "Apparently you wanted to discuss the matter of trust."

"I don't know what there is to say," Iris muttered. "It's obvious you don't trust me."

Again James was relieved that Eleanore had an answer. "Your behavior lately has not inspired trust, Iris. You're being secretive and closed, and not very kind. We feel concerned, and don't want you to get into a situation that could create difficulties for you."

"I'm not stupid," Iris snapped.

With forced control, James said, "Do *not* speak to your mother that way. I don't care how angry you are, you will not—"

"She is *not* my mother!" Iris snarled, turning toward them with fire in her eyes and a defensive stance that left James wondering what kind of evil spell had come over his daughter. He heard Eleanore gasp and could almost feel the way Iris's words had stung her, even before the girl added, "My mother is *dead,* and you can stop pretending that you *are* my mother because you're *not,* and I don't have to listen to you."

James stood to face Iris and managed to keep from shouting back. "She has been a better mother to you than your own mother ever tried to be, and you will show her the respect she deserves. If you don't apologize to her, you will not leave this room." Iris's eyes blazed more intently. "Apologize," he repeated, low and firm.

Iris sighed loudly. "I'm sorry," she said to Eleanore, but she said it snidely. A quick glance showed that Eleanore had a glisten of tears in her horrified eyes, and she was fighting not to weep openly.

James turned back to Iris and added, "Like it or not, I *am* your father, and you're going to listen to me. If spending time with Dillon is going to make you behave this way, then you won't be seeing him any more."

Iris made an appalled noise. "You can't keep me from having friends and—"

"You are more than welcome to have friends, male or female, but not when their being around makes you behave this way. Your attitude is a clear indication that something isn't right, and I'm not going to tolerate circumstances that could put you at risk."

"Risk?" she countered as if she didn't know what the word meant. "I'm not at *risk*. He's nice to me. You don't even know him!"

"Not for lack of trying," James retorted. "We couldn't get a word out of him at dinner."

"He's shy!"

"Perhaps, but not enough to justify his behaving as if every question we asked were an insult and an inconvenience. He's said nothing polite or gracious in our presence, and we have no reason to believe that he has the character to be trusted with our daughter's well-being."

"You don't know what you're talking about."

"I'm not nearly as stupid as you seem to think, young lady. I've been around long enough to discern a person's character, given a chance. I have too much evidence that I can't trust him, and that means I can't trust you if you're siding with him against your family."

"I'm not *siding* with him!"

"You talk to him cheerfully and nonstop, and yet you behave as if being in the same room with any one of us is beneath you. Yes, that clearly indicates who you are siding with."

James felt Eleanore beside him when she put her hand on his arm, silently cautioning him not to take this too far. He swallowed carefully and added in a voice that was more even, "If you want to see Dillon, you will do so here at home, and you will stay where we can see you. If you can't accept that, then you don't need to see him."

"That is the most ridiculous thing I've ever—"

"Why?" James asked. "If you weren't trying to do something wrong, then why would you want so desperately to be alone with him?"

Iris's inability to answer the question left James feeling a little sick. He hurried to add, "You know where I stand. If you want to discuss this further, you know where to find me."

James guided Eleanore out of the room, half expecting Iris to bring up more protest or toss more hurtful comments at them, but she said nothing as they left the room and closed the door. Once they were in the hall, Eleanore rushed into their bedroom as if she couldn't get there fast enough. He entered a few steps behind her and found her sobbing.

"I'm so sorry," he said and wrapped his arms around her.

"It's all right, really." She stepped back and wiped at her tears. "I'm not as hurt as you might think. And I'm not angry. I'm more just . . . concerned, James. I can't believe this is Iris talking."

"Neither can I," he said, feeling hurt *and* angry enough for both of them.

"What's gotten into her?"

"It's obvious, isn't it?"

"Is it?" Eleanore asked, sitting on the edge of the bed.

"I believe her passion has been awakened," James said, sitting beside her.

"Good heavens!" Eleanore gasped. "You don't think that she's . . . really . . . trying to get away with . . ." She didn't even want to say it. "She knows better than that!"

"Yes, she does," he said. "But she's infatuated with this boy, and I think she's taken complete leave of her senses. And I don't know what to do about it."

Eleanore saw him turn toward her as if she might spout off some glorious advice. "What?" she demanded.

"Well, you're a woman. Surely you have some insight into this that could help."

"Forgive me, Mr. Barrington," she said with subtle sarcasm, "but my *passion was not awakened* until I was married. I went through my first—and last—infatuation over my husband, a man with whom I was already having an intimate relationship. I have no advice to give you. I can only say that I believe she's been taught correctly and she'll come around so long as we keep an eye on her and let her know that we love her, no matter how she behaves. I believe anger will only drive her further away, and we need to be careful that we don't let our emotions get out of hand with her."

James exhaled loudly. "Yes, I'm sure you're right. It would be well for you to stay close by when I talk to her, even if she *is* being cruel to you."

"I can survive *that,* James. I assure you that I am not intimidated by Iris's memories of her mother. They had no positive experiences whatsoever. She's simply digging for a reason to be difficult."

"But *why?* Why would she *want* to be difficult?"

"I don't know that she *wants* to. She probably just really likes Dillon and she wants to please him, and since we are countering their spending time alone, it's making her angry."

James thought about that a moment and said, "So you *do* have insight on the matter. You always were instinctively wise."

Eleanore shrugged and leaned her head on his shoulder. "I don't know about that. Truly, I think the best thing we can do is pray for her."

"Of course." He put his arm around her and pressed a kiss into her hair. "I'm grateful to not be raising her alone. I would surely be lost."

"It's a pleasure being Iris's mother—even if she doesn't like me right now." She looked up at him and touched his face. "There are many benefits to the position."

She kissed him, and he asked, "Like what?"

"Like being married to Iris's father."

Chapter Nine
DANGLING

Throughout the remainder of the day, Iris didn't say a word, but she *did* come to supper, and she completed her evening chores without being asked. When she was on her way to bed after the family had gathered for prayer, James told her that he loved her. She didn't so much as glance in his direction, but he knew she wasn't deaf, and with any luck it would stick somewhere in her memory.

Late that night, James was staring into the darkness, futilely attempting to sleep, well aware that Eleanore was doing the same. He finally broke the silence and asked, "Tell me what you're thinking about. Maybe if we talk we'll get sleepy."

"I was just thinking about the first time I ever encountered you."

"In the library," he said.

"Yes."

"The night Caroline died."

"No. That was the first time we ever spoke. But weeks before that I overheard you arguing with her. You didn't know I was there. I told you about it later."

James groaned. "I've tried to forget about that. I was behaving very badly."

"She did have a way of bringing out the worst in you."

"Yes, she did!" He took her hand beneath the covers. "And you have a way of bringing out the best in me. You always have."

"And vice versa," she said, finding his face with her hand so she could kiss him. She settled her head on his shoulder. "It's strange, you know, how life can change. It's difficult to believe that you can not even know someone at all, then you wake up one day and realize they're the most important person in your life."

"Are you referring to someone in particular?" he asked then chuckled when she playfully hit him.

"You know very well I'm referring to you. I can assure you that when I heard you and your wife arguing, it would not have entered my mind that she would die and I would be your next wife."

"The idea certainly didn't occur to me when I caught you in the library trying to read my Bible."

"I thought you were going to dismiss me from my position and have me removed from the household for breaking the rules."

"Truthfully, I didn't know there was a rule about servants not going into the library."

"We were only allowed to clean it," she said.

"Well, it was a silly rule. If I could go back I would let *all* of the servants know that they were welcome to borrow books from the library. Better than having them collect dust."

"Are you sleepy yet?" she asked and kissed him.

"Not even a little," he said and kissed her back.

* * * * *

The following day Iris was still silent at breakfast; then she did her chores. And sometime in the afternoon she took a horse and ran off, leaving only a note on the kitchen table for explanation. *I've gone into town. I'll be home by dark. Iris.*

She *wasn't* home by dark; in fact it was more than an hour later when she showed up. At Eleanore's suggestion, James simply said to her, "A note is not good enough, young lady. You talk to one of us and get permission before you run off alone. And since you can add being late on top of leaving without permission, you'll have some extra work to complete before you get any more free time."

Iris glared at him but said nothing. The next day she did the extra work, even though she griped most of the time. James finally told her that if she didn't stop complaining he was going to add even more extra hours. In the evening she endured family prayer as if it were torture, then she slithered to her room and stayed there until James peeked in later to find her sleeping. Or at least she was pretending to sleep, likely to avoid a goodnight kiss from her father. The thought made him feel a bit mischievous, and he couldn't resist taking advantage of the opportunity. At the risk of having her wake up and catch him—or get angry because she was actually awake—he tucked the blanket up around her and kissed her forehead, whispering gently, "I love you, Iris. I'll always love you." He crept quietly out of the room, hoping she'd been awake to hear his declaration. Or if she'd been sleeping, that perhaps her spirit had sensed his love for her, and she might feel it in her dreams.

Nothing changed with Iris for a number of weeks. Dillon did come to visit occasionally, but he didn't become any more sociable, in spite of a genuine effort on the part of James and Eleanore to make him feel included. When the weather was nice, Iris would sit in the yard with him. At other times they would sit in the library or parlor, always with the door open. She didn't complain, and she did all that was expected of her, but she was aloof and almost cold to everyone *except* Dillon. James and Eleanore both continued to feel concerned, but as long as Iris wasn't breaking any rules, there was little they could do. They felt as if she were dangling at the edge of some dangerous precipice and there was nothing they could do to save her. Together they prayed morning and night, and individually a great deal in between, that Iris would come to see reason over Dillon without getting hurt too badly, or before some disaster occurred. James admitted that one of his greatest fears was that his daughter would run off and marry this young man, giving little thought to the future, and she would end up living a difficult life with a husband who had challenges in his character. While it was true that they knew very little about Dillon, Iris's behavior as a result of their acquaintance seemed a testament of something amiss. James and Eleanore even made an attempt to devise a connection with Dillon's parents, making it a point to cross paths with them at church. But they were apparently not interested in socializing with anyone who was not already included in their circle. They came across as being judgmental and pious, and they either believed Dillon was a saint, or they preferred to remain ignorant of what he was doing because it was too much bother.

James commented to Eleanore one evening while Iris and Dillon were walking along the perimeter of the woods, holding hands, "Do you have any idea how different Iris's life would be if we were living among the Saints?" He turned from the office window where he was watching the object of his concern.

"I've thought about that. Dillon has no idea of her religious beliefs."

"Better that way."

"Yes, but shouldn't she marry someone who shares those beliefs?"

"Yes, she should. But that's hardly possible under the circumstances, when there's no one around here who does." He leaned against the edge of the desk and folded his arms. "I want to think she's far too young to get married, but as you once pointed out, she's not much younger than you were when you married me. The very idea makes me feel like a hypocrite."

"I believe I was ready," Eleanore said. "Iris is different from me in many ways. But perhaps it's not so much her age as the fact that she's not giving her attention to the right kind of man. He's more immature than she is. She needs someone who is in a position to take care of her; someone who doesn't provoke her to be her worst self."

"Amen," James said and sighed loudly. "Maybe we should move, take her away from here. If we were living among the Saints, she could socialize among her own kind, and this sort of problem could be avoided."

"I'm certain that not every eligible Mormon young man is necessarily exemplary."

"No, but it would be better than this. Perhaps it's time."

"Perhaps it is," Eleanore agreed. "But you told me you were going to stop asking."

"That was before my daughter fell into this hideous trap. I'm asking."

But a few days later, once again, they both knew beyond any doubt that it *wasn't* time. They needed to stay where they were, and they had to keep believing that the prophet's promise in regard to their staying would come to pass. In the meantime, they could only keep praying that Iris would come to her senses and they could have their daughter back. Eventually they hoped to see her married to the right man for the right reasons.

* * * * *

Eleanore got up in the night when she heard Joseph fussing. It was common for him to still wake up once during the night, but a drink of water and a little cuddling soon had him back to sleep. And as always, Eleanore peeked into the rooms of the other children just enough to see that they were safe and sleeping. It was a common habit, but something the children would be unaware of, since they were always asleep—which would explain why Iris might never consider that Eleanore would realize she was gone in the middle of the night.

"James!" Eleanore said, turning the lamp up high as she rushed into the bedroom. "James! Wake up!"

"What is it?" he asked, sitting up abruptly.

"Iris is gone. Her bed's not been slept in."

"Heaven help us," he muttered and pulled on breeches and boots. Eleanore followed him down the stairs while he buttoned a shirt, but he said, "You stay here with the children. I'll get Frederick to help me look for her."

"I'll be praying," she said and watched him leave, wondering how he would ever know where to look.

James checked the barn first before waking Frederick. But she wasn't there, and a horse was missing. The painful knot in his stomach tightened with unfathomable dread. He couldn't even think about the possibilities of where she might be, and what she might be doing. He was running toward Frederick's house when he heard a horse and hesitated. He actually felt lightheaded when he realized it was Iris.

"Oh, thank you, God," he muttered and stepped into her path, taking the horse by the reins, startling her.

"You were coming to look for me?" she asked, almost sounding hopeful. He'd not heard any tone from her but cynical or angry for months.

"Fat lot of good it would have done me when I had no idea where you were, or where to begin looking. And I might not have even known you were gone until morning." He heard her sniffle loudly, and he demanded with the panic he was still feeling, "Are you crying? What's happened?"

Iris slid down from the horse's bare back and fell into his arms, sobbing. He inhaled deeply and took a moment to absorb the shock before he wrapped her in a tight embrace and pondered the possible sources of such emotion. He noticed movement from the corner of his eye and turned to see Eleanore on the porch with a lamp.

"She's here," he called. "Go back to bed. I'll be up soon."

Eleanore nodded and went back into the house. James urged Iris to walk beside him while he kept his arm around her and led the horse into the barn. Iris sat on a bale of straw and kept crying more softly while James lit a lamp, silently praying for guidance in this crucial moment. He unbridled the horse and settled it into a stall before he sat beside her and said, "Do you want to talk about it?"

"I feel like such a fool, so humiliated."

James took a deep breath. "Iris, no matter what's happened, or what you've done, your mother and I will always love you. If you're in trouble, you need to tell me so we can help you get through it."

She looked up at him. "You really mean that?"

"I really do."

"Even though I've been so . . . horrible."

He shrugged. "We all have tough times and things to learn, Iris. I've been horrible more than once in my life. That's why we have the principle of forgiveness." He put his arm around her, relieved beyond words to feel her snuggle into his embrace in a way that had once been so familiar. His little girl was back. He hoped that she would stay. "Do you want to talk about it?"

"Not really, but I probably should." Her tears increased again.

"We could wait until you get some sleep."

"No, I think it would be better to get it over with."

James feared that the worst had happened. Was she pregnant? Did she fear that it might be possible? He held his breath as she said, "He tried to have his way with me, Papa." He could barely understand her as the confession came out on a wave of fresh sobs.

"Tried?" he asked, taking her shoulders to force her to look at him.

She nodded. "When I realized he had no intention of stopping, I . . . I . . . kicked him hard. I knew it hurt him enough that he couldn't come after me. And I ran. But I shouldn't have even been there, and . . ."

"No, you shouldn't have. But we can thank God it wasn't any worse. I'm just grateful you're safe, Iris. And that he *didn't* have his way with you."

"So am I." She sniffled loudly. "I never really believed he would try something like that, in spite of . . ."

"In spite of what?" he pressed when she hesitated. "You used to tell me everything, you know."

"I know. I'm so sorry, Papa . . . that I stopped talking to you . . . and to Mama." He breathed in relief on Eleanore's behalf as well as his own. He needed her to finish that crucial sentence, and asked again, "In spite of what?"

"In spite of how much we were kissing," she admitted timidly.

"Just tonight?" he asked.

"No. Other times, too."

He wondered how she had managed to have time alone with Dillon when he thought he'd kept such a good eye on her. Then he realized that if a child was determined to be disobedient, they would surely find a way. He knew he'd done the best he could do, but he still felt like he'd failed her somehow.

He asked her some difficult questions, and she gave him straight-forward answers. He talked to her about the spiritual and physical consequences of what she'd done, and delicately reminded her of how bad it could have been if she'd not left the situation when she had. She cried long and hard once there was nothing more to say. He just held her and thanked God that she had seen reason, and that she'd been spared from far worse consequences.

When she'd calmed down he said gently, "You should save yourself for marriage, Iris. The relationship you share with your husband someday has more value than you could ever comprehend until it's a part of your life."

"Did you save yourself for marriage?"

"I did," he said and was glad to be able to answer that question without guilt or explanation.

"And my mother?" she asked.

He was going to ask which one, then he realized the answer was the same for both of the women she'd called Mother. "Yes," he said.

"So it was after you'd married her that she became unfaithful?" she asked, and James's mouth went dry. "My blood mother, I mean."

"I know who you mean," he said. "I'm just wondering how you knew. You were so young when she died. I thought I'd protected you from that."

"I heard servants talking and put pieces together. At the time I didn't fully understand what it meant. Years after she died it just came together in my head and made sense." Her eyes showed a long-absent compassion, and she took his hand. "The baby that died with her wasn't yours."

"No, it wasn't," James said, wondering why that fact still caused pain.

"Am *I* yours?" she asked, and James gasped.

"Of course you are!"

"Are you sure?" she asked, and he realized the issue had truly concerned her. He also knew that a completely honest answer was best.

"Iris," he held her hand, "obviously you're old enough to discuss this frankly. I must admit that there was a time when I wondered if you and David were mine." Her eyes widened, but she let him go on. "She was pregnant with you when I found out about the affair. I think she wanted me to believe that you and David were *not* mine. Once the truth of her indiscretions came out, she became horribly cruel."

"Yes, I know," she said. "I overheard the way she talked to you. Even as young as I was, I remember thinking that she was even more cruel to you than she was to me and David."

"Truthfully, I couldn't be sure. But I decided that it didn't matter. You were born with my name and in my marriage, and you would be my children regardless. It was your mother . . . Eleanore, who—"

"My *real* mother."

"Yes, your real mother. Right after we were married, when David was sick before we left England, she told me how much she'd seen a resemblance to me in both of you. And she meant it. I knew she was telling the truth. I guess it's harder for me to see it myself. But I'll tell you something, Iris, when I realized you and David really were my children, it didn't change the way I felt about either of you, but it changed the way I felt about myself. Being your father is one of the most important things in my life."

"Oh!" She put her head on his shoulder again. "I'm sorry I've been so awful. And I'm sorry about what I said to Mother."

"I'll let you tell her that yourself."

"I will."

"I think we could both use some sleep," he said and urged her to her feet, guiding her into the house.

Eleanore met them in the hall, where she'd been pacing. "You should be in bed," he told her.

"I couldn't possibly sleep. Is everything all right?" She took notice of James's arm around Iris.

"It is now," James said, and Iris let go of him to hug Eleanore tightly.

Eleanore cried as she held Iris close. "Oh, my darling!" she said. "I've been so terribly worried."

"I know," Iris murmured tearfully. "I'm so sorry. And I'm sorry for what I said to you. It was a horrible thing to say."

"It's all right," Eleanore said, taking Iris's face into her hands. "It doesn't matter what you say, or think, or feel. I will always be your mother, and I will always love you."

Iris nodded, too emotional to speak.

"Come along," James said. "We could all use some sleep."

"So what happened?" Eleanore asked Iris on their way up the stairs. "Unless you don't want me to know, of course."

"No, I want you to know," Iris said. "But I'll let Papa tell you."

James tucked Iris into bed, then looked in on the other children and went back to bed himself. He was barely comfortable when Eleanore said, "Are you too tired to tell me now?"

"I'm exhausted, but I know I can't sleep until I *do* tell you." He repeated everything Iris had told him, and tearfully expressed his gratitude to have her back—physically as well as emotionally—and to know that the situation hadn't been any worse.

When he told Eleanore how angry to he felt toward Dillon, she reminded him that Iris had voluntarily become involved with this young man, and had led him to believe by her behavior that she would go along with such things. He knew she was right, but he still felt angry. He wanted to go drag the boy out of his bed and give him a bloody nose for taking advantage of his daughter that way, and he told

Eleanore so. She thought he was joking, or at least she passed it off lightly, expressing her confidence in him to behave in a more Christian manner than that. At the moment he didn't feel very Christian, but he focused his thoughts on the positive outcome of the situation. His daughter was back.

Eleanore fell back to sleep, but James couldn't. He was startled to find his thoughts wandering into territory left avoided for years. But Dillon's taking unfair advantage of Iris had led him into memories of all he knew that had happened to Mormon women and children throughout the reign of Mormon persecution. And he felt haunted. He told himself the Saints were continuing to gather in a place where they could be safe and free, but the past didn't feel so far in the past as he thought of all he'd heard Ben repeat, and the boy was still so young.

James finally slept, but his sleep was troubled with dreams. He saw Iris being hurt, screaming and begging for her father to help her. He saw himself retaliating against a faceless man who had done harm to someone he loved. And then he was hanging on the edge of a cliff, clinging to the ground beneath his fingers, struggling to drag himself up. But the ground was loose and he could feel his hands losing strength. He woke up before he fell, but he went back to sleep and dreamt again of dangling at the edge of a cliff, struggling to come up. And again he woke before he fell. With a hint of light filling the room, James decided against going back to sleep, and instead prayed for peace with his feelings. He expressed gratitude for Iris's safe return, and for the preservation of her virtue. He prayed that his ill feelings would relent, but he found his mind wandering into long walks with those feelings until he heard Joseph fussing, then he went to get him. He changed the baby's diaper and let him toddle to the bed, where Eleanore laughed softly as she reached out to pick him up. She greeted Joseph with kisses and tickles, then she held a hand out to James, saying, "Good morning, my love."

"Good morning," he said, praying with all his heart that his family would remain protected from the evils of the world. If anything horrible happened to those he loved most, he felt certain he would fall off the edge of that cliff.

* * * * *

James looked up from the weeds he was pulling in the garden and saw Mr. Pitt with one of his two sons riding slowly toward him. "Great," he mumbled under his breath with sarcasm. The three men lived in the home where Andy and Miriam Plummer had once lived. They were barely friendly and leaned toward vulgar conversation, which had motivated James to avoid them. About twice a year Mr. Pitt showed up to ask a question or chat about seemingly senseless things, and James did his best to be polite and neighborly. He didn't have any reason to believe that the Pitt men weren't basically respectable, but they were brash and annoying, and he had nothing in common with them beyond actually being neighbors and planting things in the same kind of soil.

"Good morning," James said as they approached and dismounted. "What brings you out this way?" he added, stepping out of the garden.

"Just wondering if you knew about the town meeting," Mr. Pitt said.

"Town meeting?" James asked, not certain what he meant exactly.

The son responded, although James couldn't remember if this was Clint or Harry. "It's a chance for the local folk to express their opinion about things that are going on, and sometimes cast a vote. We've heard a rumor that there might be some changes come up that could affect us out here, and we thought you should know about it."

"Thank you," James said, not certain if he wanted to go to a town meeting or not, but his neighbors' motives seemed nice enough. "When is this meeting?" he asked, wondering if it might not be good for him to be informed of such things, and perhaps be involved if he felt the need.

"Tonight at 7:30," Mr. Pitt said. "At the city hall."

"I might just show up," James said. "I appreciate your letting me know."

"Not a problem," Mr. Pitt said, and James hoped they would leave, but he dismounted and pointed behind James.

"How's the garden coming along?"

"Very well," James said, and the son got down from his horse as well.

The three of them walked through the garden and chatted about growing things for nearly half an hour before the Pitts finally left.

James felt relieved when they were gone, especially because their language could tend to run off-color at times. He reminded himself that they were likely good men who simply had a much different upbringing. But he found it difficult to completely trust them. He wasn't certain if his lack of trust was based on any valid cause for concern, or if he simply felt uncomfortable with them and was jumping to conclusions.

A while later James told Eleanore about their visit and the town meeting. "Do you think I should go?"

"That's up to you," she said while trying to thread a needle.

"I don't really *want* to, but maybe I should."

"It's up to you," she repeated. "Perhaps Frederick might want to go with you."

"I'll ask him," James said, thinking it would be more enjoyable if Frederick did go, but his friend had promised to help Lizzie with something that evening and declined. James figured that was reason enough to stay at home himself, but he kept thinking about it and finally decided that he would go, if only to become a little more aware of the community and the people in it.

At the city hall there were more people than he'd expected, and most of them were men. He saw the Pitt brothers without their father, but they only waved and sat elsewhere, much to James's relief. Beyond them he didn't see anyone he knew well, only a handful of familiar faces that he'd seen in town over the years. The meeting was noisy and not very productive, in James's opinion. There was some debating over petty issues, and more than once some joking completely derailed the topic for several minutes. He heard nothing discussed that directly affected him or his family one way or another.

James was considering leaving when the man sitting next to him leaned over and started chatting. He was an older man who introduced himself simply as Leonard. He proved rather amiable and it was much more enjoyable to visit with him than to pay attention to the noisy discussions taking place.

When the meeting ended, Leonard asked James if he was going down the street a ways to a tavern, where many gathered after these meetings for a drink. James didn't drink, but he did occasionally enjoy socializing with others in the community. Perhaps the tavern would be more enjoyable than the meeting had been, and it might make the trip to town worthwhile.

At the tavern, James quickly felt disappointed and wondered what on earth he was doing there. Leonard was telling ridiculous stories to someone else, but James couldn't avoid hearing them since they were sitting next to each other. James was preparing to say good night to Leonard when a nearby conversation caught his attention. Before he consciously realized what he was hearing, he became thoroughly encompassed with a sense that he'd lived this moment before. He became so distracted by the memory of an event so similar that an eery chill rushed over his shoulders. Then, just as now, it was that word *Mormon* spoken with a drunken slur that caught his ear. He immediately felt as sick as he had the last time he'd overheard a conversation about the fact that some people didn't like Mormons at all, and that they lowered themselves to hideous methods of getting rid of them.

James heard a voice in his head, nearly as clear as the ones speaking nearby, telling him to get up and leave. His deepest instincts warned him that he did not need to overhear this conversation, and his ending up in this place at this time was not a blessing as it had been before, but rather the opposite.

Get up and leave, James repeated to himself, knowing it was the best choice. But a dark kind of curiosity battled with the edict of wisdom that lured him to remove himself from this place where men got drunk, then rambled, spilling deplorable secrets. The last time this had happened, James had eventually felt grateful for the warning he'd gotten that had prevented him from exposing his family to danger. But what purpose could possibly be served in overhearing such a conversation a second time? It couldn't *possibly* be coincidence! Considering his thoughts and ill feelings on the matter, which had come to the surface again recently, he felt certain the devil himself had lured him to this place, and he would be hanging on the edge of a cliff if he remained another minute.

Leonard said goodbye and left, and once again James told himself to do the same. But just as in his dream, he couldn't find the strength to do anything but dangle there helplessly. Then he heard something that pierced his heart and turned his entire body to lead. He felt a solid shift take place in his brain, and he didn't *want* to leave. His spirit darkened, and he felt a sick need to sit there long enough to come to believe that what he was hearing had actually transpired. He felt nauseous and woozy and almost feared he'd lose consciousness as the reality of this man's bragging meshed with connections in his own life. The monster knew too many details and names for his story to be empty boasting just for the sake of it, and James felt unfathomable anger surge to his every nerve, eradicating any other possible emotion or sense of reason.

When the conversation shifted to other deplorable topics, James finally found the strength to get up and leave, doing his best to appear nonchalant and not draw any attention to himself. Once outside he immediately turned down an alley in order to avoid the attention of those walking up and down the street. He gasped for breath and hung his head, struggling to comprehend the enormity and the horror of what he'd just learned. He fought the urge to sob, just wanting to be home where he could find sanctity and peace—if such a thing might ever be possible again. He felt angry with himself for ever leaving the house this evening, angry at the injustice of life and the persecution of innocent people. And most especially, he felt angry with the man he'd just heard bragging about the atrocities he had personally inflicted upon Mark and Sally Jensen and their family—a family who had lived in the home James was living in now with his own family. The two families had become dear friends, even across a great distance. Eleanore had been writing to Sally for years, they'd all spent time together in Nauvoo, and James had helped build them their home in Winter Quarters. James and Eleanore had known that the Jensens had left quickly, but Sally had never told Eleanore the reasons. She'd only eluded to a situation that had been horrible and difficult. And now James knew. He knew what had happened, and the question that screamed silently through his mind was a gut-wrenching, *What if it happened to us?*

James was startled by a couple of men coming down the alley. He pressed his back against the brick wall behind him, grateful to note that they'd not even seen him. Only lanterns hanging at each end of the alley illuminated enough to show the way, but the darkness hid these men from his view, as much as he was hidden from theirs once they'd come a short distance between the two buildings. More men came a few minutes later, and James realized this was a common route to one of the liveries where men left their horses while they went to the tavern. As emotional as he was, he was grateful to have gone unobserved, but he knew he needed to get home. And then he heard that voice. That horrible, grating voice. He'd never heard it before tonight, and now he feared he would never forget how it sounded. The man he'd just heard bragging about his evil doings against people James cared about was standing at the head of the alley, laughing with two other men. They were all too drunk to stand up straight, or to realize how loud and obnoxious they were. The men talked for a few minutes, and James could only watch and listen, hidden in the shadows, while his anger festered and grew until he couldn't even recognize his own thoughts. He heard one of the men call the culprit Ned, the other called him Weller. *Weller.* Where had he heard that name? The answer came quickly in association with the memory James had been contending with a short while ago regarding the first time this had happened. How could he ever forget what he'd heard then? *I guess a little harassment goes a long way in keeping the filthy scum from getting too comfortable around here. I hear the Weller boys roughed up his wife pretty good.*

James was glad there were three of them. Only the logic of knowing he was outnumbered kept him from boldly unleashing his anger on this man. Then the other two left, and Ned Weller staggered down the alley, directly past James. He held his breath and willed himself to stay calm and control his temper. But something akin to a deeply wounded animal rose to the surface and erupted in a way that James couldn't even recognize in himself. He hit Weller hard in the face, then in the belly, amazed at how much it hurt his own hand. Weller was taken so off guard that he had no opportunity to retaliate before James took him by the collar and slammed him against the wall, lowering his voice to disguise it as he told this man what he thought of him, without reference to his specific reasons. He wasn't going to reveal anything of his identity—or his religion. He would not have his own family subjected to the barbaric behavior of such a monster.

James hit him twice more, with more strength than he knew he'd possessed. A voice of reason appeared from somewhere in his head, bringing him back to his senses. He stepped back and let go of Weller with the intention of leaving before this got any worse. It was too dark to see what happened, but James felt the blade of a knife plunge deep into his thigh before Weller slithered to the ground with a groan and stayed there, grumbling unintelligibly. James cursed under his breath and hurried out of the alley, grateful the pain wasn't impeding his ability to walk, albeit with difficulty. Once in the light at the back end of the alley, James was grateful to be alone, but was alarmed to see the trail of blood he was leaving behind. He removed his jacket, folded it and pressed it over the wound, praying he would make it home before he lost consciousness—and without being followed.

He passed no one before coming to the place he'd tethered his horse. He'd left no trail from the alley, and managed to keep one hand pressed firmly over the wound while he mounted and rode toward home. His relief at arriving there was beyond description, and when he realized he'd kept any blood from leaking out of the wound to leave a trail, he felt doubly grateful. He verbally thanked God for helping him get safely home, and in the same breath he had to beg forgiveness for what he'd just done.

Chapter Ten

THE REPRIMAND

Eleanore felt mildly concerned that when it came time for the family to gather for prayer before bedtime, James still wasn't home. But she reasoned that the meeting had been long, or perhaps he was talking and had lost track of the time. Once the children were in bed, she began to feel worried. He'd told her he wouldn't be late. She paced the hall, then checked on the children and found them all asleep. With the house completely quiet, her concern exploded into panic. She paced and stewed and wrung her hands, praying while she attempted to convince herself that there was a logical explanation for her husband being so ridiculously late. Surely everything was fine. She looked at the clock and decided that if he wasn't home in ten minutes she was going to enlist Frederick's assistance, even if she had to wake him. A minute later she heard a horse and rushed out the back door just in time to see James ride into the barn.

"Oh, thank you, Father," she muttered and leaned against the door, knowing that once he unsaddled the horse he would hurry into the house. Then too many minutes passed and she wondered what he might be doing. She stepped down from the porch to go and see just as he came out of the barn door. Peering through the darkness, she saw him lean against the barn for a long moment before he started toward the house—with a definite limp.

"James!" she said, startling him. "What's happened?"

"I'm hurt," he muttered. "Help me."

Eleanore hurried to his side, vaguely able to see that he was holding something folded over his thigh. He draped his other arm around her shoulders and leaned into her enough to take the pressure off the ailing leg as they moved toward the house. "What's happened?" she repeated.

James didn't know what to tell her. He couldn't be dishonest with his wife, but he was still in shock over what had happened. He was grateful she couldn't see the guilt in his eyes, but that wouldn't last long. "Just . . . help me inside," he said.

Once they were through the door, the lamp burning in the hall illuminated the amount of blood on the folded jacket and the hand that held it in place. "What in the world . . ." Eleanore gasped.

"Just . . . help me," he muttered, clearly in pain. "I'll explain later."

Eleanore forced reason to suppress her concern, but something in his attitude left her uneasy. "Let's go in the kitchen and—"

"No," he said. "Help me upstairs. I don't want anyone but you to know about this."

Eleanore's uneasiness increased, but she only glared at him and took up the lamp with her free hand. On the stairs, James took hold of the stair rail and managed to get to the top without too much help from his wife. Eleanore's stomach churned over the possible reasons for such behavior while she guided him into the bathing room, where he sat on the edge of the tub. She set down the lamp and turned up the wick before she found a bottle of disinfectant. He peeled away the jacket he'd used for a compress just as she turned toward him, and she had to take hold of the wall to keep from teetering. She actually felt a little faint.

"What have you done?" she muttered hotly.

"Just . . . help me get out of these clothes . . . and . . ."

"It's still bleeding," she said, pulling off his boots. He groaned when she removed the one on his afflicted leg.

"Yes, it's still bleeding. At least that will help clean out the wound."

When the bloody clothes had been tossed aside, Eleanore sponged the blood away enough to pour disinfectant into the wound. James hissed and clenched his teeth, holding to the edge of the tub so tightly that his hands turned as ashen as his face. She bandaged the wound with a tight compress of clean gauze, then helped him into a clean nightshirt.

"Burn those clothes," he ordered, hobbling to the bed.

"I can soak the blood out and—"

"I don't want you to. Burn them. I don't want any sign of blood in the house."

"Why not?" she demanded as he eased onto his side of the bed and put a pillow beneath his thigh.

"Just do it!" he insisted in a hushed shout.

"Give me a reason," she countered.

"I don't want anyone in the household to have to lie on my behalf."

"Except *me?*" she asked, but he said nothing. "What are you hiding, James? Why don't you want anyone to know?"

He drew a deep breath and sought for an even temper. "I don't want anyone to know because the man who did this to me hates Mormons and will do anything to get rid of them, and I don't want him to know it was me."

Eleanore took in the implication and once again felt faint. "Someone *stabbed* you?"

James nodded.

"How could a man not know who it was that he stabbed in the leg?"

"It was dark."

"But he knows you're a Mormon?"

"No. He doesn't know who I am; that's the point."

"Then why did he stab you, James?" she asked, trying not to sound as infuriated as she felt.

He blew out a ragged breath and resigned himself to getting this over with. "Because I was hitting him."

Eleanore took a step backward. Telling herself not to jump to conclusions, she ignored the guilt in her husband's eyes and simply asked, "Why?"

"Why what?"

"Why were you hitting him?" James hesitated, and she spoke with more anger than he'd ever heard. "Tell me, James!"

"I had my reasons. Maybe it's better if I don't—"

"You tell me—now. What good reason could there be to hit a man who had a knife?"

"I didn't know he had a knife."

"Oh, that's right," she said with sarcasm, "it was dark. Why were you hitting him?"

He sighed and looked away.

"Was it self-defense?"

He sighed again and hung his head. "No."

Eleanore gasped and took another step back. "Then there is *no* good reason for you to be hitting another man." She put a hand to her chest, finding it difficult to breathe. "Do I understand this correctly? You started hitting another man—in the dark—which made *him* act in self-defense and stab you in the leg?"

James looked up at her and snarled, "He got only a taste of what he deserves."

Eleanore took *another* step back, reminded of the dramatic changes that had once occurred in Iris, changing her personality almost overnight. "How old are you, exactly?" she asked. "Because you're talking like a child."

"I'm a grown man, Eleanore. I'm old enough to admit that what I did was stupid, but it was still justified—and I'd do it again."

"I can't believe what I'm hearing. I've never known you to be even the slightest bit violent. How can you sit there and admit that you were hitting someone and not feel any remorse?"

"Don't stand there and judge me when you have no idea of what was really going on."

"And I never will, if you don't tell me," she said, provoking another weighted sigh from him. "Make me believe that what you did was right, James. Convince me. I'm waiting." He said nothing, and she blurted in a loud whisper, not wanting to wake the children. "He could have *killed* you! What if the knife had gone into your belly, or your chest? You'd be lying dead in the street right now, and where would that leave us?"

James felt his guilt rise, but he still couldn't find regret.

"You could have been dead, James. Dead! Do you hear what I'm saying?" Her voice cracked. "You broke your promise to me."

He snapped his eyes to hers. "What promise?"

"You promised me you would do everything in your power to stay safe and healthy. How *dare* you do something like this and put my husband, and the father of my children, at such a ridiculous risk?

Whatever happened, you had no business provoking such a situation."
She started crying, with a fist pressed over her heart. "You should
have walked away and stayed . . . safe." The last word choked out on
a sob, and she left the room as if staying might expose him to some
unleashed fury.

James sank back into the bed and moaned, more from his wife's
emotion than the raging pain in his leg. If he could have chased her
down he would have, but he'd used his last bit of strength to get where
he was. He *had* promised her he would do everything in his power to
remain safe and healthy. It had come up numerous times, but with the
most impact when Andy had died and Eleanore had struggled with
wondering how she would cope if it happened to them. And not so long
afterward, Eleanore had struggled through a difficult labor and delivery,
putting him on the other side of the issue, leaving him to wonder how
he would ever survive without her. His own internal battle heightened as
he considered the risk he had subjected himself to, and how he might
feel if Eleanore had done something equivalent. He would surely be at
least as upset as she was. Still, he had trouble feeling any regret. Even
now, as he thought of what this man had done—and that he then had
the audacity to sit in a tavern and boast about it ten years after the
fact—his anger toward Ned Weller consumed him. James thought about
it until the anger became almost as painful as the bleeding wound, and
he had to will himself to steer his thoughts elsewhere. His wife was
furious with him, and understandably so. But he'd done what he'd done,
and he wasn't sure if he'd go back and change it if he could—although
he would have preferred to avoid being wounded. He wondered how he
could help her understand why he'd done it without exposing her to
what he'd overheard. Thinking of that made his head hurt, and he realized how thoroughly exhausted he was. But he wasn't certain he could
sleep with such throbbing pain. He couldn't recall anything ever hurting
so much in his life, but then he'd never been this severely injured. He
prayed for strength and healing, and for some relief from this pain, then
wondered if he deserved to have any prayer answered at all. He quickly
smothered his own guilt with a silent rationalization that any man in his
situation would have done the same.

* * * * *

Eleanore ran down the stairs, knowing James could never follow her. She felt her way through the dark into the library and closed the door, struggling to breathe once she knew she was completely alone and the children couldn't overhear her even if they did wake up. "Oh, help," she cried and sank to her knees. "Oh, help me." She gasped and sobbed and fought away images of James lying dead with a knife through his heart. If it had been self-defense, or an injury from some kind of accident, she would have been able to understand that such things happen and just be grateful it wasn't worse. But he had *provoked* this.

When her tears had been vented enough that she believed she could remain composed, Eleanore reminded herself that James was likely in agony and incapable of caring for himself. She put her fear and anger aside and resigned herself to taking care of him. She entered the bedroom quietly and could tell just from looking at him that he was in pain. His eyes were closed, but his expression was tight and strained. She wondered if he was asleep until she noticed how his fist was clenched onto the sheet that covered him.

"It's bad, isn't it," she said, and he looked at her.

James hesitated, trying to gauge her mood. Her concern was somewhat comforting. "I'm certain I'll be fine."

"That's a prideful statement if I've ever heard one. You're in pain. Admit it."

"Yes, I admit it. I'm in pain, but I don't need a lecture on how my pain is my fault."

She let out a disgusted sigh. "I have some laudanum left from my last childbirth. It's not much, but maybe it will help you get some rest for the first few days."

"Thank you," he said, wondering if God had heard his prayers after all.

She left and came back with the bottle of brown liquid and a spoon. Sitting on the edge of the bed, she poured out a careful amount and offered it to him. He took it and coughed at the horrible taste, and she provided a glass of water.

"Thank you," he said again and dropped back onto the pillow.

Before the drug might take affect, Eleanore felt compelled to say, "I think you need to tell me what happened."

James thought about it and said firmly, "I can't, Eleanore. It's better this way."

"Better? Better for your wife to have no idea what—"

"Eleanore," he took hold of her arm, "we just need to forget this ever happened. I assure you it's for the best."

"Well, forgive me if I'm not entirely confident in your judgment, considering your present frame of mind."

"That's your problem, not mine."

He said it with rancor, and Eleanore couldn't believe what she was hearing. "And I'm not supposed to wonder what happened since you left home earlier that has suddenly divided my problems from yours?" He looked away, and the muscles in his face twitched. "Why is it that I sense no remorse from you?"

"Because I don't feel any." He snapped his head back to face her with hard eyes. Eleanore knew her shock must have startled him by the way he softened slightly and added, "I'm sorry I broke my promise to you. It won't happen again. But I do not regret what I did."

"Now you're contradicting yourself in the same sentence, as well as separating my problems from yours. Should I not be concerned?"

"You're going to have to trust me."

"Trust you?" She let out a scoffing laugh. "I trust the man who knows how to have a reasonable conversation with me concerning any problem that might arise. I do not see any sign of that man now." She stood up and motioned with her arm. "I only see some stranger with angry eyes and too many secrets in my bed." He said nothing, and she added, "Go to sleep, James, before I slap your face and take your mind off your other pain."

Eleanore left him to rest, wishing that he would call her back and retract all the awful things he'd said. But he didn't make a sound. She cleaned up the blood and did as he'd asked, tossing his bloody clothes into the fire, wondering with a heavy heart what her husband was trying to hide. She cried as she watched the fabric smolder, more afraid than she wanted to admit.

Eleanore tried to sleep, conscious of James's even breathing, grateful for the medicine she'd had on hand that allowed him to rest without the intervention of a doctor. She was still stewing over the situation when he began to stir. Even before he was awake she could tell that it was pain forcing him toward consciousness. When she knew he wasn't sleeping, she lit a lamp and said, "Let me check the dressing on the wound." He threw back the covers, and she found the gauze soaked with blood, nearly to the point of getting blood on the sheets. She took care of it, but there was no conversation between them, and since enough time had passed, she gave him another dose of medicine.

"Thank you," he said after he took it. "I'm grateful for the way you take care of me."

"You would do the same for me," she said, but couldn't keep the edge out of her voice.

"What's wrong, Eleanore?" James asked reluctantly.

"Is it the laudanum that's addled your brain enough that you don't know the answer to that question?"

"Just tell me what's wrong."

"I need to know what happened."

He blew out a harsh breath. "Maybe it *has* addled my brain. I can't tell you, Eleanore."

"Why not?"

"It doesn't matter. Just . . . forget about it."

"Oh, I'll do that," she said with sarcasm and tossed the bloodied gauze into the fire.

"I don't understand why you're so upset."

"Upset? I've never felt so completely furious in my life!"

"Well, at least we agree on *something*."

"What do you mean by that?"

"*I* have never been so completely furious in my life. That's why I hit the guy. So now that you understand such fury, just let it go and move on, all right?"

"How can I let it go when it makes no sense whatsoever? I still just . . . can't believe it, James. I've been your wife for more than ten years, and I can't believe you would do something like this." She shook her head, peering at her husband as if she'd never seen him before. "This is not like you, James. What were you thinking?"

"I don't know." He rubbed a hand over his face. "I just . . . I just . . ." He couldn't finish.

"Just what? Completely lost control of your senses?"

"Yes, that's exactly it. And what man wouldn't, Eleanore? What I heard was . . . horrific." Anger penetrated his voice. "There's no excuse for a man to do the things he did. How could I possibly just stand by and let him get away with such unspeakable things?"

Eleanore felt an inkling of understanding, but she felt the need to point out, "Because it's not your place to mete out judgment *or* justice. You need to swallow your pride and anger and allow justice to take its proper course."

"Justice? Since when have the Mormons ever gotten justice?"

"If not in this life, then in the next. I can assure you that God does not condone vengeance. What kind of man are *you* to think that you can mete it out? What will your children think if they know that their father—"

"They never need to know about this, Eleanore. *No one* ever needs to know. No one."

"*I* know. *God* knows. How can you possibly live with such a secret? With the guilt?"

"I'm not certain I feel any guilt. If he were—"

"You *have* taken leave of your senses. How can you assault a man and have no guilt? It was not self-defense. You attacked him. It's not right—not in the eyes of the law, or of God. You can't justify this away for any reason, James. And when you get over this ludicrous anger you're feeling, you'll realize that." He glared at her but said nothing. She added more softly, "No secret can remain a secret forever, James. Somehow people always find out."

James wanted to argue the point, but he couldn't. He wondered if that also meant it was inevitable for people to find out they were Mormons. If that were the case, then it was only a matter of time before they ended up suffering the same fate as Mark and Sally. Or worse.

Eleanore convinced herself to stop arguing, knowing it would do no good. She just doused the lamp and got back into bed, wanting once again to slap her husband. She wondered if that proved right what he'd said about fury feeding his violence. She was finally able to get some sleep and woke up to daylight while James slept on. After quietly getting dressed and putting up her hair, she checked on the children and returned just as James swung his legs over the edge of the bed.

"What are you doing?" she asked.

"Now that I've had some sleep, I'm capable of getting up and least taking care of myself."

"While you limp around the house with no strength and cause everyone to question the reasons. Or did you forget that you didn't want anyone to know?" Eleanore wasn't keen on keeping it a secret, but she was all for keeping him in bed so that he could recover properly.

James sighed and laid back down, throwing the covers over himself with a disgruntled huff. He didn't want to admit how badly it hurt just to have the leg lower than his heart.

"I'll just tell them you're not feeling well," Eleanore said. "You need to stay down and keep that leg up." She left the room, saying over her shoulder, "I'll get you something to eat."

James resisted admitting how badly he hurt when Eleanore brought him some breakfast. She changed the bandaging before he ate, which made the pain worse. She was polite and considerate, seeing to it that he had everything he needed. But she treated him like a stranger—or worse, someone she loved who had made her angry. Her voice was cool and controlled, and her eyes were flinty. But he didn't question her because he didn't want to bring it up at all. He had no desire whatsoever to talk about it. He just hoped this leg would heal quickly, and they could forget this had ever happened. He sighed at the thought. If only he *could* forget. If only he could go back and never hear what he'd heard. If only he'd gotten up and left the tavern when he'd first felt compelled to do so. But as long as he lived he would never be able to think of what he'd heard and not feel sick. Memories of repeatedly hitting Ned Weller gave him an odd sense of gratification, but it certainly didn't erase what he knew.

The children came in the room while he was eating, and Eleanore skillfully kept them from getting anywhere near his leg while they each got hugs from him and questioned his reason for being in bed. They'd likely never seen him in bed due to any physical ailment. Eleanore gracefully soothed their concerns, saying that Papa had hurt his leg but he was going to be fine in a few days. After they'd left the room, he asked, "Why didn't you just tell them I was ill?"

"Because you're not ill, and I don't lie to my children. Even when you're strong enough to get out of bed, do you think they won't notice that something's wrong? I think this is a lot more serious than you want to believe."

James didn't comment, but Eleanore felt concerned when he refused any more laudanum. He told her he wanted to save what there was for night when he needed to sleep. She wondered if his theory would be dashed when pain overruled his pride through the course of the day. And she had her doubts that they could get through this without a doctor's attention.

She left him to finish his breakfast and went straight to find Frederick and Lizzie, who were in the library, working together to dust away cobwebs from the ceiling and upper shelves. They often found a way to help with each other's work in order to spend more time together, although when Eleanore entered the room, they were actually ignoring their work and sharing a lengthy kiss. Eleanore attempted to back away and not embarrass them, but she wasn't quiet enough and they both turned toward her.

"Hello," she said. They returned greetings and hurried back to work, exchanging a mischievous glance.

While Eleanore was considering how to say what needed to be said without breaking James's confidence—however ridiculous she considered it to be—Frederick asked, "So, what exactly is wrong with James? It's not like him to miss breakfast or . . ." He stopped when Eleanore couldn't hold back her tears, and they both turned abruptly toward her.

"What in the world is wrong?" Lizzie asked and crossed the room while Frederick stepped down from the chair he'd been standing on.

Eleanore drew strength from Lizzie's familiar embrace, but she cried for a couple of minutes before she could regain her composure. The constancy of the unconditional support and genuine caring of her dear friends immediately dissolved her attempt to put on a brave face. She felt Frederick's hand on her shoulder and knew he had his arm around his wife.

"What is it?" Frederick finally asked, his voice typically kind and concerned.

"I can't say." Eleanore drew back and pressed her handkerchief beneath her nose.

"You can't *say?*" Frederick repeated. His astonishment wasn't a surprise considering that James Barrington had not kept a secret from Frederick in the all the many years they'd known each other.

She drew a sustaining breath and repeated all she felt she could, under the circumstances. "He's not feeling well, and he's upset over something. He doesn't want to talk about it, even to me. And what little I know he's asked me not to repeat. I wonder if you could give him a blessing."

"Certainly," Frederick said without hesitation. He gave Eleanore a searching gaze, as if he might find answers there that she couldn't verbalize. She felt his concern, as well as Lizzie's, but they both graciously avoided pressing her any further, and she was relieved.

Eleanore returned to the bedroom and told James, "I've asked Frederick to give you a blessing."

"Why?" he demanded in a voice that was very unlike him.

"Because you're injured, and in spite of the circumstances, we can hope that God will see fit to keep your wound from getting infected or causing any permanent damage."

"It's not that serious," he insisted.

"Oh? Like the little cut on Iris's foot that went unattended and would have killed her if not for a miracle?"

"That was unattended. This is not."

"*This,*" she motioned toward his leg, "is as deep as a knife blade. No matter how justified you feel in whatever provoked you to do something so utterly stupid, I would hope you can come up with enough humility to want to stay alive and be healthy for the sake of your family."

James wanted to insist that assuming he would feel any other way was ludicrous, but she hurried on more calmly. "So I've asked Frederick to give you a blessing. He doesn't know what happened. I just told him you weren't feeling well, and that you were also upset about something that you didn't want to talk about. That's it."

He felt tempted to scold her for telling Frederick even that much, or for soliciting the blessing, but her points were valid, and the present situation did not change the fact that Frederick had always been one of his closest confidants. She was not out of line to share this burden with him. "Fine," was all he said, and she opened the door, ushering Frederick into the room.

"Not feeling well, I hear," he said. Eleanore closed the door and took a seat.

"No," James said and nothing more.

"Want to talk?"

"No," James repeated.

"Right. Then . . . we'll just proceed."

Frederick set his hands on James's head and there was a long silence before he began the blessing. James prayed that he would be receptive to whatever he might be told, and that God might give him some indication that he'd been justified in what he'd done. He was pleasantly surprised to hear a declaration of God's unconditional love for him, then it was followed with a gentle reprimand for allowing anger to rule his actions and cloud his judgment. Scriptures were quoted with a fluency that Frederick didn't normally possess. James was told that vengeance belonged only to the Lord, and that he was required to forgive all men. He felt sick inside and frightened over what he was hearing. It was too accurate and forceful not to be real. Frederick had no idea there was an issue of vengeance. James was then told that as he forgave others and humbly sought to make restitution for what he'd done, he would be forgiven. He was also told that he would return to full health, but not without his reliance on his Father in Heaven to intervene on his behalf against the infection that was already festering in his body. He was told that his family and many others, some who had not yet come into their lives, needed him to be strong physically, as well as spiritually—to be a leader who stood as a firm example of living the gospel of Jesus Christ in every facet of his life. It was evident that God still had much work for him to do in building the kingdom, and he needed to use this experience to become more humble and faithful.

James heard his own breathing become labored as the words flowed out of Frederick's mouth. He'd never felt so thoroughly humbled—nor humiliated—in his entire life. His own rationalizations and justifications melted beneath the weight of Frederick's hands and the power of the words coursing through him. Again James was reminded of God's love for him, and of the atoning power of Christ that could make all things right.

James felt stunned and barely able to breathe as Frederick closed the blessing, then placed a firm hand on James's shoulder. James looked up at him, surprised to see such perfect acceptance and genuine concern. "If you need me . . . need anything at all . . . I won't be far."

James nodded, too overwhelmed to speak. He glanced toward Eleanore to see tears running down her face. Their eyes met for barely a moment before she left the room. Frederick followed her out and closed the door. He wondered if they wanted to talk privately, or if they figured he needed to be alone. Perhaps he did. The moment the door closed, his own emotion swelled out of him, and he fought to keep his tears and his words from being overheard while he begged God's forgiveness and wept like a baby.

* * * * *

Eleanore motioned for Frederick to follow her a short way down the hall. Wiping her tears she said, "You didn't know . . . what happened, did you? Did James tell you or—"

"You know very well I have no idea what's going on. I only know what you told me."

"I know very little. He won't talk about what happened. Perhaps you know more than I do—now."

"Well," he drawled, "assuming the power of the priesthood is real and I wasn't making it up as I went along . . ."

"Don't be flippant!"

"I'm not being flippant. I'm just trying to clarify that something very profound happened in there, Eleanore. And it happened because in spite of whatever mistake James made last night, he's a good man, and everything's going to be all right. From what little I know and what I just learned with my hands on his head, he did something based on anger that's left him wounded . . . some kind of fight, I would guess. And apparently he's going to get worse before he gets better."

Eleanore groaned at the thought and pressed her face into her hands. "But he *will* get better," he added. "You must remember that." She nodded and expected him to ask her questions. Instead he said, "This is simply some advice from a friend, Eleanore, but I think you need to ask him what *really* happened and *why*. And you need to *really* listen."

"I've asked. He won't tell me."

"And you're going to settle for that? He's your husband. Why do you think he would want to keep something from you, knowing what you know about him?"

Eleanore thought about that and was ashamed at how long it took her to come up with the answer. "To protect me?" Frederick shrugged. "But he's being so stubborn and angry and—"

"Oh, I think he's likely gotten over that now. Will you?"

"What are you saying?"

"I'm just a friend."

"What are you saying?" she repeated.

"Perhaps he's not the only one who has been stubborn and angry."

Eleanore took a deep breath and leaned back against the wall as his words penetrated her spirit. She was so upset over James being controlled by his anger that she hadn't stopped to consider that the same thing was happening to her. During the blessing she'd only been able to hope that the words of guidance and wisdom would soak into James and soften his pride and anger. She'd not even considered that the same principle applied to her.

"Of course," she said and quickly squeezed Frederick's hand.

"And, Eleanore," he added, "I assume you've been very upset, and perhaps you've not paused to analyze all of this, but . . . it's occurred to me just now that . . . we both know James Barrington very well. Such irrational behavior is not in his character. Have you considered what might actually spur a man like him to pick a fight?"

Again Eleanore felt humbled and ashamed. She'd certainly acknowledged that his behavior was out of character, but she'd become so caught up in her own fears that she hadn't stopped to look at what was most important. James *had* been angry and stubborn, but he still deserved her respect and trust. He'd certainly earned that through the years. "You're right," she said. "Thank you . . . for being friend enough to say what I needed to hear."

He smiled and kissed her hand and walked away.

Chapter Eleven
C O N F E S S I O N S

Eleanore drew courage and uttered a silent prayer before she returned to the bedroom and closed the door behind her. She found James sitting on the edge of the bed, his head in his hands. She couldn't tell if he was crying or struggling to breathe until he glanced toward her, then she could see that it was both. He looked away abruptly, ashamed and uncertain. Since she'd seen him cry before, she had to assume it was for different reasons. She knew they had much to talk about, and she knew she needed to start with an apology. She sat beside him and cleared her throat gently. "There's something I need to say."

"Yes, I would think so." He sniffled and wiped a sleeve over his face.

"It's not like that. I need to apologize."

Astonished eyes darted towards her. "Apologize?" He stood up and took a few labored steps, clearly in pain.

"Should you be doing that?" she asked and stood beside him, taking his arm.

He ignored her. "Weren't you listening, Eleanore?"

"Doesn't that hurt when you—"

"Yes, it hurts!" He sat down and groaned. "Would you stay with the subject please? Didn't you hear what that blessing said? I was chastened by God Almighty for the very thing you've been angry about. You don't owe me an apology. It's the other way around, I can assure you. You were right. I was wrong."

"Not entirely right," she said and slid an ottoman in front of him. She lifted his foot onto it, then sat beside it to face him. "What I'm trying to say is that . . . I still don't agree with what you did, but I was wrong to be so . . . condemning. I was upset . . . and scared. I still am. But . . . I should have considered that someone with your character would not have done such a thing without a good reason, or at least what you considered at the time to be a good reason."

"It wasn't a good reason, Eleanore. There's no disputing that now. I have absolutely no doubt that the words Frederick spoke to me were real. I was wrong."

"But before the blessing you felt justified in doing what you'd done. You told me you felt no remorse."

"Well, I feel it now."

"I understand, but . . . what I'm trying to say is . . . I realize there *is* a reason. I want to understand that reason. I need to know what would make you that upset. And I need to apologize for not being willing to really hear what you were telling me. I was wrong to get so angry."

James brushed a hand over his face. "That applies to me as well." He pressed both hands tightly into his hair and let out an anguished moan. "You've got to help me, Eleanore. I've obviously done something wrong . . . horribly wrong, but . . . I'm having trouble being rational here. Oh!" He moaned again. "God help me . . . forgive me."

"He *will* forgive you, James," she said. "You simply need to . . . make proper restitution and then—"

James trembled from deep inside at the very thought. He had to admit, "I don't know how to make restitution, Eleanore, without putting my family in danger."

"What are you saying?" she asked, trying not to sound as alarmed as she felt.

"I can't very well walk up to the man and say, 'I'm sorry for attacking you the way I did. I was angry because you hate Mormons and do deplorable things to them. Is there any way I can make it up to you because I really am a Christian in spite of all outward appearances?'"

Eleanore took that in, filtering the information through the need to remain calm if she expected him to tell her everything that had happened. He'd said as much before, but she hadn't really heard it.

Frederick's advice came back to her, and she felt ashamed that she'd let anger cloud her judgment so much that she'd overlooked what her husband had been trying to tell her. "So, that's it. You . . . what? Overheard the man talking about something he'd done . . . to Mormons?"

"That's right."

"Like before . . . in the tavern."

"In the tavern, yes. But not like before. Before, it was vague. This was overt bragging in hideous detail."

"Why didn't you just get up and leave?"

"I've asked myself that. I don't know. I should have. I wish I *would* have. But I can't go back and change it now. I stayed. I heard it. And I reacted very poorly."

"So, what did he say?"

James hesitated. "I don't need to tell you that. I've explained why I did what I did. I don't need to tell you what I heard." His voice became hard again, and his eyes acrid.

Eleanore felt the need to say, "You're angry again."

"Yes. Yes, I am. When I think of what he did . . . I want to go back and finish what I started."

"A minute ago you said you felt remorse; now you're angry."

"I *am* angry, Ellie. I know I'm not supposed to be, but I am. I realize I need to contend with that and get over it, but I can't simply snap my fingers and make it go away just because I know it's wrong."

"This has been going on for years, you know."

"What has?"

"This festering anger that you can't seem to be free of. You've struggled with anger toward those who have persecuted the Mormons ever since you went to Winter Quarters."

"No, it was before that," he admitted. "I felt it first when I realized it was legal to kill Mormons in Missouri, and my wife had just been baptized."

"I thought that was fear."

"Well, it didn't start becoming anger until we went to Nauvoo and heard our friends talking about what they'd been through, and what others had been through. And it's clear they hadn't told us a tenth of their own suffering."

"Why is *that* clear?" Eleanore asked.

James looked away and said, "I realize I have a problem with this. And maybe . . . all the anger and fear that's been rolling around inside of me all this time just . . . rushed out when I heard this guy bragging about what he'd done." He exhaled raggedly. "I didn't *intend* to take it out on him. It just kind of . . . happened. I went into the alley because I was upset and I needed to be alone. Then I realized that I couldn't be seen, and he was going to walk right past me. There was no one else around. It just came out of me, Eleanore. I know it was wrong, but it didn't feel wrong at the time. When I think of what *he* did, I still can't entirely regret what *I* did."

Eleanore subdued her temptation to get angry and turn this into yet another argument. He was admitting honestly to his feelings, and he had a right to them. But her concern over them—and the way he'd acted on them—left her frightened. She prayed silently for guidance in this conversation, but she still struggled to come up with the right words.

"James," she put a hand on his arm, "I know the injustice of what our people have been through is horrible, and it's impossible for it not to feel personal." She heard him take a sharp breath and asked, "What?"

"Nothing," he insisted, but she sensed it was that word *personal* he didn't like.

"I can understand your anger, James, but—"

"No, I'm not sure you can." His eyes took on a recently familiar hardness that made her realize getting beyond this was not going to be quick or easy. "I'm responsible for you, Eleanore, for our children. If something were to happen to any one of you, I could never live with that."

"You *could* live with it. You wouldn't *want* to; none of us would. But the Atonement is in place for these very things, James; the things that don't make sense in life are the ones that most require Christ's greatest miracle. If something were to happen to any one of us, we would find a way to make peace with it and move on."

"It's easy to say," he growled, "when it's not staring you in the face. When Andy died you nearly fell apart just *thinking* of how you'd feel if you lost me. You can't possibly judge or understand how I feel, given a similar dose of empathy."

"What empathy?" she asked, wondering if he would ever fully admit to what had provoked him to such an enraged act.

"The *what* doesn't matter, El. It's the principle. In theory I believe we could survive whatever might happen. We've survived the death of a child and much heartache on behalf of our friends. But comparatively, we've been very blessed. We truly have no idea what it would be like to face great losses because of our religious convictions. *Ben* knows, but *we* don't."

"Yet Ben has found peace over it."

"Ben had nightmares for weeks. Ben still cries because he misses his family. And you know that faraway look he gets in eyes, when his brow wrinkles and his eyes look like an old man who has lived through a war."

"Yes, I know that look. And I know it's left scars on him. Still, he's at peace. The difficult feelings and memories don't keep him from being happy."

"Well, I'm happy too, Eleanore. But I have some difficult feelings and memories. And fears. I admit it. I fear that our cozy little existence here will end, that we will yet be required to face the horrors that others have faced."

"And fear is the very thing that got you in trouble, James. It's fear beneath your anger." It wasn't a question. "That's what it's been all along. You're afraid it's going to happen to us." He pressed his face into his hands, and she knew he was crying again. She'd touched the painful spot at he core of the problem, but she wasn't sure what to do now except try to understand and guide him. "I know that fear, James; I do. But I do my best to pray it away, to give my fears to God. That was the only way I could cope with my fear of losing you when Andy died. These matters are in God's hands. We must trust Him."

"So it's God's will for His people to be subjected to barbaric abuse and unspeakable suffering?" He sounded angry again.

"We can't possibly understand God's purposes."

"Well, that's true," James said, but he said it bitterly.

"Does this mean you're angry with God?"

He sighed. "Maybe I am." New tears came. She'd rarely seen him cry so much. "Oh, Ellie, I'm just . . . confused. I've never felt so confused in my life. Help me make some sense of this. I don't *want* to be angry—especially with God. And I certainly don't want God to be unhappy with me. Clearly He is."

"And clearly He loves you and will help you through this. You've always been a humble, prayerful man, a man who relies on the scriptures and the guidance of the Holy Spirit. That's all you need to get through this, James. You can be forgiven, and you can find peace with these feelings; I know you can, if you will only trust Him!"

James tried to let that settle into his ailing spirit, but a pause in the conversation brought his attention to the rising intensity of the pain in his leg, and he suddenly felt a little woozy. "I think I need to go back to bed," he muttered and put his left foot on the floor. Eleanore rose to help him stand, and he felt embarrassed by how heavily he leaned on her. But she held him steady and guided him to the bed. With her arms firmly around him, and her strength compensating for his weakness, he was struck with a sudden thought that was accompanied by an unexpected warmth in his chest. The impression came to him that in every way his sweet wife would help keep him steady and guide him back to the good graces of Almighty God. She was wise and insightful; she always had been. And he needed to trust her. If he remained focused on his own wounded pride and humiliation in needing her help so completely, and the fact that he'd brought this suffering on himself, he would never get past it. In the same moment, he realized that the exact principle applied to his relationship with God. Eleanore was right. He needed to humbly and prayerfully turn to God to help him through this, and trust Him in the steps that needed to be taken. He couldn't allow his pride and anger to lure him away from God in, embarrassment and shame. In fact, those were the very reasons that he needed to turn to God more than he ever had before.

"I love you, Eleanore," he said as she helped him into bed. "Thank you . . . for being here for me . . . for loving me . . . for taking such good care of me . . . even when I don't deserve it."

"It's impossible for you to not deserve my love and care, James. If marriage isn't standing by each other through our human error, then what good would there be in it?" James felt too emotional to answer, but she pressed a hand to his face and a kiss to his brow. "I love you too—and we're going to get through this . . . together. I think you need to rest. And I think you need some more medicine so that you *can* rest. I know you're trying to be brave, but you can't fool me. You're in a great deal of pain, and I can tell."

James didn't argue. Again he was too emotional to speak. He took the medicine she offered, praying it would hold out until he could get past the worst of this. By the time she had changed the bandage on his leg, cleaning the wound carefully with disinfectant, he was starting to feel some relief and the sleepiness that came with it. He drifted off with her hand on his face and a prayer in his heart that he could be forgiven for his rash behavior, and that he could find peace over the feelings that had spurred it.

As soon as James was asleep, Eleanore checked on the children and made certain all was well with the household. Lizzie and Stella had everything under control, so she returned to her husband's side and sat with him while he slept. She turned to a lifetime habit of perusing the scriptures in search of peace and understanding. Long before the Book of Mormon had come into her life, she had randomly flipped through pages of the Bible, opening herself to any passage she might feel drawn to. And often it had been an answer she'd been seeking. She'd come to do the same with the Book of Mormon in the years since it had come into her possession, and now she actively perused both, going back and forth from one to the other, praying for guidance that might help her husband—and herself—to get through this. She didn't want to use the scriptures to condemn James in the choice he'd made. She felt certain the consequences of his actions would happen without any encouragement from her. And with time she felt sure his confusion would cease and he would clearly see his mistake; then his own remorse would prove to be self-punishment enough. Rather, she wanted to find passages that would help him see perspective and hope. After much reading she set the books aside with a few places marked, and she turned her mind to prayer and contemplation. James shifted in his sleep, and she wondered if he would wake up, but he didn't. It did, however, draw her attention to his right hand, which was discolored with bruising. The evidence that her husband had used his fist to harm another man increased her uneasiness over the situation. James had said he couldn't make restitution without putting them all in danger. Did that mean if this man found out who had attacked him in the dark, he might come after James and do him more harm? Or the family? Eleanore felt angry again as the ramifications of his poor choice became blatantly clear. She'd been angry before because James had put his own life at risk over gratifying his anger. Now she felt doubly angry to consider that his actions may have threatened their family's security. They'd worked very hard to keep their religious beliefs private in order to avoid this very thing. Now someone who hated Mormons had reason to be angry, specifically with James. Eleanore prayed that James had been right when he'd said that this man didn't know who he'd been fighting with. Then the matter of restitution came to the forefront of her mind. How *could* they make restitution and protect their anonymity? Perhaps they couldn't. Fear of what might happen chilled her, momentarily tempting her to ignore any need for restitution and simply keep the matter a secret, just as James had initially suggested. But in the next breath she knew they couldn't do it that way. They had to follow the guidance of the Spirit and trust that all would be well. She wondered if this might be the catalyst to change their lives. Perhaps joining the Saints in order to avoid persecution would become mandatory.

As James began to stir, Eleanore eased onto the bed, close to his right side in order to avoid the wounded thigh. He opened his eyes for a moment as she settled her head on his shoulder, and he shifted his arm around her. "I love you, James," she said.

He pressed a kiss to her brow and muttered sleepily, "I love you too."

"I just want you to know . . . whatever needs to be done for you to make restitution, I will be there beside you."

James twisted his head around to look at her, unable to believe what he was hearing. Even with the evidence he'd had of her strength of character when he'd proposed marriage to her, he never would have imagined such loyalty, especially when he knew she was unhappy with what he'd done.

"Don't look so surprised," she said. "You would do the same for me."

"Would I? Are you sure?"

"Yes, I'm sure. Perhaps I'll get even one day."

"So . . . one day you might just . . . get angry and impulsively do something stupid that endangers your life and puts the entire family at risk? And I'm just supposed to accept that and stand by you no matter what?"

"That's right," she said, tightening her arm around his chest.

James relaxed back onto the pillow. "In that case, I guess I'm going to have to completely swallow my pride, admit I was wrong, and do everything in my power to make it right—with you, and with that Mormon-hating—"

"Don't you say it!"

"I wasn't going to, but I have to admit that I thought it. I said some awful things to him when I was hitting him, Eleanore. And I meant them. I admit it was the wrong way to handle it, but it's going to take some time to come to terms with the way I feel."

"I believe if you act appropriately in spite of such feelings, you will be blessed. And with time, as you pray for compassion and healing and forgiveness, those things will come."

"I'm going to have to take your word for it. All I can do now is go through the motions, because I'm still angry."

"I understand."

There was a quiet moment before James said, "I keep hearing phrases from the Bible in my head. I guess that would be my guilty conscience telling me that no matter how justified I felt, it was wrong, and I knew it was wrong."

"What phrases?" Eleanore asked, certain her prayers were being heard. In a matter of hours she had seen his heart soften and his spirit become receptive.

"*Love your enemies, bless them that curse you, do good to them that hate you, and pray for them which despitefully use you, and persecute you.*" His voice broke as he repeated the words of Jesus, then he added humbly, "I think that pretty much puts me in my place."

"I'm proud of you, James."

"Proud?" he scoffed.

"For coming so quickly to the things you're saying. You're a good man who made a mistake. We're only human, after all. If we didn't make mistakes, there would be no need for an Atonement."

"I know that, Ellie; I do. But my human side is struggling with this. I hope you can be patient with me."

"I can. And God will too, I'm certain."

When it became evident he was in pain, Eleanore got up to give him a small dose of laudanum and something to eat. He wanted enough medicine to take the edge off the pain, but not enough to put him to sleep. While she was changing the bandage he said, "I'm scared, Eleanore. I have to face this man, and when I think of what he's done . . . and what I've done . . . it scares me."

"You're not well enough to face him now. Give the matter some time and prayer, and you'll know what to do. The Spirit will guide you. Perhaps God will provide an answer that won't put you in a precarious situation."

"Perhaps, but I'm not counting on it. I think I'm just going to have to . . . trust that God will protect me . . . us . . . and do what has to be done."

"What *are* we going to do, James?" his wife asked a moment later as she stood to look out the window. He felt the most regret for how this was affecting her.

"I don't know," he said, trying not to sound as upset as he felt.

"Perhaps you should have—"

"Forgive me, Eleanore, but what I should have done is not going to help solve this. We need to talk about what can be done *now.*"

"Right." Eleanore tried to adjust the idea to work in the present. "Then . . . perhaps . . . when you're feeling better . . . you should talk to the sheriff and tell him what you know. Report what this man did. It was obviously against the law. Perhaps they can—"

"Forgive me if I don't have a great deal of faith in the law protecting Mormons," James snapped, back in that angry mode instantaneously. She had a feeling she would see a lot of vacillating back and forth until he could fully come to terms with this. But she was completely unprepared for the words that flew unheeded out of his mouth. "I can't very well report the rape of a woman who left here more than ten years ago. 'Oh, and by the way, Sheriff, the entire family was beaten the same night, in the house that I now live in. Could you do something about it ten years after the fact?'"

James didn't realize what he'd said until the color drained from Eleanore's face. Her eyes widened, and her hand went to her heart the same moment his own heart began to pound and his stomach tightened. He regretted saying it as much as he felt relieved to have it over with. In his deepest self he'd known that he needed to tell her, but he hadn't wanted to, and hadn't known how. Now it had jumped out of him without premeditation. He didn't have to carry the burden alone.

James watched as his own pain became visible in Eleanore's countenance. She took two unsteady steps and wilted onto a chair. Huge tears welled in her eyes, then spilled. She looked toward him as if he might somehow be able to take away her pain. His view of her clouded behind the hot mist in his own eyes, and his heart threatened to crumble.

"Sally?" she whimpered, barely audible.

He nodded and looked down. "He . . . said her name."

Eleanore made a noise of anguish, then he heard her sniffling. "She . . . never told me . . . what happened, why . . . they left . . . so quickly."

"I know." He blew out a controlled breath that did little to ease the heat in his throat. "I know . . . how dear she is . . . to you. I kept thinking . . . of being with her and her family . . . in Winter Quarters and Nauvoo. And I thought of her . . . living here, and . . ." A wave of anger pushed his emotion fully into the open. "They lived *here*, Eleanore! This was *their* home, and the reasons for what happened apply to us every bit as much as to them." He sobbed and coughed. "How could I not think of . . . what I would do . . . if it happened to you . . . and . . ." He coughed again. "That's why I did what I did. I know it's not my place to retaliate or seek vengeance. I know it was wrong in the eyes of God—and the law. But not as wrong as what he's done."

He wiped his tears and looked at Eleanore, who was crying with a handkerchief pressed over her mouth while she stared at nothing with horrified eyes.

"I'm so sorry," he said, and she looked at him. "I'm sorry for what happened to Sally . . . and her family. I'm sorry that you had to even know about it. And I'm sorry that I've created this disaster when I should have left well enough alone. Now I've got to find a way to make restitution with this man and . . ."

"I don't know how it could ever be possible," she muttered, her voice strained with barely controlled fury. "How can you ever face him without wanting to . . ."

"Kill him?"

"Yes!" she said through clenched teeth. "Forgive me," she added more softly. "I think it's going to take some time to contend with these feelings. I know we need to forgive him, but . . ." She sobbed and wiped frantically at the ongoing flow of tears. "Forgive me," she said again, looking at him with firm resolve in her eyes, "for jumping to conclusions about what you did. I cannot condone it, and I know we must make it right. But . . . if I had been a man in your position, I probably would have been sorely tempted to do the same thing."

James breathed in her validation and empathy, feeling it soothe his troubled spirit, but he hurried to say, "I'm glad you understand . . . more than I could ever tell you. But what I did was not right, Eleanore. I should have walked away and left the matter in God's hands. And that's what we have to do now."

She nodded and took a deep breath to sustain her emotions. "I know. I just . . ."

A knock at the door interrupted the conversation, and they both hurried to appear composed.

"Come in," Eleanore called, and Frederick opened the door, peered in, then entered the room.

"How are you?" he asked James, glancing suspiciously at both of them. It would have been impossible not to notice they'd been crying.

"I've had better days," he answered, "but thank you for asking."

Frederick then reported the things he'd taken care of on James's behalf, and the errands he'd seen to in town.

"Thank you," James said. "As always, I don't know what I'd do without you."

"A pleasure," Frederick said on his way out the door. "Actually, I've got the greatest job in the world." He stepped out and almost had the door closed before he opened it again and said, "Oh, I almost forgot. Do you know a Ned Weller?"

Eleanore had never heard the name before, but the change in James's countenance sent her heart pounding. He was trying to mask his reaction, but she knew him too well. Apparently Frederick picked up on it too by the way his brows rose, and he became more attentive in waiting for James's answer.

"I know *of* him," James said. "Why?"

"There's quite a stir in town today. Apparently he was killed last night; found murdered in an alley."

Eleanore felt a jolt of shock when James sucked in a harsh breath and couldn't let it go. His expression alone left her wondering if what they'd just heard would be the undoing of all of them. She was vaguely aware of Frederick closing the door behind him, saying quietly, "Is there something you'd like to tell me?"

James turned frightened eyes to her, to Frederick, then back to her. "I swear to you that he was alive when I left him."

"It was *him?*" Eleanore demanded, knowing it was a rhetorical question.

"Yes, but . . ." James swung his legs over the edge of the bed and hung his head lower than his knees, as if he feared losing consciousness. He gasped for breath and gripped the edge of the bed.

"Do you want me to leave?" Frederick asked.

"No!" James nearly shouted, then he groaned and hung his head lower. "I need your help . . . your perspective. I . . . I can't believe it." He groaned again. "What have I done? Heaven help us. What have I done?"

"James." Eleanore sat beside him after tossing Frederick a pleading glance, silently asking him to help her. "You need to tell us everything. Everything!"

James only shook his head as he lifted it just a little. He squeezed his eyes closed, and Eleanore put a hand on his shoulder. Trying to be more specific, she asked in a gentle voice that barely masked the terror in her heart, "Is there anything you did to him that could have possibly injured him enough to—"

"No!" James insisted. He looked up at Eleanore, then Frederick, who was clearly baffled. "I hit the guy a few times. I left him on the ground. I could hear him moaning when I left. He was strong enough to stab me *after* I'd hit him. I did *not* kill him."

"Forgive me if I offer a grim perspective," Frederick said, "but I think we need to consider every possibility. Maybe this guy had a heart problem or some other health matter, and what you did was just enough to . . . well, kill him."

"Oh, help," James muttered. "Does that still constitute murder?"

Frederick proved himself as calm and rational as always. "That would be for the law to decide."

"And if they decide he's guilty of murder?" Eleanore erupted to her feet. "Then what? What?" she demanded as if getting an answer out of Frederick might change the outcome. "Will they hang him?" She sobbed, then gulped for air. "Will this one mistake be the end of him . . . of us?"

"We can't just assume the worst," Frederick said.

"And we can't just assume that I'm going to get out of this unscathed," James said.

"Is there any possible way that anyone knows it was you?" Frederick asked.

"No," James answered firmly, "but keeping this to ourselves is not an option."

Eleanore wanted to protest as her conscience was hotly attacked by her need for James to survive this. But she knew he was right when he added, "We all heard that blessing I was given earlier. God has made it clear to me, in no uncertain terms, that I must make restitution. I've got to come clean."

Eleanore put a hand over her mouth, barely suppressing a harsh whimper.

"I agree," Frederick said, "but you also need to remember that the blessing indicated a future for you in building the kingdom and being an example to others."

Eleanore breathed in Frederick's reminder and found some peace from it. She sat beside James and took his hand. Their eyes met, and she saw a glimmer of hope, but she also saw her own fear reflected there. While he was looking at her he said, "Frederick, can you take me to talk with the sheriff?"

"Right now?" she asked, fearing he would be arrested and never come home.

"The sooner I report what I know," James said, "the less guilty I'll look. I have to hope that it will go in my favor."

"I agree," Frederick said again, "but I don't think you should be up and about. I'll go and get him."

Eleanore liked that better. At least this conversation could take place in their home.

"Thank you," James said. "Before you leave, would you . . ." his voice broke, "would you pray with us?"

"Of course," Frederick said. He and Eleanore knelt beside the bed where James remained sitting. They held hands, and Frederick prayed aloud on James's behalf, repeatedly petitioning for the sheriff's heart to be softened, and for their conversation to go well.

After Frederick left, a dark pall settled over the room while James and Eleanore both remained eerily silent. "I can't believe it," he finally said. "I just . . . I don't know what to say. I never dreamed that something so horrible would happen."

"You didn't kill him."

"No, but I left him there in the alley to die. However he might have died, I had a hand in it." He shook his head and squeezed his eyes closed. "I just can't believe it."

With this new realization, James felt a fresh rise of anger over the circumstances. He knew he'd made a mistake, and he *did* regret what he'd done. But that human part of him was glad to know Ned Weller was dead. And he didn't feel at all compassionate while he hoped the man was already rotting in hell for what he'd done to Sally and her family.

Iris came to the bedroom with the children, saying they all wanted to see their father and find out how he was doing. Eleanore saw his countenance completely change when they were present. He'd once told her that he was a good actor, and she could see evidence of that now in his desire to not alarm his children or mar their time together. She was surprised to hear him say that he needed to tell them something very important. Iris, Ben, and Jamie sat on the bed, while Isaac and Joseph played nearby with some toys they'd brought in with them, oblivious to the conversation. James admitted to his children in vague terms that he'd done something wrong. He'd become angry with someone and had gotten in a fight, and that's why he'd hurt his leg. He told them the sheriff was coming to talk to him, and that he needed to be accountable for what he'd done in order to be forgiven and make it right. He told them that something had happened to this man since the fight and he was now dead, and there was cause for concern in wondering if what James had done might have something to do with the death. And whether or not that was true, perhaps people might believe that to be the case. The children asked a few questions, and he answered them with simple honesty. Eleanore was moved to see his humble admission to his children, and his concern over the example he was setting. He'd come far in the hours since he'd been determined to keep it a secret. When he finished and the silence became mildly awkward, Eleanore added, "You must all pray for your father. Not only that he will be guided in making the situation right, but that his leg will heal, and he will be well."

They all agreed, and Iris asked if they could pray together right then. They did so, with Iris offering the prayer. Eleanore was holding James's hand and felt him squeeze it more than once, silently sharing what she knew to be gratitude and awe over this amazing young woman. Once the prayer was over, each of the children hugged James, then Eleanore. They left the room, with Iris and Ben looking after the little ones, and Eleanore prayed that the adverse impact of this would not affect their children too deeply.

Chapter Twelve

THE PURGING

James diverted any possible conversation with Eleanore by saying, "Help me get dressed and go downstairs. I'm not having the sheriff find me in bed in a nightshirt."

"I don't know how you can possibly make it down those stairs without dying from the pain."

"I don't know either, but I'm going to do it anyway. Please help me."

Eleanore did as he'd asked and helped him wash up and put on clean clothes. She saw him grimace as he pulled clothing on over the wounded leg, and he clenched his teeth and groaned as he pulled a boot onto his foot. But he stubbornly insisted that he would face the sheriff with dignity. After the exertion of getting dressed, he declared that he had to rest a few minutes before endeavoring to get to the parlor. It took such a ridiculous effort for him to get down the stairs that Eleanore tried to convince him to go back to the bedroom and let the sheriff visit him there.

"What if he can't come right now?" she asked. "You'll be wasting your time and strength."

"And if he does, I won't be caught lying down."

"Well, at least you can rest on the couch before you try to make it back up."

"Or maybe I'll stay on the couch until this heals," he said facetiously.

They were nearly to the bottom of the stairs when Frederick found them and said he'd spoken to the sheriff, who would be coming in a short while, once he took care of a matter of business. Frederick also announced that he and Lizzie were taking the children out of the house for a little impromptu picnic. Stella was going with them as well. They felt it would be best to leave James and Eleanore alone during the sheriff's visit, and Eleanore thanked him for his insight.

In the parlor, Eleanore helped James prop his booted foot up on a pillow placed on the table in front of the couch. Once he was situated, she started to pace the room, wringing a lace handkerchief in her hands. "Would you please sit down," he said.

"Sorry." She sat beside him and took his hand. "Are you nervous?"

"Scared out of my mind," he admitted. "At least we know the sheriff. I never thought I'd be glad to say that we'd had him come to our home on multiple occasions."

"I believe he's a good man. That should surely work in our favor."

"I wonder how Ralph and Lu are doing. And Amanda."

"I miss them," Eleanore said.

"So do I. Maybe it's time we joined them."

Eleanore turned to him abruptly, not hesitating to say, "I confess I've had the same thought." She rose and started pacing again. "Do you think it will come to being forced from our home once all of this comes out? Better to leave than have you arrested or . . . maybe we should have put off talking to the sheriff and start packing instead or—"

"Sit down, Eleanore," he said and again she did.

"We both know we can't run from doing the right thing. I have to face this. I'm only sorry you have to face it with me."

"It's all right," she said, taking his hand. "Somehow we'll get through this."

"If you can sit still and stop driving me crazy with your nerves," he said, then chuckled. But seeing a glimpse of his usual self helped calm Eleanore, and she put her head on his shoulder.

"Why don't you read to me while we're waiting," James suggested a minute later, and Eleanore got up to retrieve the Book of Mormon. She read the entire book of Enos and was starting into Jarom before the sheriff came.

Hearing the knock on the front door, they shared a gaze of trepidation before Eleanore took a deep breath, set the book aside, and went to answer it. She willed her heart and stomach to be calm, and forced a pleasant expression before she pulled the door open to see Sheriff Willis on the porch with his hat in his hand.

"Thank you so much for coming," Eleanore said. "I know how busy you must be."

"Not a problem, Mrs. Barrington," he said as she motioned him inside and closed the door. "Frederick tells me your husband might have some insight as to what happened to Ned Weller."

"That's right. He's in here." She led the way into the parlor while she prayed with all her soul that this man's heart would be softened, and that he might have discernment over the situation.

"Hello, Sheriff," James said and made no effort to move beyond holding out his hand. "Forgive me if I don't get up. I'm contending with an injury."

"No worries," Willis said and shook his hand firmly.

"Have a seat," Eleanore said. The sheriff took a chair across the room, and Eleanore sat down again next to James on the couch.

She wondered how James might work his way into his confession. He sent her heart pounding when he said straightaway, "The injury I speak of is due to Ned Weller stabbing me in the leg."

"Is that right?" Willis asked, one eyebrow going up. "And when did this occur?"

"Last night."

"I'm listening."

"Before we begin, I must tell you that I don't know if I had anything to do with his death. That certainly wasn't my intention, and he was very much alive when I left him. If he had some heart condition or something I was unaware of, I suppose the fact that I hit him five or six times could have injured him enough to kill him. But again, that was not my intention."

The sheriff leaned forward and put his forearms on his thighs, intensifying his focus on James as he repeated, "I'm listening."

"I went to the meeting at city hall," James said. "Afterward, I was asked by a man I met there to join some others for a drink at the tavern. I don't drink, but I sometimes enjoy the socializing, so I went along. I overheard Ned Weller, who had obviously had too much to drink, bragging about something horrible he'd done. A name came up. It was a family I know well that he'd done this to, which was their reason for leaving the area many years ago."

Eleanore listened to him speak with a steady voice while she could feel a slight trembling in the hand she was holding. Her own nervousness heightened as she heard details of the event that he'd not shared with her previously. Combined with her hammering heart and sweating palms, the reality of what he'd overheard made her feel physically ill.

"When he changed the subject I left, but I was terribly upset. I went down the alley to avoid anyone seeing me because . . . well, I was upset." The sheriff nodded, and James went on. "When some men went down the alley, I realized no one could see me because where I was, it was completely dark. I was trying to get my composure and start for home when Weller and a couple of other men stopped at the top of the alley, talking and laughing before they parted company. Next thing I know, Weller's walking right past me, all alone, and I just . . . lost control of my anger toward him. It was too dark for him to know who it was. I hit him five or six times. He knifed me in the leg. I left him on the ground next to the wall. He was groaning and cursing when I left."

James took a sustaining breath and squeezed Eleanore's hand, so grateful to have that out in the open. Now he only had to add the moral issue. "I know what I did was wrong, Sheriff, and I'm prepared to take the consequences for that. But I did not kill that man. I can only pray that you believe me."

The sheriff said nothing for an excruciatingly long minute while he appeared to be deep in thought. He finally said, "Let me ask you a few questions."

"Anything," James said eagerly, not wanting any room for misunderstanding.

"Did you know Ned Weller prior to encountering him last night?"

"No, but I'd heard his name come up once before in a conversation several years ago."

"What did you hear?"

"I just heard some men in the same tavern talking about some trouble they'd caused for a family of . . . a certain religion. I heard one of them say that the Weller boys had roughed up the wife. That's it."

Eleanore felt astonished. She'd not realized the connection. It all seemed too eery to be coincidence.

"Well," the sheriff said, "Ned Weller and his brother did have a reputation for stirring up trouble, and they were certainly the most bigoted men I've ever known."

"*Were?*" Eleanore asked.

"Ned's gone now, and their father, who was certainly the example for all this trouble, passed on a few years back. Rufus is still around, but he tended to be more of a follower. Now that Ned's gone, maybe he'll calm down."

Eleanore exchanged a discreet glance with James, wondering if he shared her thoughts. She couldn't help being concerned to know that this Rufus Weller was still around, since he carried such bigoted attitudes. But it seemed that Sheriff Willis sounded relieved to have Ned Weller dead. As if to confirm that, he said, "Of course I can't condone murder, or any other violence for that matter, but if I'd ever been able to prove that Ned and Rufus were responsible for half of what they'd done, they'd have been done away with by the law a long time ago. Now I've got one less problem on my hands, although I'm not sure his wife and children will see it that way. I barely know them."

James took a sharp breath at the thought. A wife and children? No matter what kind of man Ned Weller might have been, a family had been left without a husband and father. He felt sick at the thought and wondered if his restitution might involve making it right with them. He still found it difficult to accept that he was responsible for a man's death, even if indirectly. With that thought uppermost in his mind, James said, "I don't know what happened to Ned Weller, but if my leaving him there contributed to his death, I need to know."

"We're working on that," the sheriff said. "What time did you leave?"

"I . . . don't know . . . exactly."

"He arrived home with the wound before midnight," Eleanore said.

"Are you certain?" Willis asked.

"Absolutely," Eleanore said. "I was worried about him, pacing and checking the clock every few minutes."

"Did anyone else know you were there?"

"No," James said. "Only Frederick knows anything at all, except for the explanation I gave my children a short while ago."

"And what time did you tell Frederick?"

James felt confused by the question. "Er . . . just before he came to get you; that's when he told me he'd been in town and had heard that Weller was dead. What does this have to do with—"

"It's evident you're innocent, Mr. Barrington," the sheriff said with a matter-of-fact shrug.

"It is?" James asked, a little breathless. Eleanore put a hand to her heart.

"If I put a man behind bars for throwing a few punches, we'd have to get a much bigger jail."

"But Weller is dead and—"

"That's right, and if you had been the man to pull the trigger, I think I would have been able to see through what you just told me."

"Trigger?" James echoed.

"That's right. He was shot, right through the heart. Bartender heard the shot about three in the morning while he was cleaning up after his late-night customers. He's the one that found him."

James sighed so loudly it filled the room. He dropped his head forward, and Eleanore started to cry.

"You were worried," the sheriff observed.

"Yes, very," James said with a little chuckle.

"But you asked me to come here. If no one saw you, why did you feel the need to even tell me this?"

"Because it's the right thing to do," James said.

Sheriff Willis chuckled and shook his head. "It's a rare form of honesty; I'll tell you that. At least now I know why there was a knife with blood on it near the body, and why he had some bruising on his face. My guess is he passed out from the drinking after you left him there. It wouldn't be the first time he'd been found passed out drunk somewhere in town. The man's got a lot of enemies. We may never find who did it."

"And when you do?"

"With enough evidence, they'll hang for murder," he answered straightly and came to his feet. Motioning toward James's leg, he added, "Has a doctor looked at that?"

"No, it's fine," James said, still stunned with relief.

Eleanore stood. "Thank you, Sheriff. Your kindness and understanding mean more than we could ever tell you."

"Well, you're good folks. Always have been as long as I've known you. Have you heard from Ralph and that sweet Bailey girl he ran off with?"

"Not recently," Eleanore said, "but according to their last letter they were doing well."

"That's good then." He sighed and rocked on his heels. "You know, those Weller boys just always had it in for anyone who was different. I'll never understand such bigotry. Anyone Jewish, Negro, or Mormon, those boys could practically sniff them out, and next thing you know some of the best folks around are up and leaving." He shook his head. "I'll never understand it." He smiled slightly and looked directly at James. "You folks wouldn't be Jewish, would you?"

James glanced at Eleanore, then at the sheriff. This conversation had been completely honest up to this point; he couldn't break his record now. Perhaps this was the moment of reckoning. As much as they'd felt prompted to remain quiet and protect themselves, perhaps the time had come to be willing to declare their beliefs openly, even if it meant being exposed to possible trouble.

"No, Sheriff," James said, "we're not Jewish; you know very well that we're not."

The sheriff's smile appeared again. "And obviously not Negro."

"Obviously not," James said, and wondered if he would come right out and ask.

Sheriff Willis rocked on his heels again and said, "I've known a few Mormon folks in my day. Never had any cause to complain or believe they would cause trouble, in spite of rumors. Good, God-fearing people from what I can tell. I'd be happy to see more of them around here." He looked again at James with a directness that echoed his message. "If Rufus Weller or anyone else even shows his face around here or hints at giving you trouble, I want to know about it."

"Thank you, Sheriff," James said. "That means more than you will ever know."

"Maybe, but I could probably guess," he replied then thanked James again for his honesty and the information that would help the investigation. He spoke his goodbyes, then said on his way out the door, "I'll send the doctor to have a look at that leg." He didn't wait for a protest.

Eleanore closed the door behind the sheriff and returned to the parlor to find tears on her husband's face that quickly urged her own to the surface again. She sat beside him, and they embraced each other tightly. James muttered close to her ear, "We've been blessed with a miracle, my dear."

"Yes. Yes, we have. And when you get back on your feet, we'll find a way to help Mrs. Weller and her children."

"My exact thought," James said and drew back, touching the tears on her face. "You are so precious to me, Ellie. Thank you . . . for standing by me."

"Like I said," she smiled, "you would do the same for me."

Once they had recounted all they'd just learned, and the relief they felt, James admitted that he wasn't feeling well, that the pain was making him feel unsteady. Eleanore helped him back up the stairs, which proved to be more of a challenge than his getting down them. Arriving at the bed, he sat down carefully, then lay back with a breathless moan. Eleanore pulled off his boots just before she heard a loud knock at the front door.

"I wonder who that could be," she said and hurried down the stairs. Surely it was too soon for the doctor to arrive, even if the sheriff had gone straight to find him. But that's exactly who she saw when she opened the door. Her relief made her realize how worried she had been, but talking with the sheriff had overshadowed her concern for James's health.

"Oh, hello," she said. "How good of you to come so quickly."

"Sheriff Willis told me I should hurry. I had no patients needing me, so I came right away."

"Thank you," Eleanore said and motioned for him to follow her. "He's upstairs. Did the sheriff tell you what happened?"

"He did," the doctor said, then grumbled something about the Weller boys and the trouble they caused.

"My husband did start this fight," Eleanore pointed out.

"I'll wager he had good cause, knowing Ned Weller."

"Still, not a very Christian way to handle the problem, as James will readily admit."

"Yes," the doctor sighed, "you're right. Still. . . ."

They arrived at the bedroom door that had been left open. Eleanore found James right where she'd left him, laying back sideways on the bed with his feet dangling over the edge. She knocked on the open door, and he turned toward her. "The doctor is here," she said. "I'll leave the two of you alone."

She closed the door and faced the empty hallway just as a memory erupted in her mind, sending a sharp pain to her heart that made her cry out softly. "Oh, help," she muttered and leaned against the wall. She'd been so caught up in the spiritual and moral aspects of the situation that she'd completely forgotten one of the other points that had been made in the blessing Frederick had given to James. "Oh, help," she said again as the words hovered plainly in her mind. James had been told that he would return to full health, but not without his reliance on his Father in Heaven to intervene on his behalf against the infection that was already festering in his body. Eleanore clung to the promise that he would return to full health, but she wondered how bad it was going to get before he did.

The doctor came out a while later to report that, as of yet, there was no sign of infection, but he had reopened the wound and disinfected it as a precaution. Eleanore winced at the description. He said he would check back in a couple of days, or to send for him if the need arose. Eleanore showed him to the door, then hurried back to the bedroom to find James nearly as white as the sheet where he lay, with the wound on his thigh newly bandaged, and a hint of fresh blood showing through. He opened his eyes as she closed the door.

"He assured me," James said, "that what he did to me is going to help, but I still wanted to hit him."

"I think you're going to have to learn to temper such feelings," she said, trying to sound facetious, but his expression was self-incriminating. "Is there anything I can get you?" she asked, sitting on the edge of the bed.

"No thank you," he said. She pushed his hair back from his face. "He gave me something for the pain, and it's starting to make me sleepy."

"I'll get you something to eat when you wake up," she said. He nodded, and she kissed his brow. "I love you, James. I'm proud of you."

"I'm glad to hear it." He smiled faintly. "But don't speak too soon. This isn't over yet." He grimaced and shifted slightly. "It's going to get worse, isn't it?"

Eleanore swallowed carefully. "If we believe what that blessing said, then . . . yes, I fear it is." She put a hand to his face. "But I will be with you, I promise. And we'll get through it together."

James nodded, appreciating her reassurance, but certain there were aspects of what he had to face that he could only face alone.

Later that evening, Eleanore had everyone gather in the bedroom for prayer. Each of the children hugged their father before Eleanore saw them off to bed, then she returned to find James propped up against pillows, not looking well at all. The pain he felt showed in his face.

"I wish I could go back twenty-four hours," he said.

She sat beside him and put her head on his shoulder. "Well, you can't. We just need to look ahead to the time when you have recovered from this and life will return to normal."

"But it will never be the same again."

Eleanore thought about that for a moment. "No, it probably won't. But right now we're just going to get you well."

James sighed deeply. "I can't help wondering what price I'll have to pay for what I've done; even worse, I wonder how much those I love will have to pay. What if something goes wrong . . . while I'm too ill to do anything about it."

"Nothing's going to go wrong," she said. "We must trust in God. He will bless and protect us, James. He will make up the difference for our mistakes. You must rest, and we're not going to talk about it any more until you're well."

During the next couple of days, James struggled with the pain and did little but eat and sleep, due to his reliance on the pain medication. The doctor was dismayed when the wound looked worse instead of better. He lanced it again and James almost went unconscious from the pain. Later that night the fever set in.

Eleanore was awakened by James nudging her in the dark. "What is it?" she asked.

"I need your help," he muttered, his voice drained of strength. While she acclimated herself to being awake, she realized he was shaking so badly that his teeth were chattering. She rolled over abruptly and put a hand to his face, finding it fearfully hot.

"No," she whispered, having hoped it wouldn't come to this. While she got water and rags to cool him down, she tried to remember that he'd been given a promise of recovery,

With a lamp burning low in their room, she bathed his fevered body in tepid water and prayed. She couldn't help thinking of Miriam losing her dear Andy to illness, and then her mind was drawn to memories of David dying in his father's arms, hot with fever and struggling to breathe. She thought of Iris and the infection she'd once gotten after concealing an injury that had become infected. They'd been blessed with a miracle then. She could only pray that they might be blessed with a miracle now.

"I'm freezing," James barely managed to say.

"I know, but your skin is hot. We need to keep you cool or it will only get worse.

He groaned and muttered, "I hate to put you through this. You should be sleeping."

"I'm fine. I have plenty of help with my home and children, and even if I didn't, I'm certain I would manage. You've sat with me through much pain and misery."

"That's different," he said. "It was all related to childbirth. I brought this on myself."

She smiled and touched his face. "Perhaps some might say I *did* bring it on myself."

"Or maybe that was all my fault, too." He tried to smile back, but his misery was all-consuming.

Days passed while the fever rose and fell, and James became lost in a sea of suffering unlike anything he'd ever known. The doctor came every day, opening the wound to try and kill the infection there as much as possible. Eleanore applied poultices regularly that were supposed to draw the infection to the surface, but she saw no improvement. Frederick gave him two more priesthood blessings, but little was said beyond an offering of peace and hope. It seemed they needed to rely on the promise and direction of the blessing he'd been given initially.

Eleanore was grateful to have others in the house to care for her home and children so that she didn't need to leave her husband's side,

even for a moment. She did her best to make contact with the children
several times each day, but she didn't want them in the room with
James when he was so disturbingly miserable. Iris and Ben watched
out for the little ones with no complaint, and they both assured
Eleanore every day that they were praying very hard for their father,
and surely everything would be all right.

James drifted in and out of delirium while days passed in a timeless
blur. Unfathomable pain and raging fever fought together to purge his
spirit of any minuscule residue of anger or bitterness. Fear became
replaced by abject humility, and a consummate realization that his life
and the well-being of his family were in God's hands, and attempting to
manipulate any outcome contrary to God's will would only see him
condemned. James vicariously felt the helplessness of Jonah in the belly
of a whale, and the absolute debilitation of Alma the Younger, struck
down by a divine source and brought to a full awareness of his poor
choices. James knew that his sins were not of a willful and rebellious
nature, nor were they heinous or abhorrent in the sight of God. But he
also knew that a portion of his heart had remained bitter and closed
from the Almighty. That bitterness had eagerly taken hold of his fears
and anger in relation to the persecution of people he cared for. Now he
knew that if he ever hoped to face God with a clear conscience, and
make himself an instrument in his Maker's hands to do whatever was
required of him, those places in his heart needed to be completely
broken in order to be made whole again. Amidst the heights of fever
that left him drifting in and out of consciousness, writhing and
delirious, James begged forgiveness and offered a silent pledge to never
allow his actions—or his heart—to be ruled by anger or fear again.

While James had little sense of night or day, or of hours passing,
he would occasionally feel lucid enough to be aware of his surroundings. And he always found Eleanore by his side, always with concern
in her expression, and sometimes tears on her face. On one such occasion he put a hand over hers where it rested on his chest. "I'm so
sorry," he murmured.

"All is forgiven, James," she said and pressed a gentle kiss to his
lips. "Just live. You must fight to come through this. Do you hear me?"
He nodded, and she showed him a strained smile. "I love you. I love
you so much. I need you. Do you understand?" He nodded again.

"We're all praying for you, and the doctor's doing everything he can." Tears leaked from her eyes. "Everyone at church is praying for you. The minister even came by the house."

James made a scoffing noise and managed to say, "I'll gladly take the prayers of the congregation, but . . ." He ran out of strength, and Eleanore nodded. He knew she was aware of his sentiments. The man meant well, but James had never been fond of him since David's funeral when he'd had nothing to say that had given any comfort. In fact, it had been quite the opposite. Then a thought occurred to him, and he whispered, "I suppose I need to forgive him, too."

Eleanore nodded and bit her lip, and he realized she was too upset to speak. She took his face into her hands and kissed him again. His next awareness was another painful visit from the doctor, and then there was a long stretch of laudanum-induced oblivion. He wondered if he was becoming addicted to the drug; he'd heard this was common. But in his present state that was the least of his worries.

James drifted once again into painful oblivion as the fever rose. He dreamt of hanging on the edge of that cliff, struggling to hold on while the ground beneath his fingers crumbled and threatened to give way. He would come barely into consciousness and be aware of his surroundings and then drift again into the dream, over and over, clinging desperately to life and safety. Even as he dreamt, he seemed able to ponder the possible meaning. Was it simple survival he was holding on to, or did the cliff represent something deep in his spirit that he was desperately hanging on to?

Somewhere in the deepest part of his incoherence, the dream changed. *Let go,* he heard. *Trust Me.* Still James clung fearfully to the edge of the cliff, until his arms ached and his will lessened. And finally he had to accept that he didn't have the strength to lift himself up. He needed help. He shouted and begged, but no one came. Again he heard the words. *Let go. Trust Me.* With nothing left to fight with, James took a deep breath and pulled his hands away, immersed in a deep inner peace that contradicted his belief that he was bound for jagged rocks below. But the painful landing never came. Instead he had the sensation of falling back onto a soft mattress, and he thought he heard a gentle chuckle, like a father who had known all along that something was there to break the child's fall. Light surrounded him, and he allowed it to completely swallow him up, wanting never to exist outside its reach.

Eleanore's concern worsened when she watched her husband go from a state of much visible anguish to showing no response at all. When he began to look as though he were dead, she feared that the worst would happen. She wondered if they had misunderstood the blessing he'd been given, or perhaps misinterpreted its meaning. She knew in her heart that God's will had to be accepted above all else. Still, she prayed with all the energy of her heart and soul for his survival, and she fasted more than she ate.

Exhausted beyond all recognition, Eleanore glanced at the clock barely illuminated by the lamp and saw that it was just past two. She'd barely been able to rouse James enough to be assured that he was alive before she crawled into the bed next to him and put a hand against his throat to be mindful of the blood pumping through his veins. With the evidence pulsing against her fingers, she drifted to sleep. She dreamt of her husband's empty boots on the floor at the foot of the bed, and his clothes hanging unworn in the closet; of a casket being lowered into the ground next to the grave of their son, and a journey west to Salt Lake City, leaving his body behind. She dreamt of wearing black and weeping alone in her cold bed. Then she felt warmth steal over her, and she looked up to see James surrounded by light, beckoning to her. She took his hand and was lifted up, feeling his arms surround her with perfect peace, and a knowledge that they would be together forever.

Eleanore woke with a gasp and found direct sunlight warming her face. She shifted slightly and looked down to see James's arm around her waist. When she'd gone to sleep he hadn't had the strength to move, or the awareness to be mindful of her lying next to him. She rolled over carefully, holding her breath, and found him watching her, his eyes unclouded and cognizant.

"James," she whispered and turned fully to face him. He attempted to tighten his arm around her, but his weakness was readily evident.

"You were dreaming," he muttered, his voice raspy. "It sounded bad."

"I dreamt you were dead."

"Well, I'm not."

"I can see that," she said, laughing through sudden tears while she touched his face with her hands, internalizing the evidence. "The dream ended well, however. You took me up into heaven with you, and we were surrounded by light."

"That *is* a good ending," he said, and his eyelids became heavy. "I believe I had a dream something like that too. But I think we should wait a few decades before we come to that part."

"Of course," she said and laughed again. "You're tired."

"I am," he whispered. "And so weak I can hardly breathe." He rolled carefully on to his back but kept his face turned toward her. "So get me something to eat, woman. I'm starving to death here."

"Oh!" she said with glee and jumped out of bed. "I'll be right back." She turned around to press a kiss to his lips that coaxed a soft chuckle out of him. "I'll hurry."

After Eleanore had fed her husband a small portion of gruel, she gathered the family around him to offer a prayer of thanksgiving. With regular feedings of either thin porridge or broth, he gradually ate more and more and progressed to normal meals. He went through a couple of days of difficult symptoms that the doctor said were a withdrawal from the laudanum; it was a miserable interlude, but nothing to be concerned about. The wound in the leg had become a healthy color, and the doctor declared that it was healing well at last. As Eleanore watched her husband come back to life, there was no missing the light in his eyes. When she asked him about it, he simply said that he knew God had forgiven him, and that he wasn't the same man who had taken out his anger on Ned Weller. Being awake more but still very weak, James often asked his wife to read to him. She read passages from many books, but mostly from the scriptures. He requested some specific sections, but made no comment until she read the story of the conversion of Alma the Younger.

"In some small way," James said, "I feel like that's what happened to me."

Eleanore set the book aside and leaned toward him. "But Alma was doing horrible things, James. You've always been a good man with a good heart. Even your anger was grounded in good intentions."

"I understand that, Ellie, I do. I realize we're all human, with differing degrees of personal struggle. I can't judge where anyone else might stand with such issues. But for me, I know now that a piece of my heart has been angry and bitter since my childhood. I was holding on to hard feelings, if only to a degree, but it left me vulnerable to the fear and anger I've had to deal with more recently. I know we can't completely reach perfection in this life, and I may struggle with these feelings for as long as I live. But I've come to realize that to be truly Christian, we must have hearts filled with love and forgiveness, and we shouldn't even have to think about whether or not another human being deserves those things from us. God will see to justice when it's not met fully in this life. And even when consequences must be faced in this life, they should still be addressed with compassion and forgiveness." He drew a deep breath and settled more deeply against the pillows behind his head. "God really means it, Eleanore, when He says that He will forgive whom He will forgive, but for us we must forgive all men. It's not up for debate. It's not our burden to carry. And when you really think about it, why would we want to? I don't want the burden of having to judge Ned Weller's actions, or to carry the weight of what he did. The Savior has taken that burden from me, and I'm grateful."

Eleanore moved to sit on the edge of the bed, wrapping her arms around him. He returned the embrace with a glimmer of strength and said in a gentle voice, "I know what I did was stupid, Ellie, but I can't regret doing it, only in the respect that I would not trade away what I have learned and gained." He drew back and took her shoulders into his hands. "I'm only sorry that you've had to suffer with me, and that we have no way of knowing what the future will bring."

"It will be all right," she said, pressing her hand to his face. "Whatever happens, it will be all right. You're alive, and we're together, and we can get through anything."

"I believe you're right, Mrs. Barrington," he said and hugged her again.

Chapter Thirteen
RESTITUTION

The healing process for James was slow and cumbersome. But with each difficult day, he came to better understand and accept his total reliance on his Father in Heaven and his Savior. He knew his being alive was a miracle, that logically the infection should have killed him. And he'd been given a lesson in controlling his anger that he'd never forget.

James also gained a new gratitude for the life he lived. He'd never been one to take his blessings for granted, but he saw the people and circumstances surrounding him through new eyes. When he was finally strong enough to go down the stairs and just sit in the kitchen or parlor with his family, it felt like Christmas morning. And then, with some help, he was able to venture outside with the aid of a cane that Frederick had purchased in town to assist James in getting around until the leg fully healed.

Having Frederick and Lizzie and their sweet little daughter as part of their family was a rich blessing. Together they had helped and supported the family through many things, but this most recent episode that had left James completely incapacitated had made him appreciate just how much they did, and how cheerfully and eagerly they did it. Ben was also a tremendous blessing in their home. He had willingly helped Frederick see that every chore was completed while James was ill, and he had not uttered a single complaint. He had survived the ordeals of his life well, and was a fine example to James and everyone around him, and James loved him dearly. James also felt an overwhelming love for his own children. Earlier in his life he could not have comprehended having such a beautiful family. His children were healthy and strong, and the light of the gospel shone in their faces. And at the heart of his family was Eleanore; his dear, sweet Eleanore. When he'd proposed marriage to her, he had seen enough of her character to believe that she would commit herself to marriage and family with integrity and respect. He'd never imagined what an angelic gem God had guided into his life. Apart from the gospel, she was his heart and soul. Seeing how she had stood by him and nurtured him through the depths of hell, he couldn't begin to comprehend how he'd ever managed without her. And to think how different his life might have been if he'd never met her—or had the good sense to marry her—caused him to shudder and cringe.

As it was, he could look around and see himself surrounded by the beauty and wonder of a second chance at life—a life better than most men could ever dream of enjoying. When he told Eleanore he didn't understand why he was so thoroughly blessed, she looked at him straightly and said, "Yes, we are very blessed." She examined the view from the side porch where they were sitting. "There's no denying it. But you must remember, James Barrington, that much of what brings you joy is a result of the choices you've made. You're a man of morals and integrity, and you have always striven to honor God and those you love, even when it's difficult. Life can certainly bring challenges, but it's how we respond to them that truly creates the life we live. You deserve to be happy."

He took her hand and kissed it. "Well, I am." He sighed. "Even though I know I need to speak with Ned Weller's widow."

"I'm going with you."

"I would hope so," he said. "I'm going to need your woman's intuition. You're gifted at handling difficult situations. I think you brought that with you when you were born."

"Perhaps." She took in the view again. "When will we go? I think we need to take care of it so that it's not weighing on us."

"Us? This is *my* weight to carry."

"There you go again; trying to separate my problems from yours. What makes you believe this isn't weighing on me? I'm certain when we exchanged vows, it included the promise to stand beside each other while knocking on Mrs. Weller's door."

James sighed. "I'm sure you're right. I only wish that—"

"Hush." She put her fingers over his mouth. "We can't wish away what's happened or what needs to be done. We just need to take care of it the best we can."

James nodded, feeling dread tighten his chest and throat. And he knew that until he did what he had to do, the dread would never go away. "How about this afternoon?"

"Today?" she almost shrieked.

"Let's get it over with. I'm certain Ned Weller is long buried by now."

Eleanore let out a worried sigh, then bit her lip before she stood with determination. "Very well. I'll gather some things to take for the family so we don't go empty-handed."

Frederick harnessed the buggy, and James had no trouble getting in and out. He tried it a couple of times to make certain he could go out in public without making a fool of himself. Eleanore put in some baskets of various food items she'd collected from the kitchen and cellar. She climbed up beside James, and he snapped the reins.

"So, where do they live?" she asked.

He could only say, "I have no idea."

Eleanore chuckled. "Then perhaps a visit to the sheriff's office would be in order first."

They drove in silence for a few minutes before James said, "It feels good to be out . . . and with you."

"Yes, it does." She touched his face. "It's good to see you getting some color. You're almost looking like your old self."

In town they bought a few more things to add to the baskets, as long as they were there, then they stopped at the sheriff's office, and Eleanore went in. She wondered if Sheriff Willis would even be there, and hoped that whoever *was* there might be willing to give out the address for the Weller home. The sheriff was there, and he greeted her kindly. When she told him the purpose of her visit, he wrote down simple directions for a place outside of town in the opposite direction from her own home.

"And how is your husband doing?" the sheriff asked. "I hear he almost didn't make it."

"He's in the buggy right now, and doing very well. Thank you for asking. And thank you for your kindness."

Sheriff Willis walked outside with her and shook James's hand in a friendly greeting. They chatted about health and the weather for a few minutes before the sheriff said, "We never did figure out who killed Weller. But I've sure found a lot of people who are glad he's dead." Neither James nor Eleanore commented on that. The sheriff went on. "If we find out anything, I'll let you know."

"We appreciate that," James said and shook his hand again. "It's good to see you. Thank you again, for everything."

"A pleasure, Mr. Barrington. You have a nice day now." He nodded and smiled at Eleanore as James drove the buggy forward.

Nothing at all was said between them as they drove to the Weller farm. James's regret over what he'd done consumed him anew as he considered facing these people. A part of him hoped that Ned's brother wouldn't be around, but in his heart he believed he needed to face the brother as well as the wife. Getting it over with would be nice. But he couldn't deny his fear that Rufus Weller would find a way to retaliate for what James had done, or even blame him for the death.

"Wait," Eleanore said, putting a hand on his arm. "Let's stop and pray."

"Excellent idea." He guided the buggy to the edge of the road and stopped it, glad to note there wasn't another person anywhere in sight. They held hands, and James prayed aloud for this visit to go well, and for God's mercy to be extended in making right what had been wrong. He prayed for hearts to be softened, for protection from their enemies, and even for miracles to be wrought according to God's will. After sharing an amen and a firm embrace, they drove on. James still felt a tight dread, but he didn't feel afraid. He knew the matter was in God's hands and that somehow, all would be well.

They found the Weller home easily enough. It was old and in sore need of paint. The farmland and yard around it looked sorely neglected. A dog barked as they pulled up, but it was tied somewhere in the back, and they couldn't see it.

"Here goes," James said, halting the buggy. He'd intended to help Eleanore down, as he'd always done, but he was so slow getting out himself that by the time he was on two feet she was standing beside him, holding both baskets. He took one from her and drew a deep breath.

"Everything will be fine," she said and led the way to the porch.

As they went up the steps, the baskets felt awkward and Eleanore set them down to the side of the door before James muttered something about being out of his mind, then he knocked loudly. Eleanore put a hand over her quavering stomach and shared an anxious glance with her husband. They heard noise on the other side of the door, but it took a minute for someone to come. The woman who answered looked tired and unkempt, with cynical eyes and prematurely graying hair that hung freely to her shoulders. She had a baby on her hip, and a small child holding to her skirts, peering out at them. Both children had runny noses and dirty faces. Noises from the house indicated that there were other children as well. The woman looked at Eleanore and James skeptically, taking special notice of the cane James was leaning on. James and Eleanore took a step back as she stepped onto the porch, leaving the door open.

"Mrs. Weller?" James asked.

"Yes," she drawled. "Who are you?" she demanded, more skeptical than angry.

"My name is James Barrington, and this is my wife, Eleanore. We heard of your husband's death and came to—"

"My husband hurt you, didn't he." Mrs. Weller looked again at his leg and the cane in his hand. Her statement left no room for doubting her certainty over the matter.

James sought for an honest answer. "I hurt him first."

"He made a lot of people angry. I wouldn't be surprised if you were one of them. I've heard from a lot of angry people since he died, people expecting me to make things right. If that's what you've come for then—"

"No," James hurried to say. "No, of course not. We've brought some things." He motioned to the baskets they'd set on the porch. She turned to look over her shoulder, and her eyes went wide, then distrustful. "We just wanted to offer our condolences on the loss of your husband. It must surely be difficult to lose someone you love and—"

"You're serious, aren't you." Again, there was no question in her voice.

"Yes," James drawled. "Is there a problem?"

"Not with me, there's not," she said. "You folks aren't from around here, are you? England, sounds like."

"Originally, yes," James said, "but we've lived in Iowa for more than a decade now."

"Then you must know of my husband's reputation. You would or you wouldn't have aggravated him enough to get in his way."

"That's irrelevant now, Mrs. Weller. We simply wanted to bring some things that might help you and your children after the death in your family." He stretched the truth a bit when he added, "It's a tradition where we come from. Our intention is not to offend you; we only want to offer our condolences."

Mrs. Weller's eyes narrowed. "Why?"

"Why?" James echoed and looked to Eleanore, silently giving her permission to step in and say something any time now.

"Because it's the Christian thing to do," Eleanore said. "My husband *did* have an altercation with your husband, and we *did* have cause to be angry with him. But we've discussed the matter and decided that it's not our place to judge or place blame. It is only right for us to forgive. He's gone now, so we've come to you, asking that you speak on his behalf. What my husband is trying to say is . . . that he would like to ask forgiveness for what he did to your husband."

Mrs. Weller looked nothing less than astonished. "What did he do?" she asked Eleanore while she looked at James as if he'd turned an unnatural color.

"He provoked a fight with your husband." Eleanore discreetly elbowed James.

"That's right. I did. What my wife says is true. I would ask you to represent your husband in my asking forgiveness for what I did and—"

"Who's there?" a gruff male voice called from somewhere in the house.

Mrs. Weller called over her shoulder, "Some folks asking forgiveness, if you can imagine."

Rufus Weller came to the door and stood beside his sister-in-law. James fought for composure. Rufus looked so much like his brother that James's belief that he needed to face Ned Weller with this conversation suddenly became more real. "What did you do to him?" Rufus asked.

"Says he hit him, started a fight," Mrs. Weller reported.

Again James exchanged a discreet glance with Eleanore, wondering if she was as disbelieving as he was at how badly this was going. Then it took a turn for the better when Rufus said, "I hope you won. He was a mean cuss."

Before James could comment, Mrs. Weller motioned to the things on the porch and added, "They brought some stuff . . . to offer condolences."

"Why?" Rufus asked.

Again Mrs. Weller replied, "They said it was the Christian thing to do."

Rufus chuckled. "You're joking, right?"

"No, we're quite serious," Eleanore said.

"Exactly what sort of Christians are you?" Rufus asked, and James expected him to be angry or offended by their offering something that may have wounded his pride. He went on to say, "Never heard of any of the Christians around here even saying a kind word to us, especially since Ned died."

"Well, now you have," James said, hoping to divert the question.

"So, what church is it exactly you belong to? I might actually consider going to a church that teaches *that* way of being Christians."

James looked at Eleanore, uttered a silent prayer, then looked directly at Rufus Weller. He spoke with complete honesty, saying, "As we understand it, your brother didn't care much for people of our religion. It might be better if we kept that to ourselves. We simply came to offer our condolences, and to see if there's anything we can do to help since . . . the death."

Rufus screwed up his face, then blurted, "You're *Mormons?*"

James drew a deep breath, and Eleanore took his hand. "Yes, we are. But you won't find a Mormon church to attend around here, Mr. Weller. As far as we know, we're the only ones."

A tense silence descended while James wondered how to make a gracious exit. He expected some kind of outburst, some demand for them to remove themselves from the property and take their charity with them. But Rufus Weller said, "Well, I'll be hung from a rotten tree. I've never heard of such a thing."

"What haven't you heard of, Mr. Weller?" James asked.

Rufus Weller apparently couldn't answer the question. When Rufus said nothing, his sister-in-law filled the silence. "Thank you for your kindness." The baby had started to fuss, and it was evident she wanted to end the conversation and take care of her child. "We'll not forget it."

"Yes, thank you," Rufus said, still looking at them with an expression of deep contemplation.

"We'll go and leave you in peace," James said, "as soon as I clarify what I came here to say. I came to apologize for what I did to Ned, and would hope that the both of you would considering offering forgiveness on his behalf."

"Well, yeah," Rufus said at the same time that Mrs. Weller said, "Certainly."

James felt as stunned as they both looked. It couldn't be this easy. It just couldn't. He felt compelled to ask, "Is there anything we can do for you? I don't want to offend you, but . . . you have had a death in the family. Is there anything we can do to help?"

The Wellers looked at each other, then again at James, then Eleanore, then James again. Mrs. Weller shook her head while Rufus said, "No, but thanks all the same."

Awkward goodbyes were exchanged, then James and Eleanore started for home, silent for the first mile. James finally said, "I can't believe it." Then he chuckled. "That is the strangest thing I've ever encountered."

"How did Mr. Weller put it?" Eleanore laughed softly, then mimicked Rufus, "'Well, I'll be hung from a rotten tree.'"

James laughed at the imitation and the absurdity of such words coming from Eleanore's mouth. But he had to say, "Amen."

Again they stopped to pray, this time expressing gratitude for yet another miracle in helping them come through this difficulty. They prayed on behalf of the Weller family, and also prayed that no unforeseen repercussions would cause them any trouble or put them in danger. Then James drove for home, feeling more bright and happy than he perhaps ever had. A great burden had been lifted from his life. He'd finally been able to let go.

* * * * *

The following Sunday, James made certain they arrived at church early, and he asked the minister if they could briefly have a private word. Eleanore wondered what they might be talking about while she settled the children onto the usual pew and waited. By the time James returned to sit beside her, the opening hymn was being sung. She gave him a questioning gaze, but he whispered, "Later."

Not many minutes after that, the minister announced over the pulpit that on the upcoming Saturday everyone was encouraged to help with a project to help the Weller family. Eleanore tossed her husband an astonished glance. He returned her gaze with perfect innocence. A low murmur went through the congregation before the minister silenced them and gave a little speech about being kind and charitable to the widows and fatherless, regardless of the sins committed by the father. James whispered in Eleanore's ear, "That's not exactly how I put it to him."

Eleanore wanted to question him on how long he'd been planning this, and why he hadn't let her in on it, but she didn't want to miss what the minister was saying. He announced that all the materials had been provided by an anonymous donor to do some repairs and painting on the house and barn, and he strongly encouraged everyone to come, to bring food that might be shared throughout the course of the day, and to give of themselves in a charitable way that would surely bring blessings into their lives.

James was glad for a number of reasons that no one knew he was the instigator of the Weller project. He wanted to think that his greatest motivation was simply the importance of allowing the charitable act to remain between him and God. He was trying to make restitution in God's eyes, and what anyone else thought didn't matter. But he couldn't deny preferring to remain anonymous in order to avoid any undue attention—whether positive or negative. And he was glad for it after the church meeting was adjourned and the buzz among the congregation was an undercurrent of astonishment that they might be asked to help a family that had caused so much trouble in the community. The more James heard about the Wellers, the more he realized it wasn't just Jews, Mormons, and Negroes who had received their unwanted attention. These boys had been raised by a mean, drunk, bigoted father, and they had apparently taken to his ways zealously. James wondered how much Rufus had to do with all the rumors floating about of the misdeeds of "the Weller boys," as they were frequently referred to. The sheriff had told him Ned was the instigator. Rufus had responded quite positively to all that had been said when James and Eleanore had paid their visit. But James had no idea where the man's heart was. Of course, only God knew that. It wasn't up to James to figure out the accountability or motives of this man—or anyone else. His only concern was that he needed to be an instrument in God's hands to do His will. And right now, that meant seeing that the Weller family got some much-needed help. He wondered if anyone would show up for the project, given the general attitude, but he didn't worry about that either.

Throughout the week, James had Frederick go with him to discreetly get a better look at the Weller home and property to see what was needed. Then they went into town and purchased paint, lumber, and a number of odds and ends that might be needed. On Friday they left the supplies at the edge of the yard, quietly and after dark in order to go unnoticed. A note was tacked to the pile of lumber, explaining that some people would be coming to do some work on Saturday, and not to be alarmed.

When Saturday morning dawned especially warm for early autumn, Stella and Eleanore were already up and preparing food to take along to the Wellers, optimistic that there would be many workers to feed. James purposely insisted on going late. He didn't want to appear too obvious, even if he and Eleanore would likely be the only faces the Wellers would recognize.

When James *did* arrive, with his entire household and enough food to feed three times that many people, he had to fight back tears to see more people hard at work than he could count. His family and Frederick's quickly meshed into the group, each finding a task to do. The women set out food and held tools and nails for the men while they sawed, hammered, and repaired a number of things. The children were assigned various tasks according to their abilities, and James noticed Ben and Iris initiating an ambitious weed-pulling project. Then the painting began, and with so many helping hands, the house changed colors very quickly.

James felt hot and went to the well behind the house for some water. He got a drink, then splashed it on his face. He was pushing his wet hands through his hair when he heard, "I thought you might have something to do with this." James turned around to see Mrs. Weller, her hands on her hips. But she looked more amused than angry. And thankfully no one else was close enough to hear their conversation.

"It was announced at church. I just came along to help." He took another drink of water.

"Some help you are with that bum leg," she added facetiously.

"It doesn't take two good legs to work a paintbrush or a hammer."

"You *did* have something to do with this, didn't you?"

James chuckled. "I'll admit to hitting your husband, but that's all I'm going to admit to."

The light mood of their conversation dissipated as she added, "Wait a minute. I thought you said you were the only Mormons around here, and there wasn't a church to go to. So how could they announce it at church?"

James glanced around then looked at her. "Oh, these people aren't Mormons—except for the ones who live at my house. But they *are* all Christians. Or at least they try to be. You have to give them credit for that. They're here, aren't they? Most of them have good hearts and good intentions." A surprising thought occurred to him, and he felt compelled to add, "Like you."

Mrs. Weller appeared stunned before she looked away abruptly. He could hear her sniffling before she said with a cracked voice, "I didn't know what Ned was like when I married him. I can't tell you the sleepless nights I've had, wondering what kind of damage he'd done." She regained her composure somewhat and looked up. "He was so much like his father and—"

"You don't have to tell me this," James said, wondering how their brief encounters had made her want to unburden herself on him.

"But I do," she insisted. "Please . . . hear me out." James nodded, and she went on. "A couple of years back, Rufus lost his home and family because of the trouble Rufus and Ned had been causing."

James wanted to ask what she meant by *lost*, but it didn't really matter. He just listened.

"That's when he moved in with us, and Rufus tried and tried to get Ned to give up this ridiculous hatred. All that changed was that Ned and Rufus started fighting each other all the time, which I suppose is better than having them out hurting innocent people. Rufus wanted to change his ways, and he refused to be involved in Ned's mischief." She blew out a long, slow breath, as if she'd just set down a heavy load. "We're glad he's dead, Mr. Barrington. Beyond fathering these children and barely keeping food in our mouths, he never did a good thing in his life."

"Perhaps he didn't know any better."

"Perhaps. But that doesn't make it right, now, does it."

"No, it doesn't. However, I believe that many things that are wrong in this world will be made right when we get to the other side."

"I do hope so, Mr. Barrington. I believe God forgives those who are penitent. That's one thing I've gotten out of going to church alone all these years. I hope it's true, because poor, dear Rufus deserves a chance to start over. I don't think he ever knew any better. He just did what his pa and his brother did." She looked around at the bustle of activity with a glow of wonder in her eyes. "Rufus is gone for a few days. When he gets back, he won't believe this. We've been wondering how to get the money to fix things up. Rufus is managing the farm all right, but it doesn't give him much time to do the extra things, so . . ." She became too emotional to speak.

"We're glad to help, Mrs. Weller. And if you want my opinion, it's never too late for redemption. I'm certain God knows Rufus's heart."

"I believe He does," she said. "But folks have a hard time forgetting."

"That's why it's not up to them whether or not a person is forgiven."

She thought about that, then smiled. "Me and Rufus are getting married next week. It seemed the right thing to do. He's always treated me better then Ned ever did." She chuckled and wiped at the remnants of tears on her face. "I won't have to change my name."

"Congratulations are in order, then."

Again she smiled. "We'll never forget what you've done for us."

"It's nothing, Mrs. Weller; truly. I only try to do what I believe God wants me to do. I believe you should consider any blessings you receive to be from Him. The hands that do His work are merely human."

She nodded and walked away. He sensed that emotion was over-taking her and that she preferred to be alone. He stood there for a long moment, pondering the miracle. And suddenly, gone were the fear and dread that had hovered inside of him in varying degrees for longer than he could remember. Or perhaps it was not so sudden; nevertheless, their last remnants flitted away, and their absence left room for light and peace and hope to a degree he'd never imagined possible. He wondered for a moment if he should follow Mrs. Weller and clarify that it might be best if the people here didn't know he was a Mormon; then he realized he didn't care. It was time to stop hiding the fact. He'd felt completely comfortable up to this point in keeping it a secret, knowing it was with the approval of the Holy Spirit. And now he knew by the same means that it was time to go public with his beliefs and to be unafraid of the consequences. He didn't know if the timing had anything to do with Ned Weller's death. Regardless, he was done hiding. He could only pray that his family would remain protected.

The day proved to be a huge success. Not only did the necessary work get completed on the house and barn, but weeds were pulled, flowers planted, and trash removed and burned. Mrs. Weller and the children hovered at a distance until the food came out, then Eleanore ushered them into the middle of the crowd and started introducing them to people, starting with Lizzie and Stella, who hardly left her side, making certain she felt included. By evening Mrs. Weller almost blended with the others, except for her regular bouts of weeping. But her emotion got the attention of people who had likely come with an attitude that was a bit begrudging, and they were now surprised by the way their own hearts and countenances had softened throughout the day.

That night as James was crawling into bed, Eleanore asked, "Are you all right?"

"I'm exhausted, and my leg is killing me. But it was worth it."

"I can't speak for your leg, but I'll agree that it was certainly worth every bit of effort we put into what we did." She kissed his brow. "You're a brilliant man, James Barrington, to have thought of it."

"*I* didn't think of it. I was prompted. Big difference. I just did what I was told."

"Well, you're a brilliant man for doing what you're told. It's one of a million reasons why I love you."

"Tell me the others while I fall asleep," he said, and she did. But she didn't get to more than twenty.

The following day at church, the minister thanked everyone for their help and support the previous day. And he welcomed the

Weller family to church. James turned around and saw them seated a few rows back. He felt Eleanore squeeze his hand and caught her smiling.

"They might prefer being Mormons," Eleanore whispered.

"One step at a time," James whispered back.

After the meeting, the minister quietly thanked James for his insight, which made his visit later in the week even more of a surprise. He showed up at the door in the middle of the afternoon, without warning. It took no effort to sense his disgruntlement as he was offered a seat in the parlor. James and Eleanore sat across from him, and they exchanged cursory greetings. James considered his history with this man. He felt certain the minister's intentions were good, and that he genuinely cared for the people in his congregation. But James had heard him make bold accusations against other religions over the pulpit, and the man's sermons were often aimed more at guilt than hope. He preached of a God who was harsh and condemning, and he also taught that the relationships shared in this world would have no meaning in the world to come. James and Eleanore, along with everyone under their roof, had agreed from the time that they'd begun to practice their own beliefs privately that they could quietly disagree with what the minister was teaching and still be respectful to his position and the beliefs of the congregation. But James had struggled with particularly difficult feelings toward this man at the time of David's death. His words at the funeral had been devoid of any peace or hope. James had thought at the time that even the most basic Christian denomination should have common beliefs in some areas, most particularly in regard to the Resurrection and the Atonement. But this man had said nothing at David's graveside about those things, and James had come away angry and unhappy with this man and his beliefs. He'd long ago come to terms with David's death according to the truths of the gospel that he'd embraced fully in the meantime, and his more recent experiences had purged his spirit of such negative feelings toward others. He held no malice toward this man, and he respected whatever his opinions might be. But he had a hunch the feeling was not mutual as the minister looked at James and Eleanore with skeptical eyes before declaring, "I've heard the most disturbing rumor."

"Have you?" James countered coolly.

"The rumor is that your connection to the Weller family occurred because the Weller boys had a strong aversion to Mormons, and that *you* are Mormons; that this . . . grand . . . charity project," he motioned wildly with his hands, "was some effort to mend the differences between your families."

James contemplated this for a moment, more concerned with the man's tone and countenance than with what he was actually saying. He answered in a calm voice, "What difference does it make *why* something good took place? We're all Christians, and Christ's example would have us seek out opportunities to help those in need."

"Are you Mormons or not?" the minister demanded in a voice that was anything but Christlike.

"Yes," James said with no hesitation.

Astonishment flared in the man's eyes. "And how long has this been the case?"

"Many years," James said without apology.

Fury smothered the minister's astonishment in an instant. *"Years? For years* you have been secretly lurking in my congregation, hiding from everyone the evil you practice privately?"

Eleanore put a hand on James's arm as a familiar way of reminding him to remain calm. But he needed no such reminder. He felt entirely unruffled as he said, "What we believe is not evil, sir. There are not enough people who share our beliefs to constitute a congregation, and we have chosen to gather on the Sabbath among other Christians in order to—"

"Christians?" The minister rose to his feet. "You dare to call yourselves *Christians?* People who claim to have their own Bible and follow some self-made prophet like gypsies?"

James rose to face him, and Eleanore stood by his side. "I respect your right to believe whatever you want, sir. I only ask the same of you. This is America—the land of religious freedom; a land where we are given the right to worship however we choose."

"Fine," came the heated retort, "worship how you choose, but if you *choose* to hold to these heathen beliefs, you and your family are not welcome in my church."

"Your church?" James countered with a calmness that seemed to aggravate the minister further. "Should it not be God's church?" The man made a scoffing noise, and James added, "We will be happy to take our worship elsewhere, sir. And I trust that since *you*

are a Christian man, you will respect our right to do so and refrain from speaking ill of others simply because their beliefs differ from yours. If members of your congregation become suddenly poisoned against my household, I will know where the venom started, and I will not hesitate to report any harassment to the sheriff. Now, please leave my home."

The minister muttered something about the inevitable hellfire and brimstone that awaited those who were swayed by such evil designs, then he left and slammed the door. James turned to look at his wife, saying with a facetiousness that surprised even himself, "Well, at least I can stop pretending to like *him* every Sunday."

"At least you were always gracious and respectful, even though you *didn't* like him."

James sighed and sat down. "Maybe it's time, Eleanore."

"Time for what?"

"To go to Salt Lake City."

Eleanore sat down. "You really mean that."

"I really do. I know the journey could be challenging, but I'm tired of living like this. And now, who knows what will happen? The Wellers don't seem to mind that we're Mormons, but clearly there are some people who disapprove. I want my children to have friends who share their faith. I want Iris to find a man who will live the gospel with her."

"Maybe it *is* time. We both need to know . . . beyond any doubt."

"Of course. We'll pray about it . . . as we always have."

"It would be so good to live among the Saints . . . to be with Sally and Miriam."

"Yes. Yes, it would."

"However, we must remember that Brother Brigham told you there would be some purpose served in our being here."

"I'd forgotten about that," James had to admit. "Still, perhaps that purpose *has* been served somehow and we just don't know it. Maybe it was to bring Stella into the Church, or to help the Weller family."

"Perhaps," Eleanore said, hoping that was the case. Over the next couple of days, she began planning in her mind how they would go about making the move to the Salt Lake Valley. She made mental lists of what they would take, and she emotionally started to separate herself from all they would leave behind.

It was actually a relief not to have to attend church on Sunday among a congregation that would surely now be whispering about them, or worse, throwing bold accusations at them face-to-face. They held their usual worship service in the parlor, which included taking the sacrament together. And the peace they shared as a family united by gospel truths far outweighed any difficult feelings or concerns. In fact, Eleanore felt so much peace over the sweet spirit in her home that by nightfall she knew that her answer was, once again, to remain there, at least for now. She knew the time would come when they would join the Saints. But this was not that time. She went up to bed early to be alone with tears that accompanied thoughts of the distance between herself and the people she longed to live among and worship with. James found her there and held her close, whispering near her ear, "You're disappointed."

"About what?" she asked to test him.

"That it's not yet time to leave. That *is* the answer you got, isn't it?"

"Yes." She shifted in order to see his face in the lamplight. "Why, James? Why is it necessary for us to stay when the Saints are being gathered from such faraway places? I don't understand."

"I don't understand either, Ellie. But we must trust in God. One day we *will* understand. Perhaps . . ."

"Perhaps what? You can't think of anything, can you?"

"Actually . . . the thought just occurred to me that . . . well, perhaps there are people here who need the gospel in their lives, and if we leave, that won't happen. Or . . ."

"Or?"

"Well . . . what if, for instance, the man Iris is supposed to marry is someone she'll meet here. If we left too soon, such a thing might not happen."

"But there's no one here who—"

"Not now, but . . . perhaps it's someone who will come into the fold because of her influence. We simply can't predict the future, Eleanore. But God can. We must trust Him."

"I know. I know you're right. I'm just . . . disappointed."

"Yes, so am I." He kissed her. "But at least we have each other."

Chapter Fourteen

THE GATHERING

James firmly declared, once again, that he was going to stop asking if he should take his family west. He felt certain that when it was time, the Lord would let him know. With his declaration came a determination to settle into the life they enjoyed and make peace with it.

A few weeks after Rufus and Bess Weller were married, they showed up at the door of the Barrington home, looking much less unkempt than they had on previous encounters. They brought a cake and two loaves of freshly baked bread, along with an expression of appreciation. Eleanore invited them in, sensing there was more purpose in their visit than they'd initially indicated. They both seemed a bit nervous. James gathered everyone together and official introductions were made before the entire household sat down to visit with the Weller family. And that's when Rufus Weller tearfully apologized for anything he may have done to bring grief to people who were Mormons. A comfortable conversation about forgiveness and redemption naturally followed, and the Wellers' curiosity regarding Mormonism became evident as their questions began to flow more freely. Before the visit ended, James had invited them to join the family the following Sunday for their private service. Two months later, Rufus and Bess were baptized on one of the last miraculously warm days of autumn. The three older children were baptized as well. And from that time forward, the Wellers came nearly every Sunday to join their tiny congregation. They all became good friends, creating a situation that was reminiscent of the days when the Plummer family joined them every Sunday. And in the spirit of that tradition, when spring came, the Weller family moved west to Salt Lake City, taking

with them letters and small gifts to give to all the friends that James
and Eleanore had there. Rufus was especially nervous about meeting
people he might have once done harm to, but James repeatedly
assured him that his friends were the forgiving sort. And they talked
of the stories of Alma the Younger and the sons of Mosiah, who had
changed their ways and become great missionaries. Rufus loved those
stories.

Surprisingly little happened as a result of it becoming common
knowledge in the community that every member of the Barrington
household was a Mormon. They received a few odd comments and
questions when encountering people in town, but no one really
seemed to care.

The house felt quiet the first Sunday after the Wellers moved, but
James didn't even bring up whether his family should go as well. He'd
stopped asking. He sold Ralph and Amanda's home for a fair amount
to a middle-aged couple whose children were all grown and on their
own. They seemed to be good people, but they traveled quite a bit
and were not very sociable.

Occasionally someone would mention how much they missed
Ralph and Amanda, but that led to missing Miriam and Andy, and
Andy was no longer alive. The joy of seeing these friends could only
come through moving, but James had stopped asking.

Weeks and months passed, gracefully escorting the children
through the process of growing older and changing with each season.
Soon after Joseph turned four, Eleanore gave birth to an adorable
baby girl. They called her Mariah Eleanore, and she immediately
became the center of attention. Mariah's arrival marked a passage of
time for James and Eleanore, and they sat together one evening while
she fed the baby, recounting all that had happened in their lives since
they'd come to America fifteen years earlier.

Iris had many suitors, but she never showed any interest in a
particular man for more than a week or two. James told Eleanore that
he found it ironic that he'd once struggled with the idea of his little
girl growing up, marrying, and leaving his home. Now he was
becoming concerned that she might never do so. She was twenty years
old and seemed content with the life she was living as a part of the
household where she'd grown up. She was as involved in the running

of the home as Eleanore, and she continually helped look after the children. But James didn't want her being some kind of housekeeper and nanny for her siblings. He wanted her to find the kind of love he'd found with Eleanore; he wanted her to have children of her own and live a full life. Daily he prayed that the right man would come along, that perhaps someone who might also be interested in the gospel would take an interest in her. But Iris continued to be entirely indifferent to any possible suitor, and she was growing older in the process.

Ben was now seventeen and looking more like a man than a child. He was a hard worker and diligent in living the beliefs that his family had given their lives for. But James and Eleanore both sensed a growing restlessness in him. They knew he longed to be among the Saints and feared that one day he might up and leave the way Ralph had done. There had even been some joking about Iris going with him. James and Eleanore prayed that it would never come to that, but their children were getting older, and a time would come when they would need to make their own decisions. They found some comfort in knowing that both Ben and Iris would make those decisions with the careful guidance of the Spirit.

Jamie had grown into a studious but very funny child. At the age of nine, he had become good friends with his brother Isaac, who was less than two years behind in age. Isaac was also studious, and he laughed at anything Jamie said or did, which made them well matched. Joseph, who was now five and showed no inclination toward being studious at all, followed his brothers around and was generally responsible for any mischief that occurred. But his brothers were patient and looked after him well. Frederick and Lizzie's daughter, Mary Jane, was like a sister to all of them. She was now nearly fourteen and was blossoming into a lovely young woman. She often joked that with her red hair and freckled skin, she would never attract male attention the way Iris did with her unusual beauty. But Iris joked in return that she would be glad to pass along every man that came her way. She also told Mary Jane that by the time she was old enough to marry, they would all come to their senses and realize what an amazing young woman she was.

Not long after Mariah's birth, Iris came home to announce that she'd met a very nice man on a visit to town, and they had ended up

talking in the book shop for more than an hour. The subject of religion had come up, and he'd expressed an interest in knowing more of
her beliefs. Iris had invited him over for dinner on Sunday, and to
join their little service.

Miles proved to be a nice young man who was more than five
years older than Iris. He was polite and friendly and had a respectable
job at the bank. He started coming around a great deal, and after
some weeks had passed, it was evident he had a keen interest in Iris,
as well as her religious beliefs. Iris became hopeful that he would be
the one for her, and she quickly grew attached to his company. But
their courtship went on and on without anything changing, and there
was no mention of marriage.

Time continued to hurry by while the Lord sent no message for
the Barrington household to move west. Occasionally the matter was
brought up over the supper table, with speculations over what the
Lord's purposes might be. But the conclusion was always that they
could never second-guess the Lord, and that they might never know
what purpose would be served in their staying. Frederick suggested
that it could simply be their own individual test of patience and
perseverance, with nothing more to it than that. James didn't really
care about the purpose; he just knew that he needed an invitation
from the right source before he would take his family anywhere.

James began following the example of his wife and children by
writing more frequently in his journal. He wrote a brief account of
his life, his conversion to the gospel, and the experiences he'd had that
he felt might be important to pass on to his posterity. He even wrote
about his poor choice in assaulting Ned Weller, and everything that
had subsequently transpired. He felt that writing about it added
another layer of healing, and he appreciated being able to go back and
read the evolution of his coming to terms with the issue and being
forgiven. He mentioned to Eleanore that he wasn't certain he wanted
his grandchildren to know what a fool he'd been, but she felt it was
good for his descendants to know that he was human, and that he'd
had struggles and overcome them. He couldn't dispute that.

Jack, the family dog, died in his sleep and was buried close to
David in the woods. The two had shared some history together, and
it seemed only fitting. Everyone missed Jack, and many tears were

shed, but they loved to talk about images of David and Jack together in heaven.

In the autumn of 1855, Mr. Pitt, their cantankerous neighbor, passed away. They all attended the service but weren't surprised by the standoffish nature of his sons, who apparently had no intention of ever marrying.

Eleanore discovered that she was pregnant, and James started making jokes over the Prophet Joseph's declaration about Eleanore having many children. "Be careful when a prophet tells you something," James said facetiously to the children. "It will surely come to pass."

This prompted a request to tell the story for the hundredth time of when James and Eleanore had met Joseph Smith. To them it seemed a lifetime ago, and to the children the story had almost become a legend.

An upset occurred when Iris became frustrated over her relationship with Miles. She loved him, and he claimed to love her, but she felt increasingly uneasy concerning the possible reasons why he was avoiding any talk of marriage, or taking any steps in regard to the religion that he had declared to know was true. James suggested that the family participate in a fast with Iris and make it a matter of earnest prayer that she might be able to move on with her life, one way or another. Two days following the fast, James took Eleanore out for a fine dinner at a restaurant they'd never been to before. Iris had suggested it, having overhead while shopping the previous day that the food was delicious and the atmosphere quite romantic. It was her idea that her parents needed an evening away together. Before leaving, they asked if she was going to see Miles, but she reported that he had a family matter to attend to. An hour later, James and Eleanore saw him at the restaurant, sitting across a table from a garish-looking woman with far too much of herself exposed by her low-cut gown. Miles was holding the woman's hand and kissing it. Eleanore felt horrified, but James felt angry. However, he remained completely calm as he approached the table where they were sitting, and confronted Miles's guilt-ridden attempts to explain a situation that had no honorable explanation. James simply told him that if he came anywhere near his daughter again, they would have a problem.

Iris was devastated by the news, but not entirely surprised. As she cried and talked to her parents far into the night, she admitted that she'd seen hints of a lack of integrity, and she had avoided looking at evidences that the life Miles lived was contrary to the one he pretended to live. For weeks she grieved over the ending of her relationship with Miles. She said it wasn't so much that her heart was broken, as it was that she felt humiliated over being such a fool and losing several months of her life to a man who had deceived and betrayed her.

A month after the incident at the restaurant, James looked up from his desk to see Iris in the doorway of his office. "Hello," he said and leaned back in his chair. "To what do I owe this pleasure?"

"You see me all the time," she said, nonchalantly pretending to examine items on a shelf that she'd looked at a hundred times.

"Not all alone in my office," he said. "You keep yourself very busy, young lady."

"It's easier to not think about how pathetic my life is when I'm busy."

"Pathetic?" he echoed, sounding comically insulted.

She turned abruptly. "We have a good life here; that's not what I mean."

"I know what you mean," he said gently.

Iris sighed. "By the time Mother was my age, she'd been married to you for years."

"That doesn't mean being unmarried is such a bad thing. You can't compare your life to hers." He hesitated before adding, "She didn't have the heartbreak that you've had."

Iris sighed and eased into a chair. "Maybe I should just get to the point."

"Maybe you should."

"I've been thinking that . . . perhaps it would be good for me to . . . leave."

"Leave?" James countered. "To go where? Do what?"

"I don't know. Back east, perhaps, or—"

"Or perhaps it's time our family went west so that you could associate with young men who share your values and beliefs."

"You know very well it's not the right time for the family to move . . . unless something has changed in the last few days."

James sighed and had to say, "You're right. I know that. But I also know you're not going to find what you're looking for back east. And sending you away on your own is not something I feel good about."

She looked at him firmly in a way that reminded him of Eleanore, and he wondered how that could be when they shared no blood. Nevertheless, Eleanore's influence was quite evident. "Father," she said, "I know you don't like it, but I'm an adult. If I feel that it's right to go, then I need to go."

James sighed again. "You're right. I don't like it. I don't like it at all. But if I felt like your reasons for going had some substantiation, I might feel better. I'm certain you're capable of taking care of yourself, although the world can still be a difficult place for a young lady on her own. But you're telling me you don't know where you're going or what you would do. That sounds like running away to me. Maybe you *do* need a change, but I believe you need to give it some time and some serious prayer." He leaned forward. "I can let you go, Iris, if I know in my heart it's what God wants for you. There is no other way I can find peace with it. Do you understand?"

Iris nodded and sniffled, then wiped a hand over her face. "You're probably right. I probably am just running away . . . but I don't know what I'm running to . . . or from. I just. . . ." Her emotion heightened, "I just don't want to be alone any more. I see the relationship you have with Mother, and . . . I want that in my life, Papa. I feel empty inside. I want children of my own. I want a man beside me that I can trust and rely on. But I'm not so sure such a man exists."

"Come here," James said, and she stood beside him. He urged her onto his lap as if she were a little girl again, and the moment his arms came around her she started to sob against his shoulder. "You'll find your way, Iris. I know you will. I don't know how, but you will."

Once she'd calmed down he said, "Why don't you give the matter some time and thought. And prayer, of course. You can't go running off during the winter months anyway, when the weather is so harsh and unpredictable. If you can come up with a feasible plan, then we'll discuss options—in the spring. Fair enough?"

"More than fair enough," she said, but James already dreaded the arrival of spring when she might actually make the decision to set out on her own.

A week later Eleanore miscarried. The ordeal proved to be more painful than it had been in the past, but she got through it without any real drama beyond the usual emotional loss. She grieved for the loss of yet another unborn child gone, but she found peace and joy in the beautiful children they had. Mariah was strong and lovely, with dark hair like her brothers. But she actually looked a great deal like Iris. Since Eleanore and Iris shared no blood, it was evident the resemblance came through their father. The boys were growing quickly and were full of energy, and Ben was approaching adulthood far too fast.

With the onset of winter, Stella began to complain about arthritis in her knees. No one in the household had even known of the problem prior to then, but it had suddenly worsened with the cold weather, and she reluctantly admitted that going up and down the stairs to her apartment had become very difficult. She apologized profusely for causing an upset, but Eleanore and James both assured her that she was a part of their family now, and they were glad to be able to help her with whatever problem might come up. James had the doctor come and check her, and he believed that if she could avoid stairs and stay out of the cold, she would manage fairly well. Stella was upset with the diagnosis, since she lived in the attic apartment over Frederick and Lizzie's house, and she also needed to traverse the distance between the houses each day. It was James who came up with the idea to move his desk into the library, which had more than ample room for a little more furniture. He could easily do his paperwork there, and that freed up the office as a bedroom for Stella. She would be right across the hall from the kitchen, with no need to go up and down stairs during her normal routine, and no need to go outside unless she wanted to. Since other people in the house took care of all of the errands and shopping, and their church services were held in the home, Stella gratefully declared that she might never go outside in the winter again.

With everyone pitching in to help, the changes were made in the course of a day. The office was thoroughly cleaned once James's belongings were all moved out and placed in the library, which had only needed some minor rearranging. Then all of Stella's things were moved from the attic apartment into her new room. That very day James ordered another bed for the apartment, simply to have it available should the need ever arise for someone to stay there. He offered it to Ben on the chance that sharing space with his younger brothers might be making him a little crazy. But Ben assured him that he liked being with his brothers, and it wasn't a problem. So, the apartment would sit empty for the time being, but James just had a feeling that it would be needed again, and he wanted to have it ready for unexpected guests.

Throughout the winter months, Iris said nothing more about her desire to start a new life on her own, but James knew it was brewing inside her. He sensed her restlessness, but knew it was beyond his control. With the approach of spring he felt perhaps more unsettled than he ever had over the apparent need to be kept away from the body of the Saints in Salt Lake City. He knew that members were continually joining the Church and then traveling great distances to live in Zion. But his household remained aloof and separate, while his children had no peers to associate with who shared their beliefs. Since their religion had become public, they had all made more of an effort to express those beliefs to people they encountered, hoping they might add to their little flock. But no one seemed interested, and nothing changed. James began to wonder if he was really getting the right answers, when there seemed to be no answer at all. He even considered the possibility that perhaps the Lord just expected him to use his own brain and assess that the move needed to be made. But Eleanore discounted that theory when she told him she knew in her own heart they were meant to stay. He began to wonder if they would grow old and die in this place, while each of their own children left, one by one.

On a cold day in March, the sheriff came to the house, asking to speak privately to James. They went into the library and closed the door, exchanging pleasant chitchat until they were seated across from each other.

"So, what brings you all the way out here?" James asked.

"Two things," the sheriff said, reaching into his coat to pull out an envelope. "First off, I wonder if I could get you to send that to Lu Bailey; I guess it's Mrs. Leichty now. I assume you would know where to send it."

"I do, yes." James took the envelope. "May I ask what it is?"

"Her uncle passed on."

"Did he? I hadn't heard."

"He did little but drink, you know."

"I had heard that." James thought of the numerous times he and Eleanore had left food for Mr. Bailey. He wished they could have done more.

"He's been gone for some time, actually; a few months now." The sheriff set his hat on the couch beside him. "Anyway, as far as we know, Lu was his only living relative. That's the money from selling his property."

"Oh?" James couldn't help being pleased. "I'm certain they'll be glad to get it. I'm sure they can use it."

"I'm sure they can. How are they anyway?"

"Doing well, last we heard," James said. "They've got three children now."

The sheriff chuckled. "Well, that's fine, isn't it."

"Yes, it is." James stood up and put the envelope in a secure place in his desk. "I'll send it off right away. Thank you for bringing it out. I'm sure you didn't need to see to it personally."

James sat back down to face the sheriff as he said, "There was something else I needed to tell you."

"All right," James said.

"Your neighbor, Mr. Pitt. He passed on a while back."

"Yes," James drawled, wondering what the point might be. "I did know *that.*"

"Did you know him well?"

"Not very. He stopped by very rarely with one of his boys, or sometimes alone. I probably only spoke with him once or twice a year. The boys have hardly said a word to me. Why?"

"His boys came to see me yesterday. Apparently they had some need for a clear conscience. Seems their father had some grievance with Ned Weller."

James was assaulted with a quickened heartbeat. "Really?" he asked, not betraying his emotional response to hearing the name.

"They told me their father had killed Weller."

James swallowed carefully and closed his eyes, feeling a little woozy as his experience surrounding Ned Weller's death came back to him. When he couldn't find voice enough to respond, James was glad the sheriff went on to explain.

"They say the old man confessed it on his death bed. The boys didn't say anything before now because they didn't want their father's name tarnished. But I guess the guilt got to them. They wanted me to know. I assured them I would close the case and not discuss it with anyone except those who were personally affected and needed to know. I consider you one of those people. I'm sure you'll respect their wishes."

"Of course," James managed. "Do you know what happened? Why it happened?"

"I don't. I think the boys knew more than they were saying. They just told me their pa had a grievance with Weller, and it had been a problem for a long time; I believe it actually started with Old Man Weller, the boys' father. The Pitt family lived on the other side of town for many years before they bought the Plummer farm."

"I didn't realize that."

"So whatever this problem is, it could have gone back to before you were born."

James chuckled. "That *is* a long time."

"I just thought you should know."

"Yes, thank you." He wanted to say he was glad the mystery had been solved, but it didn't feel solved. Mr. Pitt was dead, and so was Ned Weller. But the issue between them remained a mystery. And James knew that opening up a conversation with the Pitt brothers would be completely inappropriate. The matter was closed.

The sheriff stayed a few more minutes, exchanging friendly small talk. As soon as he left, James found his wife in the kitchen and asked her to take a walk with him. He told her of the sheriff's report and how he felt about it. She had little to say, but she listened and held his hand and told him how she loved him. For that and many other reasons, he was glad to know that he'd made right his mistakes—with God *and* the law.

Just a few days later, James was helping the children clear the table after supper when a firm knock sounded at the front door.

"I'll get it," Ben said, and a moment later James heard a deep voice ask, "Is your father at home, young man?"

"Yes, I'll get him," Ben said just before James stepped into the hallway to see two men framed by the front door, holding hats in their hands. He knew immediately they were not from around here. His heart quickened as something familiar in their aura struck him.

"Hello," James said, stepping forward. The men both looked toward him, and his spirit became illogically alert. "What can I do for you?"

"James Barrington?" one of them said, and he wondered for a second if his reaction was meant to warn him. But another second's thought left him undoubtedly certain that what he felt was good.

"That's right," James said.

The men exchanged a quick glance and a smile, as if their finding him meant something. One man stepped forward, holding out an eager hand. "A pleasure, Brother Barrington," he said, and that word *brother* spurred a further quickening of James's heart. While he zealously shook James's hand, the man added, "Brother Jensen gave us excellent directions to your home."

James sucked in his breath as the reality began to sink in. Still, he had trouble believing it, even when the other gentleman stepped forward for a handshake and said, "We've come from Salt Lake City."

"Truly?" James exhaled with a breathless chuckle while Ben closed the door. He moved next to James, wearing a smile that made him glow.

"Indeed," one of them said. "Brother Brigham has sent us to take care of some business here in Iowa City."

James chuckled again, hearing disbelief in his tone. "Truly?" he asked again, more astonished.

"Truly," the other man said with a pleasant little laugh.

"Come in. Come in." James guided them to the parlor. "Are you hungry? Can I—"

"No, thank you. We've eaten."

"Something to drink? A glass of water or—"

"Thank you, we're fine," the other one said.

"Have a seat," James said, feeling flustered. "Ben, get your mother, and . . ." He chuckled. "No, you go find Frederick. I'll get your mother." To the visitors he added, "I'll just gather the family, and . . . if that's all right, and—"

"By all means, gather the family. We'd love to meet them."

James hurried down the hall and found the women in the kitchen chattering while they cleaned dishes. Mariah was playing on the floor. He could hear the boys outside.

"Who was at the door?" Eleanore asked when she saw him.

He took the pan she was drying out of her hands and set it aside, along with the towel. He laughed as he grasped both her hands in his. His behavior caught the attention of Lizzie, Stella, and Iris, but it was Eleanore he spoke to. "Oh, my darling," he said, feeling a childish excitement that surprised even himself. "It's surely a miracle."

"What? Tell me," she insisted when he had trouble catching his breath.

"It's two men . . . from Salt Lake City." Eleanore and the other women all gasped in chorus. He added, "They said Brother Jensen told them how to find the house, and Brother Brigham has sent them to Iowa City on a matter of business."

Eleanore laughed softly and drew an astonished breath before she rushed past him. "What are we doing in here?"

James picked up Mariah and followed her to the parlor, with the others following closely behind. The gentlemen stood as they entered the room. "Sister Barrington?" one of them said, extending a hand.

"Yes!" she said brightly, shaking his hand, then that of the other man. "It's so good to have you in our home. Are you hungry or—"

"No, thank you. Your husband already offered. I'm Brother Kimball, and this is Brother Grant."

"A pleasure," Eleanore said, then motioned behind her as she introduced the others. Frederick and Ben entered with the boys before she'd finished the introductions. After Brothers Kimball and Grant offered kind greetings, everyone was seated, and the children sat on the floor.

A sudden quiet except for a little squawk from Mariah made it evident that everyone was waiting to hear what these men had to say. Brother Kimball began, "First may I say that you have a beautiful family."

"Thank you," James said. "I would agree with that."

"And allow us to thank you for your gracious welcome."

"The pleasure is entirely ours," James said. "We've longed to be among the Saints, but the answer to our prayers continues to be that we need to remain here—at least for now."

The visitors exchanged a brief glance, as if they knew something that no one else did. James and Eleanore looked at each other similarly, but were more puzzled. James took her hand and felt her scoot just a bit closer to him on the sofa.

"Clearly," Brother Grant said, "the Lord has meant for you to be in this place at this time."

"Has He?" James asked, tightening his hold on Eleanore's hand. In the breadth of a moment, James felt more than saw a panoramic vision fill his mind. Each choice he and Eleanore had made to lead them to this day came back to him clearly: the struggle to understand, the elusiveness of hope and faith at times, the waiting and wondering over their purpose in remaining here in Iowa. And the words of a prophet that had kept them believing there would *be* a purpose in these things. All of it came together with such force and clarity that James found it difficult to draw his next breath. But he forced air into his lungs, feeling a dreamlike sensation that surrounded the group gathered in the parlor.

"I believe you spent some weeks in Winter Quarters," Brother Kimball said to James.

James forced another deep breath. "That's right." He motioned to Frederick. "We both did, about ten years ago."

The visitors glanced at Ben and smiled, as if their thoughts were as one. "And this must be the young man you brought back with you."

"Yes, this is Benjamin," James said.

Eyes turned again to James. Brother Kimball went on. "Brigham remembers you. He was very specific in asking us to speak with you. You are surely aware that the railroad has come to Iowa City."

"Yes," James drawled, his anticipation threatening to stop his heart.

"That is why this area has been chosen as a gathering place for the Saints who are going west. Our numbers are growing very quickly, Brother Barrington. Saints are arriving in large numbers from Europe and back east, and this is where they will be accumulating necessary supplies and preparing for the 1300-mile journey to Salt Lake City." Tears stung James's eyes and heated his throat, even before Brother Grant added, "We have come to ask your family to assist in helping the Saints in these preparations."

James heard Eleanore sob quietly, and he hurried to put a hand over his own mouth before he did the same. He felt tears slide down his cheeks in the very same moment that he heard sniffles in the room. He took in the contented expressions and peaceful eyes of their visitors and wiped at his tears, chuckling in an attempt to keep from sobbing. Hoping to explain, he said, "We've lived here for nearly seventeen years, gentlemen. And we have been members for nearly that long. We have lived our religion quietly, waiting for the day that . . . we could leave here and . . ." He swallowed a rise of emotion. Eleanore's hand trembled in his. "I don't think any of us ever imagined . . . this." He chuckled again and wiped at more tears. "Did you say . . . large numbers? The Saints? *Here?*"

"That's right," Brother Kimball said. "Matters are coming together well. We're certain that your assistance will greatly aid the situation."

"Of course," James said. "We'll do anything we can." He glanced at Frederick, silently acknowledging that he needed to speak for his own family.

"Certainly," Frederick said firmly. "Anything."

"We can help these people get what they need," James said, then clarified what he really meant, "We have money—more than plenty."

"Yes," Brother Kimball said as if they'd already known that he was a wealthy men. And apparently they had discussed the matter by the way he also said, "We advise you to tread carefully in that regard and share what you have according to the guidance of the Spirit. It would be impossible for you to help everyone who will come here in need. And the Lord surely has His plan for each of His children. For some it is important that they earn the means to acquire what they need, and to make sacrifices according to His will."

"Of course," James said again, humbled and deeply touched. His heart warmed as if to tell him that he was not only capable of doing all that was being asked of him, but that it was indeed what God had planned for them all along. The feeling quickly coincided with a series of brief thoughts apparently related to this situation that strengthened his confidence in the assignment. He couldn't put into words what he felt; he only knew that the correct attitude regarding the situation had been planted in his spirit.

Eleanore attempted to accept the reality of what she was hearing while Brothers Grant and Kimball went on to explain the preparations that had already been made in laying the foundation for moving thousands of Saints west. They described what they called a handcart, and explained how it would enable families to travel without needing to purchase oxen or horses. The handcarts were more affordable than wagons and teams, but James was struck by the implication that this meant people would be walking 1300 miles. His newfound confidence in the assignment became coupled with a surge of compassion, even awe, for what these people were willing to do.

"We've contracted for the building of a hundred handcarts," Brother Kimball said.

"A hundred?" Eleanore echoed. Her words were accompanied with a delighted laugh. A hundred Mormon families? She couldn't believe it. But these men had talked of thousands of Saints coming through here. It was incredible! A miracle! Of course, these people would all be preparing to move on, but they could be a part of that; they could associate with them, be among those who shared their beliefs.

Brother Grant went on to explain more about the handcarts, and of the prospects for work that were available in the area that would help the Saints prepare for the journey. They spoke of being well received in the area, and mentioned that they'd been aware of some persecution in the past, but it seemed not to be a problem at this time. Eleanore felt her heart would burst from her growing amazement over what she was hearing. She knew that James had likely had something to do with the softening of attitudes toward Mormons in the area, but she kept the thought to herself. And she couldn't believe what she was hearing when it became evident that a Mormon settlement was already budding nearby while they had been completely oblivious.

Once explanations were sufficiently given, Brother Grant looked squarely at James and said, "Brother Brigham asked me to speak on his behalf in requesting that you commit yourself to this work for a year's time, and then move west with the Saints when you feel prompted to do so."

"Yes, of course," James said with no hesitation, and Eleanore felt so proud of him. A year? It seemed so short a time, really, considering how long they had waited. A year and they would be joining their friends at last! She felt hope and joy beyond description.

After James and Eleanore showed their visitors to the door, they returned to the parlor to find everyone in stunned silence. Then they all started talking, and the conversation didn't run down for nearly two hours. Everyone who was old enough to understand wholeheartedly agreed that a miracle had just occurred. So much that hadn't made sense had now fallen perfectly into perspective. There was no disputing that their lives had been in God's hands all along, and His plan for them was far more incredible than they ever could have imagined.

Epilogue

James helped Eleanore out of the buggy, and they both just stood there, holding hands, unable to move, unable to speak as they took in the breadth of the Mormon camp. Eleanore finally let out a delighted laugh, inspiring him to do the same.

She said, "It's as if . . ."

"As if what?"

"As if . . . we've been searching for heaven all these years, and heaven showed up at our doorstep."

"Yes, it is like that," he said, and Eleanore tugged on his hand, suddenly impatient.

They spent the day immersing themselves in the bustle of activity. They embraced people they'd never met, and listened to stories of how the gospel had brought them from many different lands. They assessed needs while Eleanore kept careful notes and occasionally wept for no apparent reason. And James told her to write down the names of a couple of fine young men who would likely enjoy meeting Iris. She cautioned him against matchmaking, but wrote down their names anyway. And she only let out a little giggle when he told them separately that he had some work they could do on his property to earn some money, if they were interested. And they both were.

Late that evening, James and Eleanore sat on their own porch in the dark, knowing everyone else was asleep. They relived the day in words, marveling over and over at the miracle that had found them. And then they revisited each step of their lives that had brought them to this day. Looking back, they both felt certain that God had planted in their hearts the need to come here, long before either of them had ever comprehended what the feelings inside of them would come to mean. James had longed to leave behind his aristocratic upbringing and settle in America. It had been one of his deepest wishes throughout most of his life. And Eleanore had stumbled upon a discarded Book of Mormon, knowing almost immediately that she must follow where it led her. And they had come together with a common love of the Bible, and a desire to live their lives according to the direction of God and the guidance of the Spirit. And, without a doubt, that guidance had led them to this place, to a home that had connected them to people in Nauvoo who remained some of their dearest friends, even across the miles. And to a city where God would have known all along He intended as a gathering place and a way station for His people. It was as if they had been born to this mission, and nothing in their lives had been happenstance. They also found perspective for circumstances that had once been terribly difficult. Eleanore knew that if her father hadn't died when she was a child, her mother would not have gone to work for the Barrington household. And if James hadn't married Caroline, he would not have been left a widower in need of a governess for his children when Eleanore was the proper age to take the position.

"It was destiny for us to be together, Ellie," he said and kissed her hand.

"So, you're saying it was a good thing for me to sneak into your library at night and read your Bible."

"That's exactly what I'm saying."

He put his arm around her, and she leaned her head on his shoulder.

"Did I ever tell you," he said, "how I came to the decision to ask you to marry me?"

"No." She lifted her head to look at him. "How can we have been married seventeen years and you've never told me that?"

"I was saving it," he chuckled.

"So, tell me."

"Do you remember the day I came into the sitting room, and you and the children were looking at a map of the world, talking about where you would like to travel? Lizzie was there too."

"I remember it well," she said. "I was looking at New York on the map, thinking that's where the Book of Mormon had been printed, and that's where I wanted to go, to find the people who had done it."

"I asked you why you wanted to go to America. Do you remember what you told me?"

"Not exactly, no."

"You said that you would very much like the opportunity to explore new beliefs and a way of life that didn't hold some of the restrictions we had there in our society. And your words went right into my heart. I'd forgotten until that moment how deeply I'd once longed to go to America for that very reason. My marriage to Caroline had squelched that dream, and in that moment, it came back to life. And there you were in the center of it. In that same moment, I saw you with me in my mind. I saw us making that journey and working together to care for the children. It wasn't until that night when I couldn't sleep that it occurred to me that our being married was the only possible and appropriate option to make that vision come to pass. I remember gasping at the thought, and then I laughed out loud. Right there alone in my bed. Beyond anything related directly to my children, it was the first glimpse of happiness I'd felt in years. I knew it was right. It took me a few days to completely settle with the idea and work it through, but . . . I just knew it was right. You know the rest."

"Yes, I know the rest." She once again laid her head on his shoulder. "I think they call that happily ever after."

AUTHOR'S SUGGESTIONS FOR READERS GROUP DISCUSSION

1. How does the Saints' completion of the Nauvoo Temple during the evacuation apply to us in our day? Are we willing to finish what God asks of us, even if it doesn't make sense to us?

2. How does the character Benjamin represent the ongoing persecution and suffering of the Saints during this period of history?

3. What can we learn as parents in the way that James and Eleanore handled the difficult stage that Iris went through? How does Iris's behavior represent the free agency of all human beings, and the level of a parent's responsibility? How did unconditional love, forgiveness, communication, and a lack of anger all contribute to solving the problem?

4. What do you think prevented James from coming to terms with his emotional response to the persecution and struggles of others? How did harboring ill feelings lead him to make choices that were not appropriate?

5. What challenges do we face today that could bring on similar reactions to the persecution of the early Saints? How can we learn from their examples to deal more appropriately with betrayal, abuse, or disappointment in people or circumstances that have hurt us?

6. While the challenges of the early Saints often make us think we never could have survived all that they endured, what struggles do we have today that might make them feel the same way about us?

7. From Eleanore's initial reaction to the reasons for James being injured, what can we learn about judgment and anger, as opposed to compassion and understanding when those we love make mistakes?

8. Consider the series of steps that led up to James's fateful encounter with Ned Weller. At what point did he lose control of his actions, and at what point should he have made different choices?

9. What can we learn about repentance, restitution, and charity from the outcome of the situation with James and the Weller family? How does the situation illustrate the tender mercies of our Father in Heaven, and the power of the Atonement, and how can we apply them more fully in our own lives?

10. What can we learn about trusting in the Lord's timing as the purpose for the Barrington family staying in Iowa City comes to light? How might we find more patience in our present struggles and frustration if we consider that they may have a specific purpose according to God's perspective?

ABOUT THE AUTHOR

Anita Stansfield, the LDS market's number-one best-selling romance novelist, is a prolific and imaginative writer. Her novels have captivated and moved hundreds of thousands of readers, and she is a popular speaker for women's groups and in literary circles. She and her husband, Vince, are the parents of five children and grandparents of one and live in Alpine, Utah.